The Ghosts of Grand Detour

The Ghosts of Grand Detour

Rebecca Kohles

iUniverse, Inc.
New York Lincoln Shanghai

The Ghosts of Grand Detour

iUniverse books may be ordered through booksellers or by contacting:

iUniverse
2021 Pine Lake Road, Suite 100
Lincoln, NE 68512
www.iuniverse.com
1-800-Authors (1-800-288-4677)

ISBN-13: 978-0-595-33902-0 (pbk)
ISBN-13: 978-0-595-78687-9 (ebk)
ISBN-10: 0-595-33902-6 (pbk)
ISBN-10: 0-595-78687-1 (ebk)

Printed in the United States of America

AUTHOR'S DEDICATION

To my parents, who indulged me by taking me for riding lessons as a kid. I know my Mom hoped and prayed that I'd grow out of the horse thing. She bought me every doll under the sun trying to influence my nature. Too bad they didn't explain to her that there are people who love horses, and then there is everyone else. It took her a long time to realize that there are much worse things I could occupy myself with instead of horses.

For Mr. Chat Nichols, who, to my mother's dismay (and probable horror), gave me my first horse and forever changed my life. Chat began this lifelong obsession of mine with equine companionship and sent me into the wonderful world of the ever intelligent, American Saddlebred. I know that he has a very special place in heaven. For me he was the greatest man to influence my life. He wanted to remain anonymous, further testimony that he wanted no thanks or recognition. I was very surprised when a letter I wrote him many years later as a thank you showed up in the *American Saddlebred* magazine, which was delivered to my house—with his name cut out of course!

To Prince Charles (no not that one!), a.k.a. *Chuck* my first horse, who was a fiery sorrel, five-gaited giant trapped in a 14'2 body. Through him I learned humility, freedom, humility, tenacity, humility, and how to fall gracefully. Did I mention humility? Eighteen years was not enough with you, and I experienced a year of nightmares filled with grief after your loss. I can now picture you galloping in heaven, quick as the wind and bossing the other horses around. You were given to me on the condition that if I ever sold you I owed Chat $300. Chat could not have picked out a better horse to teach me manners.

For my beloved Princess Di, (no, not that one either) who was my second full-blooded American Saddlebred *horse-child.* To say that you were beautiful seems an insult—it doesn't even cover how good-natured and loving you were. You were my equine soul mate, the once-in-a-lifetime horse. You had the heart and soul of an angel. There has never been, nor will there be, a day I do not mourn your passing. You took me places I had never dreamed to go. It was an honor every time we galloped an event course. For the longest time, I often felt as though most of me died with you. I only know that upon leaving this world you became a bona fide angel, and I continually try to pass along all the important things that you taught me while you graced my life.

For my husband, Michael, who didn't desert me during this very rough time. You became my sole reason for staying here on this earth. I was so distraught and many times wished I could die, too. You are the best thing that ever happened to me, I do cherish you and your support even if I do give you a hard time about sports.

For wonderful Fox, our smiling half-Schipperke, half-Terrier, twelve-pound, little clown. You bring daily smiles to my face. I am so grateful that you graced Michael's life and mine. Thank God for dogs—I'd go crazy without them!

In honor of my onetime event coach and friend, Jane Stickland, I could never have made it to those wonderful horse shows without you. I learned so much from you. I can never thank you enough for the wonderful memories I will always treasure from showing Di.

In memory of Tom Stender, who was one of the best people I have ever known. You were one of the best friends I ever had. Tom was a man who always gave and expected nothing in return. A truly unique find these days. Your heart was as big as the outdoors that you loved so much. I am still troubled by your leaving us so soon, and I pray that you have been released from the intense pain that troubled you so often. I'm sure you are enjoying the best fishing spot in heaven.

Last, but not least, to my newest horse-child, Terpsichore (a.k.a. Cory). Aptly named for the Greek goddess of song and dance. You have been a delightful youngster to train, and it is amazing to see how intelligent you are. You put a lot of people I know to shame. Though you were a gift from my parents, I almost feel as though Di picked you out and sent you to me as my guardian angel in black horsehair. Half American Saddlebred and half Percheron, your athletic abilities are far outdistancing my riding abilities, and I find myself galloping sometimes to keep up with you. I hope that we have a long time together. Thank you for coming to care for me and giving me the desire to get this manuscript out of the trash receptacle.

My heartfelt apologies to the Cherokee language. All mistakes I have made are mine and mine alone, because I could find no one to help me with the right words. Please forgive me.

Lastly, for all those little girls who are in love with horses and dream of one day having their very own, *never, never* give up your dream!

AUTHOR'S NOTES

As an Illinois horse owner, I am very distraught over the recent defeat of an Illinois bill that would have made horse slaughter for consumption illegal in this state. Horses are spiritual, soulful creatures. We would never have advanced as far as we have without their divine intervention.

It is wrong to kill these creatures that give us their unconditional love and attempt to carry our pain. Anyone who tells you that these animals have no *soul* and are *just* animals don't even begin to know what they are talking about.

My greatest wish in life would be to get a farm and put the slaughterhouse(s) out of business. One of my best friends and I would love to bring abused horses and children together so that they can heal each other. I hope through the proceeds of this and other works to try and bring this dream to a reality. Every living thing should be allowed to live its life to the fullest. It is only the cruel and naive that can't see the forest for the trees.

According to the Full Circle lessons from our Cherokee brothers, nature is our lesson and our answer to harmony and balance; honor all life. The animals are thought of as our four-legged brothers and sisters; the horse itself is a sacred symbol of power.

Where did we lose this lesson?

1

Her eyelids fluttered, and Ivy Chesterton gradually regained consciousness. The thick, metallic taste that lingered in her mouth slowly jogged her memory to her last recollection. She had been abducted.

"Ooooooh," she groaned in a small, tired voice.

Struggling to regain her senses, Ivy heard a male voice speaking in a tongue she had never heard before. The image of her kidnapper flashed through her memory with a jolt, and her eyes snapped into focus. Now aware that she was slung over a moving horse, Ivy struggled to free herself from constricting ropes, but her labor produced no results against her heavy bonds.

"Let me go," she cried, as rough hands ripped her from atop the horse she had been tied to.

Finally able to lift her head, Ivy could see her abductors. The fire and torchlight illuminated the area, and she saw their frightening faces against the night sky. One of the larger figures drew closer to her, and she could see the face beneath the war paint.

"You," Ivy whispered in fright. "I know you. Why would you do this to me?"

The menacing figure gestured to the two men holding her, indicating that they should take her to a wooden frame constructed on the hill. Again he mumbled something in the strange language.

"Noooooo!," she screamed, struggling against them. "Somebody! There must be somebody who can help me!"

Despite her struggles, the two warriors easily maneuvered her to the odd, makeshift frame built in the middle of nowhere. They tightly secured her, spread-eagle—the restraints giving her the appearance of a living picture.

Ivy's cries for help had strained her voice. Her body shook, and she sobbed. The man she had recognized approached her with an animal skin prepared for carrying liquids.

"Why?" she whispered, tears of fear streaming down her face.

"He must have his tribute," he replied in a low voice, whispering menacingly in her ear.

"Who must?" she sobbed.

"Who must?" she shouted at him.

But her requests went unanswered. The man returned to the unknown language and forced her to swallow the contents of the skin. The taste was sickeningly sweet. Through her wild panic, she felt a calming sensation taking over her mind. With her vision impaired, she could now just barely see her captors. Ivy's mind swam with the chaos.

The fires burned, the ritual continued, and as the first morning star rose in the sky, three chosen men approached her from the group. Ivy could feel the euphoric sensations lifting from her, dumping her back in a world of blazing terror.

Catching sight of their demonic half-black, half-red faces, she struggled harder than ever against her tight bonds. The gag that had been placed in her mouth after the liquids guaranteed her silence through the ceremony.

The three warriors then produced a lit torch, an arrow, and a large, glistening dagger. The man with the torch approached first and set fire to the horrified young woman's clothing. He began an unearthly chanting, which the second man quickly joined. He then drew his bow back, sending the arrow through the woman from side to side, just underneath both arms. The third man, the man that Ivy had recognized, also picked up the ceremonial chanting. He approached Ivy with the dagger and slashed into her chest, producing a large gaping wound. He viciously thrust his fist into her chest and ripped out her heart. Turning to face his "*tribe*," he collected the blood from the organ into the palm of his hand and smeared it over his face in ecstasy.

"Aaaaaaaah," he cried out in rapture. Glancing down on his people while they took their place in the ritual, his heart filled with a rush of pleasure.

2

Rita McAllister sat in the driveway of the old Grand Detour Hotel. The rain beat against her car windows, plummeting her already foul mood to further depths. She inhaled the intoxicating aroma of new leather in her silver Lexus and tapped her well-manicured, "peach pit-stop" colored nails against her teeth. It was a bad habit that she had developed as a teenager and had never been able to avoid when she became nervous or greatly annoyed. Today Rita was both. She looked at her watch in irritation; counting how many minutes she would continue to wait for her client before she abandoned all hope and fled for the warm, dry comforts of The Blue Ram Pub.

"Five more minutes—that's it!" she exclaimed under her breath. "And the only reason I'm giving you that is that the sale of this behemoth would pay a year's salary."

Becoming a realtor in this town had not been an easy task. Rita often wondered why she had chosen to stay here at all, considering her early upbringing at an orphanage several towns away. But then, she also had to consider Ron's feelings. Ron and his father had been instrumental in bringing her to this town while she was still a teen, providing her with a home, eventually a job, and the training it had taken for her to achieve the position she was in today. She would feel guilty just leaving him after all he'd done for her.

Besides, it was a red-letter day when someone from out of state actually wanted to look at any property here; much less the old Conrad place. Why would someone want to look at that old horror of a house, it was unfathomable, even to her. The local reputation of the place was far from desirable. Between the legends and her own experience, Rita could feel her panic rising.

Sitting in silence in the car, Rita's mind wandered and her mind filled with the image of a young girl. The girl was a stranger to her, and yet she seemed so familiar. She was wearing an old-fashioned, pale pink dress, and she looked frightened.

An earsplitting clap of thunder shook her car, and the lightning eerily brightened up the sky behind one of the castle-like turrets of the old hotel. Rita jumped in fear, breaking her daydreams of the girl. For a moment, in that flash of light, Rita thought she had seen a large, menacing dog skulking behind the house. When she squinted and strained to see in the dark, the figure was gone. Smiling nervously, Rita could see that just over the hill a hint of headlights was finally coming her way.

"Great," she said sarcastically, "at least she's only thirty-five minutes late."

The dark blue car approached, and Rita got out of her car shivering. Just remembering her own experiences in this place had been enough for her to swear that she'd never come back. Yet now, here she was. She had to question her own sanity and wonder why she would risk being here again.

3

A frighteningly dramatic bolt of lightning filled the sky and the background of the old hotel. The rain had diminished to a light drizzle, and the windshield wipers were making that annoying scraping sound they make when there's not enough moisture for them to wipe away. The scene before her reminded Sarah Caldwell of all those horrible B-movies that she and Bruce used to stay up and watch every Halloween. Both would curl up with a large bowl of freshly popped popcorn and laugh at how stupid the characters were to run straight at the often not-so-scary monsters. The once happy memory made Sarah go hollow with pain.

"What am I doing here?" she asked quietly, closing the car door and looking up at the house.

Memories built up inside of her, but Sarah fought to push them away. She vowed that they would not get through to her tonight. She wouldn't allow it. Her analyst, Barbara, had been teaching her to block out those feelings when they reared their ugly head at inappropriate moments. This was an important time for her, and she needed to be strong. She needed to change her life for the better. It was now time to fulfill both a dream and a promise.

Sarah looked up again at the towering old hotel; it made her feel so tiny and defenseless. Sadly, Sarah fought to remember the future she and Bruce had wanted together.

"Hey. Are you all right?" Rita asked with concern.

"I just never realized how intimidating it is to find out that there is only so much about your own fate you actually have control over," Sarah replied blankly.

"Huh?"

"Oh, just thinking out loud," Sarah apologized. She smiled slightly. "Letting my imagination run wild."

"You got the right house for that, I'm sure," Rita replied, wrinkling her pert nose in obvious distaste. "This place is a nightmare even in the daylight."

"I'm…sorry?" Sarah stammered as she slapped herself back to reality.

"I'm Rita. Rita McAllister—your realtor," Rita said as she offered her hand in a businesslike manner.

"Forgive me," Sarah replied as she shook Rita's hand firmly. "Sarah Caldwell."

"Let's get in before it begins to rain again, okay?"

"Sounds good."

As Sarah walked towards the door, she looked up at the immenseness of the building. From where she stood, it looked at though the top floor pierced the clouds overhead. Now that she was standing here at the base of the building, it seemed much more imposing than the picture in the listing.

"Are you sure that Dracula's cousin doesn't live here?" Sarah giggled, finding herself in the dark foyer of the ancient hotel.

"Don't ever say that!" Rita exclaimed.

"Sorry," Rita added as she studied the surprised, blank look on Sarah's pale face. "This town does not have much of a sense of humor. Especially about the macabre. I can tell you firsthand just how long it takes for an outsider to be accepted by the locals. There is no shining history here in Grand Detour and they do not take kindly to people stirring up stories. Real or imagined."

"Thanks," Sarah said. She swallowed deeply and absently placed some stray blond hair behind her right ear. "I'll keep that in mind."

Rita flipped on a switch and began her carefully rehearsed tour. "It's just a friendly word of warning for you if you do plan to reside here. And now, as they say, 'On with the show.' The hotel was originally wired for electricity in 1935; however, through the stipulation of the original will that governs this property, a complete update on electrical wiring was just done last year."

"Many things," Rita said as she continued her speech "including the plumbing, heating, and the new addition of air conditioning ductwork have been installed or updated just prior to the marketed release of the property. These conditions were part of a preexisting will that was held by the late owner. All fixtures and furnishings are to be included in the final sale package, and though you are permitted to repair or reupholster, no extensive changes in decor would ever be permitted."

"You mean to tell me that these beautiful antiques go with the place?" Sarah asked incredulously as she placed her hand on an ebonized Victorian rocker.

"I'm glad that you like them," Rita scoffed. "I prefer sleek, modern lines myself. These outdated furnishing beauties are a mandatory requirement in order to purchase this place. There is and always shall be a nosy lawyer that drops in every six months or so to make sure that you are following the rules of the purchase contract. Any additions not approved and any other infractions will have to be changed on a timetable that they will give to you."

"The previous owner sounds like a real stickler for details."

"He was. From everything I've ever heard, he was that and much, much more."

Sarah inspected the place from top to bottom with Rita tagging along behind. Every room was beautiful to her; desperately in need of several coats of paint, but the potential of great beauty still resounded within the walls. Each room was unique with antique bed frames and matching dressers, and Sarah fingered every furniture piece in an appreciative awe. The private suites were huge. Sarah vigorously inspected each screened-in porch off the suites. Two of the suites had their very own kitchens; Sarah settled on the larger one for herself and mentally assigned the other, more open one to her friend Alex.

Time flew by for Sarah. Hours seemed like minutes as the hotel's essence wrapped itself around her, drawing her into another world. Momentarily lost, Sarah found herself in the massive kitchen.

"Can't you just see a kitchen staff hard at work in here?" Sarah asked. "I love it, but Alex wouldn't be caught dead in here."

Rita smiled as her conscience fought violently within her. After following Sarah through the house, Rita had truly come to like her. Sarah had proven to be very genuine; this was a rare quality for Rita to encounter. How would she be able to sleep nights after selling this ark of dread to such a nice lady?

"This Alex…is that your husband?" Rita asked.

"Alex?" Sarah said absently. "No, Alex is my best friend."

"Why would you think of taking this on alone?" Rita questioned, sounding more nervous than she meant to.

"My husband and I always dreamed of an old-fashioned bed and breakfast out in the country."

"Then your husband will be joining you eventually?"

"No," Sarah replied sadly, her throat constricting in grief.

Rita noticed Sarah's sudden change and thought that the petite woman suddenly looked frail and tragic.

"You see, my husband Bruce…well, he died not too long ago."

"Honey, I'm so sorry. I didn't know," Rita said as she slid a sympathetic arm around Sarah's shoulders, in a show of support.

"It's all right," Sarah said, wiping away a small trail of tears that had spilled over from her eyes. "At least his pain is over. He is…I mean…was suffering terribly from a rare form of bone cancer."

"Then you're taking on this project alone?"

"No. As I said, I have Alex. She is my best friend; we've known each other since we were ten." Sarah finally brightened, giving a brave smile. "Alexandra Markum. Perhaps you've heard of her? She has spent the last two Olympics coaching several of the U.S. equestrian riders."

"Actually, I'm not much into the Olympics, but I think that I have heard her name somewhere before."

"I hope you can keep a secret?" Sarah whispered childlike.

"Sure, shoot," Rita replied, anxious to be privy to any good secrets.

"Well, we really wanted to keep this quiet, but I feel like I can tell you. Alex and I want to make this more or less an equestrian retreat where people can come for as long as they like and bring their own horses for extensive riding clinics. We would also like to have some lesson horses here that Alex would train herself. They would be available for anyone from beginners to advanced riders who just want to get away for some R and R. But, the real hush-hush part of it is that she will also be training the next U.S. equestrian team here."

"Wow, that really is a fantastic concept, but are you sure that this is the place? I know we'd really love to have an Olympic-caliber celebrity in residence here, but do you think she'd go for such a little place?"

Sarah giggled. "Alex? She'd think living in a barn would be a pleasure. If she had it her way, she would strap a hammock in the stall with her horse, Peverell. She claims that he is her brother. She won her gold medal on him."

"She'd really like that?" Rita asked incredulously because her idea of roughing it was a four-star hotel.

"Believe me, she would be in seventh heaven. Sometimes I swear that the woman lives on carrots, hay, and sweet feed."

The rest of the tour went fairly quietly. Rita was relieved when it was completed. All except one room in the main house had been accessible, and Rita promised to return with a skeleton key the following morning so Sarah could see it and walk the rest of the property, the barns, and the other outbuildings. Rita sighed thankfully; at least this could be done in the daylight.

Rita was delighted to get back behind the wheel of her car. She held the wheel firmly in her hands. It felt familiar, like an old friend. Old friends. Now why did she have to come up with that thought tonight of all nights? Thankful at last to be leaving the old Conrad place, Rita involuntarily shuddered.

During the drive home, Rita played devil's advocate with her conscience. When she had finally shaken off the chill of the visit, her mind was firmly made up. She would do her best to discourage Sarah from purchasing the Conrad place. Although it meant losing a sizable commission, Sarah was just too nice of a lady to be put through the dread surrounding that place. Besides, Rita was sure that there were other properties that Sarah would like as much. This place would bring her nothing but misery and perhaps much more than Rita cared to think about. She was thankful there had been no ghostly shrieks there tonight. Rita knew for a fact they existed. She had heard them with her own ears the night she and a bunch of her pals from the orphanage had taken a dare to stay one night in the old place. The group had not made it through more than just a few hours and they had all been scared witless. They had all been huddled together in raging fear by the end. Rita remembered that she had never been so frightened. Her best friend, Suzy Parker, had just disappeared that night. Rita and her friends had called and searched everywhere; none of them could find any trace of her.

The sheriff's office had put it down to a runaway. Rita and her friends had known better. Suzy Parker had been stolen out of this world by the ghost—the legendary ghost of Grand Detour. Parking her car in the garage and hitting the automatic door closer, Rita got the house keys out of her purse. As she exited the car to go inside the automatic garage door opener lights burnt out leaving Rita in the dark.

"Marvelous," she exclaimed.

Feeling her way along in the dark she bumped her shin on something and felt a small trickle of blood run down her right calf.

"Damn," she swore.

Reaching the doorknob, she felt for the key opening and inserted the key into the hole. Rita gasped and turned around quickly in the dark. A noise startled her and a small breeze brushed against the right side of her face, blowing her hair slightly.

"Is someone there?" she stammered. Neither hearing nor feeling anything, else Rita marked the episode off to nerves.

"That old house would upset Gandhi," she chided herself.

Turning the key inside the lock Rita opened the door and walked into her house. She flicked on the lights and was shocked to see her small fish bowl overturned on the floor. It was not broken, just carefully placed on its side after someone had purposely dumped her pets all over the floor. From all appearances, it had been done quite a while ago because the goldfish and the spilled water were all dried up.

Suddenly, she had an odd sense of déjà vu. Instantly, Rita's body was overcome while a cold, unpleasant shiver ran through her, the likes of which she had never before experienced.

Her vision from earlier in the evening returned to her. Once again she could imagine seeing the young girl with the long, blond hair and pale, pink dress. The image flashed dreamlike as she whispered, "Samantha".

Rita and this girl from the past became one. It was as if Rita were seeing through Samantha's eyes as they journeyed down a cobblestone street past an alley entrance. A large dog passed the width of the alley, and Rita could feel the girl's fright. A gloved hand clamped over Samantha's mouth and forcibly drew her into the alley. It was dark, and Rita could no longer see but she could hear cloth tearing and a girl's muffled scream. Then the large dog passed again, except this time there was a pile of pink cloth torn to shreds and covered in blood.

Rita drew her black wool sport coat tightly around her. It was the same dream she had experienced many times before as a little girl in the orphanage. Although she could never understand it, she felt that it was a warning.

The howl of a large dog in her backyard panicked her. Rita's eyes filled with terror, and she gasped.

Her large, green eyes widened with fear as she was suddenly, violently grabbed from behind. The thrust of the motion made her green-tinted contacts fly out in two different directions. Her mind cried out that this could not be happening. But then she saw it. She knew instantly she was going to die. In the reflection of her kitchen window, she could see that a gloved hand held a large, glistening, eight-inch blade, poised and ready to strike. The last thing Rita McAllister felt was a burning sensation in her chest. The last thing she would ever feel was immense fear. She would never be able to warn Sarah.

The nightmare would begin again.

4

Time was passing too slowly for Sarah. She grew claustrophobic in the front seat of her car after just five minutes of waiting. The early morning sun was shining over the green lawn, and she suspected that there was a glorious fresh smell about the place after the storm of last night.

"How could a night so awful make way for such a beautiful day?" she wondered. Stepping outside of the car, Sarah closed her eyes and inhaled the clean smell of the countryside and was just thankful that she did not have to wait in the pouring rain. The sun felt so warm and refreshing to her after the long drive that all Sarah could do was smile in satisfaction after her first deep breath of air. Hands on hips, tapping her fingers lightly, she stood waiting in anticipation.

Glancing at her watch, she noted that a half an hour had already passed and she was beginning to feel antsy about seeing the rest of the property. After just a few moments of sitting in the grass, Sarah became uncomfortable. Restlessly, she began to slap at bugs, whether real or imagined, and long stalks of green grass that tickled her exposed skin. For Sarah, it was understandably normal to feel this anxious about what she felt would be the conclusive decision of her destiny. If only Rita would hurry.

Fantasizing about the house, Sarah's blue eyes fell on those big, white wicker chairs on the wraparound porch. It would be a glorious day to sit on this grandiose porch and watch the clouds roll by in the blue sky. The chairs looked terribly inviting all of a sudden, and she felt that there was no harm in making herself comfortable while waiting. Just like a proverbial Goldilocks, Sarah passed over into a comfortable nap after ten minutes in the comfortable Victorian wicker rocker. A golden sunbeam warmed her as she slept.

For the next two hours, anyone passing the old hotel grounds would see a napping figure on the porch and a beautiful sunny day. They would hear the birds singing that all in life was good.

Little did Sarah know that this would be the last truly peaceful moment she would know for a long time to come.

Someone was shaking her shoulder roughly. Sarah's brain raced to send that message to the rest of the body in an effort to rouse itself. She could feel the sensation as it shook her from a deep sleep. She sleepily stretched, opened her eyes, and saw a figure standing just behind her left shoulder. She turned to greet the figure she assumed was Rita. What she saw instead gave her quite a shock. The figure which stood to her side was not Rita McAllister, but another, younger woman. Although she had the same red hair that Rita sported, she was dressed in clothes from decades ago; her face was young and beautiful, but it also held something else there. Sarah could feel it. It was something dreadful.

"Hello," Sarah said as she tried to break the trancelike spell that had settled in.

The figure shook her head from side to side, eyes closed and face drawn in an expression of extreme pain.

"Can I help you?" Sarah asked, standing and taking a step toward the woman.

In the blink of an eye, the woman changed into a bleeding mass of torn body parts. Blood was everywhere that the horrified Sarah looked, including all over herself and her clothes. After gazing down at her bloody hands, Sarah forced herself to look back in the direction of the woman. Sarah could see tears glimmered in the apparition's eyes. Then, along with the spattering of blood, the mysterious woman faded from view within seconds.

With a nasty start, Sarah bolted upright from her chair. Her heart was pounding and she began to gasp for breath.

"It was only a dream," she whispered. "But a nasty dream. It seemed so real."

Looking at her watch, Sarah realized that it was nearly two hours past the time she was scheduled to meet Rita. Sarah suddenly felt very alone and vulnerable out here and what she wanted most was to hear the sound of another human voice. Anyone at all would do for the moment.

Rummaging around in her large handbag, she finally came up with her small flip phone. Quickly she punched in the numbers for the Van Allen real estate office and, as a voice answered, she tried to hide the traces of panic in her voice.

"Rita McAllister, please."

"I'm sorry, Rita is not in the office right now. She's due back from a viewing at any time," replied the young woman. "Could she call you?"

"I think that there is some kind of mix up," Sarah said. "She was supposed to be showing me the old Grand Detour Hotel, but that was two hours ago. She still is not here."

"Not there?" The voice seemed genuinely surprised. "Excuse me for saying so, but that's just not like Rita at all. I'm sorry. Well…let me get you Mr. Van Allen."

The line went quiet for a moment, then annoying music replaced the silence.

"Come on, come on," Sarah chanted as she glanced around nervously. "Pick up. Hurry."

Sarah, now pacing on the porch, waited while a few more moments ticked by. The bad tenor singing to the music clicked off suddenly, and a man's voice came on the line.

"Sarah Caldwell?"

"Yes, this is."

"Ron Van Allen, here. I'm sorry about any confusion there may be. I assure you that Rita is not one to forget appointments. Fact is, she's never had a sick day here in five years."

"I hope that there is nothing seriously wrong."

Sarah had lost some of her anxiety by this time. It was a comfort just to be listening to another person's voice—even if that voice was suspiciously trying to hide concern.

"Perhaps I should just try and reschedule with her? Being as reliable as you say, she must have had some kind of emergency."

"Tell you what I'll do," Van Allen said. "I have one more phone call to make and I'll drive out there myself. It will take me about twenty more minutes or less if that's all right."

"Well, I've waited this long. Certainly twenty more minutes won't make much difference," she said, sighing.

"Thanks for understanding, I'll be there in about twenty minutes."

"Okay," Sarah replied limply, then added in a thin whisper as she switched off the power to the phone, "Please make it sooner."

Van Allen hung up the phone and just as quickly snatched it back up and dialed in another local number. Had it been his imagination or had the Caldwell woman sounded nervous?

"Sheriff's office."

"Hi, Donna. Ron Van Allen. Is Ian there?"

"Sure, hang on," the cheery voice replied. A few moments of silence and then…

"Ron, what can I do for you?"

"Ian, I need a favor."

"Sure, shoot, but don't think I'm going to buy one of your high-priced homes on my salary."

"I'm serious, Ian," Van Allen snapped nervously.

"Sorry, Ron, take it easy. What's wrong?"

"Rita didn't show up for a client today, and she didn't call in either."

"Ron, maybe she's just got the flu or something." Ian suggested.

"No, not Rita. She's showing the Grand Detour Hotel today. Do you have any idea just how much coin is involved in selling the old Conrad place? Rita would be showing it on two crutches with an IV in her arm if that was what it took. This was a final showing and she was ninety-nine percent sure it was going to be a done deal."

"Maybe the client canceled?" Ian asked.

"No, I just heard from the client. In fact, I've got to run out there and break every speed law to do it so she won't walk. Besides, she sounded a little nervous, and I cannot say that I blame her—sitting out at that old place for two hours alone."

"Sounds like you just want to distract me so you won't get a speeding ticket, Ron," Ian chirped.

"Listen, Ian, I need a favor. While I go meet with this client, I need you to go check on Rita at her home."

"Sure, if you think that's necessary. I've got to go make rounds anyway. I can just leave a little early."

"I'd appreciate it if you left now. Right now! Rita wouldn't miss a sale or an appointment even if she had to get out of her deathbed to do it."

"Okay, I'll leave right now, Ron."

"Thanks, Ian," Ron said sounding relieved. "Call me as soon as you do. My cell phone. Not the office. I want to know what's going on."

"I promise."

"Just as soon as you know anything!"

"Ron, I promise that the second I know something I will give you a call on your private line."

"I appreciate it," came the final, slightly shaky reply. Ron Van Allen then quickly hung up the receiver.

Gathering up his briefcase and cell phone, Van Allen made for the parking lot. As he passed by the secretary's desk he told her where he was going and to call him for anything important. His hands shook violently as he tried to put the key in the door to his car. Something was wrong; he could feel it.

"Get hold of yourself, Ron," he commanded.

Finally getting the door open on the navy blue Lincoln, Ron climbed in, started the car, and drove off towards the waiting client.

Ian hung up the phone, and sensed that Ron was starting to panic. It was so unlike him to fly off the handle and jump to any conclusions. Ian's attempt at levity had certainly not helped the conversation at all. Ron's voice had been cracking, showing Ian just how concerned Ron was. Above all, Ian knew that Van Allen was a rock solid man when it came to sound judgment. In fact, he had been so serious when they had attended high school together that the other kids had teased Ron, telling him he was downright grim.

"Well, at least it is sunny today," Sarah mumbled, reminding herself for about the millionth time since she'd hung up the phone.

She was concerned that Rita had not shown up. Then there was that daytime nightmare that had shaken her up considerably. Since Bruce's death she had suffered from many nightmares, but none had ever been so brutal. Waiting had given her time to analyze her dream, and Sarah could justify it right down to almost the very last detail. For some reason she must have replaced Bruce with this unknown woman. Possibly it was just to distance herself from the horrible pain that Bruce had felt. The blood on her hands? Simple enough; she had felt helpless, ineffectual, unable to ease his suffering and therefore she had laid a heavy load of guilt on her own shoulders.

Feeling a little less burdened now that she had psychoanalyzed her frightening dream, she sat and inhaled the fresh air around her. Sarah knew that her decision about the property had been made.

It was just about thirty minutes later when Sarah saw the outline of a navy blue car barreling up the driveway to the hotel.

After pulling up alongside her car a tall, a strawberry-blond man with a nicely manicured mustache and beard practically jumped out of the car.

"Ron Van Allen," he said as he smiled and extended his hand.

"Sarah Caldwell."

"I apologize again for whatever misunderstanding has taken place. And I'm also very sorry that I am later than I had promised."

"No need," Sarah reassured him. "From the way you describe Rita, and I must include my own impressions of her as well, I'm sure that whatever has delayed her must be very important. I assure you she was extremely professional last evening. As a matter of fact, I kept her waiting last night and she never said a word. The least that I can do is give her the same courtesy."

There was an uncomfortable silence, and Sarah noted that Van Allen appeared to be very pale underneath his fairly health tan. Worry was written all over his face, and Sarah felt that it was up to her to try to lighten the moments to follow.

"How about we start with the barns?" Sarah suggested.

"F-fine," he stammered.

"I'd like to go over the grounds first and then look at the boundary maps one last time, if that's all right."

"Whatever you would like," Ron said, forcing a smile. "You're the customer."

Sarah secretly thought that hiking around the property first might loosen the tension she knew he had to be feeling.

In a short time she proved herself to be correct. Van Allen began to get a little color back in his face, almost to the point of being robust. The only feature that did not leave him was the furrowed brow of deep worry.

Sarah found it is very difficult to be gloomy on a sunny day in the country. The songbirds alone were almost deafening. Instead of letting the afternoon pass in a gloomy silence, Sarah rattled on and on about Alex's huge plans for the equestrian center. She could tell that her inane prattling had helped lighten Van Allen's mood.

Although Sarah was herself merely a weekend rider at best, she bragged about her friend, Alexandra Markum, and her plans to have a fully equipped, three-day event center. He definitely showed some interest in the fact that the U.S. equestrian team would train here in town. Judging from some of his confused looks, Sarah could tell that he had no knowledge at all of the horse world.

"I understand that a lawyer comes every six months to check up on me er, us?"

"Yes," Van Allen answered. "There is a clause in the will that states that the property must be kept to the period."

"Alex will want to put in both indoor and outdoor riding arenas. Of that I'm sure," Sarah stated. "In addition, I know that she will have plans for cross-country obstacles. Before any final paperwork is done, I will need to know if the firm handling the contract for the sale will accept the additions we want to add. I can assure them that we would adhere to any exterior plans so it would not look out of place on the estate."

"I promise to find out the details of anything you want," Van Allen offered. "Why don't you make a list of improvements you would like to make as we walk around? Then I can fax it to the law firm this afternoon to see if the changes you would like to make would be in the realm of possibility."

"That would be marvelous!"

"I'd like to thank you," Ron said after an uncomfortable silence.

"For what?" Sarah replied innocently.

"For rambling on about nothing in particular. I know what you have been trying to do, and it has helped me. I apologize if I seemed grim and unfriendly."

"Oh, that," she replied with a smirk. "I dabble in psychology when I get the urge, but I'm not licensed so you can't sue me."

"I'll do better than that. I'll just go over these blueprints with you, but not here."

"Where did you have in mind?"

"The Blue Ram, for lunch."

"The Blue Ram?" she questioned. "What's that?"

"A nice little outdoor cafe that doubles at night for the local tavern. I was thinking that this afternoon we could go over this in more detail. You can meet me at the office and we can walk there together. I think that it is the least I can do for your doctor bill," he said with a smile.

"That looks nice."

"What does?"

"A genuine smile! Don't lose it because I'd like to think I had one friend in this town."

While Ron had quickly gathered up his briefcase and had begun the drive out to meet Sarah, Ian had sped out in the squad car to check up on Rita. It had bothered Ian immensely that Ron had been so agitated about the entire Rita thing. No matter how many times he turned it over in his head, he could never remember Ron displaying such edgy characteristics.

Ian had spent enough time with the two of them to know that there could be no relationship between Ron and Rita except the professional one that they shared. Ron behaved in a manner more characteristic of a big brother, and Ian fervently hoped that Rita was home with nothing more than a bad flu bug.

Pulling into her driveway, he slammed the squad car door solidly and walked casually over to the garage window. Peeking quickly through the windowpanes, Ian could make out the familiar lines of a Lexus through the sheers hung on the inside of the windows. Seeing that Rita's car stood silently in the garage, he breathed a quick sigh of relief.

"Curtains in a garage! Women!"

With the car present, Ian figured that the circumstances must be illness related as he had first suspected. As long as he was here, Ian decided that he would alleviate Ron's fears and check up on her anyway. Still, it did strike Ian as strange that if Rita was indeed home with a cold or flu she hadn't at least called in to the office. The facts were just not adding up correctly, and he hated that.

Just a quick knock on the door, he thought. Check up on Rita; then call Ron. He should make sure that everything was all right and that she did not need any medical help. He withdrew his face from the glass and began his walk to the front door.

Arriving at the front door, he rang the bell. Mentally, he quickly drew up a vivid picture of Rita answering the door in pink curlers and a matching pink fuzzy bathrobe and smelling distinctly of Vicks.

When no answer came in a reasonable amount of time, he began knocking on the door.

"Rita," he called loudly.

Worry flooded back to haunt him as seconds flew by and his knocking had turned into almost a frenzied pounding accompanied with the occasional shouts.

As quickly as the pink flu scenario had come to Ian's mind, it had vanished. Now, in its stead, rose the possibility of a sudden stroke, seizure, or perhaps something worse.

Unable to rouse any answer to his increasingly demanding summons, Ian began a systematic inspection through all the windows, hoping to catch a glimpse of the occupant. He forcibly rattled any and all doors. Still there was no answer.

Lastly, he came to the kitchen window. All he could see on the floor was an overturned fish bowl. The frown on his face turned into a full-blown scowl, and he found himself back at the front door.

He began an immediate, intensified search of the front door area. Only this time he was searching for something. A key. A hidden key. Under the mat—no. On top of the porch light, the door frame—no and no.

In utter frustration, he picked up a large stone from her rock garden by the door and was about to fling it through a window when he realized what sat next to the rocks. Ian beheld a large pile of dog poop underneath those neatly trimmed hedges. Grinning, he remembered that Rita had no dog, and that he knew for a fact that she would be scared to death of any dog that could make a pile of this size. Likewise, she would be appalled to find that this was present in her meticulously cared for garden.

Lightly, Ian tapped the suspect pile with the toe of his police-issued shoes. Sure enough, it was one of those plastic piles for hiding a spare key in. A dual purpose, he thought, because burglars would see the large pile and expect a very large dog to go with it. Feeling a little stupid, he felt that he should have guessed as much. Rita was a known junk magazine addict. If an item had the slightest use, it was certain that Rita owned it.

Inserting the key in the lock, Ian opened the door.

"Rita," he called cautiously.

There was no answer. The house produced nothing but nerve-racking silence. It was all too quiet to suit Ian's tastes.

Ian roamed stealthily from room to room, until all that remained to search was the kitchen and the basement, the door of which was just off the kitchen. A nagging feeling that something was horribly wrong continued to plague him, and he took great care not to touch anything and smear any possible fingerprints. Fearing a possible abduction, he did not want to ruin any clues that might be there, waiting to be discovered.

Noting quickly the dried, curled up fish on the floor, Ian stepped gingerly around them, jerked open the door, and switched on the lights leading down the stairs of the basement. He called out Rita's name several times and descended the stairs. After checking every corner of the basement, Ian turned in hesitation and slowly walked over to the dark crawl space. Pulling out his flashlight, he poured a large ray of light into the black hole and peered inside. He breathed an audible sigh of relief. It was empty, except for a few cobwebs in the corners.

Puzzled, he returned to the main floor and then noticed that the door to the garage did not give the appearance of being shut properly. Upon closer investigation, he found the keys were still in the other side of the lock.

Ian turned, he noticed that next to one of the dried up fish lay something small and green. Curious, he bent down for a closer examination. Ian recognized the item. It was one of Rita's contact lenses. Now fearing that some sort of abduction must have indeed taken place, Ian ran to the squad car and radioed in that he would like to request a team from the state police, including a crime scene investigator, for a possible kidnapping. The address was given, and the wait until their arrival began.

Ian walked back through the door, and an unnatural chill ran up his spine, ending by making the small hairs on the back of his neck stand up on end. Had he just heard something? No, surely that was just the sound of the furnace kicking on. This empty house and the circumstances surrounding it were beginning to make him jumpy.

Taking a clean cloth from his back pocket, he began to make a second, more intensive and careful search of the house for any signs of Rita. This time he would not only open every closet, he would check behind every hatbox as well.

A search of the bedroom, closets, and bathroom yielded nothing that he did not already know. For example, Rita was the worse kind of clotheshorse in existence. Her shoes alone would put that Marcos woman to shame. It also appeared that Rita never threw anything away, even if it had been out of style for the last ten years. Her bell-bottoms from high school were even still here. Naturally they were in style again, except the kids insisted that they were "flares" and not at all like the bell-bottoms of earlier years. Yeah right; and he was Superman in emergencies and mild-mannered Clark Kent during the day.

Judging from the contents of her closet and the full set of luggage that sat boldly in residence, he arrived at another fact. No one had picked her up, and Rita had no emergencies to run off to. Although Ian felt it a futile avenue, he made a mental note to run a check at the local cab company to see if it was a possibility that someone had driven here and picked her up.

The evidence, or rather the lack thereof, in the bathroom, made it even more conclusive that Rita had not left willingly. Nothing was missing. From her contact solution to her toothbrush and toothpaste, everything that would need to be taken was present. No one has such an emergency that they cannot at least grab their toothbrush on their way out the door.

It was definitely looking more and more like an abduction or foul play to him. Glancing out the bathroom window, Ian thought he saw the tail end of a large dog and heard a low, menacing growl to go along with the retreating figure.

"Glad I tested that pile first," he said. "Looks like maybe Rita had a large dog visitor after all."

Lastly, Ian headed for the one place he had not checked out—the hall closet. Ian approached the door and twisted the knob. As he opened the door, Ian caught something out of the corner of his eye. It was long, glistening of silver, and moving swiftly. The object surprised him as it flew out of the closet, rushing at his face. Ian threw his arms up as a natural reflex to cover his face and redirect the oncoming blow.

His heart pounded so loudly he thought it would burst as he threw himself backwards to miss the expected impact.

* * *

He laughed a little at the start he had given himself and picked himself up off the floor.

"Jesus!" Ian swore. "I wonder if she could fit any more in this closet!"

Ian bent over to pick up the errant vacuum arm that had fallen straight out at him. His rapid breathing had returned to normal, and he carefully placed the metal pole back into the closet so it would not repeat that fall for the state cops. Upon further investigation of the closet he found nothing but coats, more shoes, and a wide array of things that obviously Rita could find no other place for in the house.

Promptly, Ian heard many vehicles pull up into the driveway. Walking outside, he saw the familiar caravan of faces belonging to the state csi boys. The entourage came complete with flashing lights but no sirens.

It was just as well, he figured, because he could not possibly look at those dried up fish on the kitchen floor another minute. He could only hope that Rita did not resemble her pets in any way.

Ian hoped that the crime lab pros could make some sense out of all of this. He would make himself available as the state cops combed the home, car, and surrounding area. They would perhaps need some background information that he could provide.

At the very least, the lab rats would need him to speak to old Harold Anderson next door. Harold was the kind of man who always came to the front door prepared. Prepared that is, with a hunting rifle large enough to shoot an elephant, unless he knew you.

Ian hoped that a clue of some kind could be turned up. Rita had no family to demand a ransom from. She had come to town early on as an orphan. Ron Van Allen had taken her in and given her a real life, but she really had no one. The thing that bothered him most was that there was no note. Things just were not adding up for him. Cops liked things to add up. Otherwise, they tended not to sleep until the facts did add up. It was a stubborn trait that had been passed down through the heredity lines of his family, or so he'd been told.

Inner cop intuition told Ian that he would be getting precious little sleep from now on. Another worry echoed in his brain. Just what was he going to tell Ron about all of this? Ron's fears had proven to be well-founded, but how would he take the news? And what exactly was the news?

People just don't disappear off the face of the earth.

Or did they?

In this town, as history proclaimed, anything unfortunate was possible.

7

The smoky interior of The Blue Ram was dark and depressing. Upon entering, Sarah's first impression had been to turn immediately around and leave. Uncomfortable vibes sent warnings out to her that this location had not been a very good idea. She could feel a chill from the damp air of the place, and noticed that the decor was like an old stone cellar. Pictured upon a pillar that Sarah passed was a weathered relief of a grotesque and frightening gargoyle-type figure with a ram's head. Sarah gasped in alarm while her eyes stared at the twisted features. She could feel her blood curdle just looking at it. Sarah recognized the blue coloring; it resembled the original blue indigo ink used to reflect bugs away from the doors of houses in the southern states. If one looked closely beneath the flaked off bits of blue there was a slight hint of gold underneath. The outline of the beast gave Sarah a wicked chill, and she turned her back on the picture quickly. Sarah could not find a reason, but she found the image of the beast horrid and bothersome.

With a silent sigh of relief, Sarah found the exterior to be the total opposite from what she had previewed inside. The sidewalk cafe boasted a bright cheery atmosphere with the outdoor tables of white and blue topped with blue umbrellas. The chipper little waitress awarded them with their menus, announced her name as Carol, and whisked away to get them both a tall glass of ice tea.

"I must tell you that for a minute I was worried when I saw the inside of this place," Sarah said as she sat at the table.

"Yes, the inside is rather depressing. I make it a practice to only sit out here. During the winter months I don't even frequent here because the inside tends to make me overly melancholy. Perhaps it is the owner that depresses me even more," Ron said.

"You sound jealous," Sarah chided him.

"Maybe. I don't really know. Jack Darwin is probably the most prosperous man I have ever had the misfortune to know."

"I take it he's the owner?"

"Forgive me," Ron apologized. "Yes, he is and he has the most uncanny stroke of luck I have ever known. Nice enough fellow, I suppose, but for some reason always rubbed me the wrong way."

As if on a stage cue, a tall, dark, thin and rather handsome man appeared at their tableside.

"Allow me to introduce myself," he said, addressing Sarah only. "Jack Darwin."

The stranger bent forward from the waist, grasped her hand and kissed it. Embarrassed, Sarah pulled her hand away quickly, startling the newcomer.

"I'm s-s-sorry," she stammered. "I just don't know what came over me. Forgive me, it was very rude of me."

"Please," he pleaded. "Think nothing of it. It is I who should apologize to you. Somehow I have upset you and I only hope that you will forgive me and give me a chance to make it up to you. Often my attention to proper treatment of a true lady is thought of as old-fashioned."

"Of course," Sarah stuttered.

"I merely concluded that a woman as beautiful as yourself was used to being treated—how shall I say?—in a more civilized fashion."

"Don't scare her off before she gets a chance to sign on the line for contract for deed, Darwin," Van Allen scolded.

"Oh, she is a client," Darwin replied while smirking elegantly. "That explains it; I thought your taste in women was finally improving."

Again, directing his full attention to Sarah, Darwin ignored the indignant look of outrage he had purposely put on Van Allen's face.

"Are you interested in purchasing a local business, young lady?"

"The Grand Detour Hotel," Sarah answered rather breathlessly. "Hopefully, if all goes well."

"Congratulations," Darwin beamed. "That is a fine old place. I have tried to purchase it many times myself, but I have not been able to come up with just enough capitol at the correct time. For years, there has been a tie up of some kind or another with the will of the previous owner. Perhaps in the future we could discuss the plans you have made for it?"

"Perhaps," Sarah replied uncomfortably, not wanting to seem rude.

"The plans are to make it into an equestrian retreat," Van Allen said hotly. "Miss Caldwell is a close friend of the Olympic equestrian coach and gold-medal winner, Alexandra Markum."

"How very interesting," Darwin replied. "Miss Caldwell, you must bring Miss Markum with you when she arrives. A celebrity of her stature would be a most welcome addition to our little community. I would love to entertain you both sometime over lunch."

"Thank you," Sarah replied meekly.

"If you will excuse me now, I have other guests to see to. Enjoy your meal."

Jack Darwin walked away and Sarah caught herself holding her breath. She quickly exhaled and smiled in discomfort.

"Is he always that charming?" she asked.

"Yes. Perhaps that's why all the men in town have some unseen grudge against him. Forgive me for spouting off at him. It gave me a great deal of satisfaction to finally know something before he did."

"Oh, it's okay. Only I wonder how he knew?"

"Knew what?"

"That Alex isn't here yet?" Sarah questioned. "Maybe I'm just being silly. He probably decided if she were here, she would be here." Indicating the table with her outstretched hands.

As if on cue, Carol, their waitress, arrived, pad in hand to take their luncheon selections. Scribbling down a chef salad for Sarah, and a fish and chips basket for Ron, she scurried away to attend to her other waitress duties.

After ordering, they brought out the blueprints, spread them over the table, and talked them over in great detail. Sarah was able to give Ron a short but detailed list of changes she and Alex would wish to make along with a basic sketch of some of the obstacles that would be required for the equine training facility.

Ron excused himself and walked next door to his office so he could fax all of the details and sketches to the lawyers' office. He hoped that yet this afternoon Sarah could have her answers.

Lunch arrived at the same time that Ron returned to the table, and the pair ate and discussed plans.

"I think you'll find that your business and yourselves will be readily welcomed here in Grand Detour," Ron said. "You will find the residents friendly and helpful."

"I'm happy to hear that they will welcome a new business and new people," Sarah replied. "Sometimes when you move and start over you find that you are treated like outsiders. I lived in a town for several years and found that I never fit in."

"This town has always been one step behind the eight-ball. They will see your business venture as a way to get some wealth back into the city coffers. The celebrity status of Miss Markum will give the community a jolt. Of that I'm certain."

"You know, Ron, Alex perceives herself to be an average person. She tends to shy away from any notoriety. The last thing she wants is to be treated differently."

"Surely with all of her wonderful accomplishments she has been able to embrace her more public status?"

"Alex," Sarah laughed, "is just this side of a recluse. She will only stick her nose out of the front door if it has something to do with a horse or a person in trouble. For all the stink she makes about people in general, she'll gallop across the country to help someone who's desperate."

"I've read some of the articles. I think she's amazingly gifted. I can't wait to meet her myself."

Carol reappeared and asked about dessert; Ron's phone rang.

"Ron Van Allen," he answered nervously.

Hearing the stress in his voice, Sarah could also see Ron's calm exterior draining away. Van Allen's coloring faded, and his eyes showed that he was becoming increasingly upset by the second as he listened intently to the person on the other end of the phone. He said "uh-huh" several times in response before speaking again.

"Right now I'm finishing lunch up at The Blue Ram," Van Allen said into the cell phone. "Could you come over here and go into it in more detail? Uh-huh. Okay. I'll see you then in a few minutes."

"Anything I can do to help?" Sarah asked.

"No, I'm afraid not at this time," Van Allen said quietly. "Will you be all right finding your way back to your accommodations? I'm afraid that I have a rather urgent meeting to attend to right now."

"I'm sure that I will be just fine," Sarah replied. "But, if you don't mind an outsider saying so, you look right now like you could use the support of a friend. If you don't mind me being a little nosy, was that call about Rita?"

"Yes, it was," he said hesitantly. "That call was from a friend of mine, Ian. He's the sheriff here now, but the two of us went all through school together. He's known Rita since she came here from the orphanage. Ian and I are not the closest of friends, but he has always been a straight shooter when you've needed someone you could count on."

"The sheriff? Oh no. Nothing dreadful has happened, has it?" Sarah quickly pictured in her mind the woman from the previous night. She had seemed a genuinely likable person with obviously dedicated compassion for her clients.

"They think that it is some kind of random abduction. Ian didn't want to go over it on the phone. When the news is solemn, I think he likes to deliver it in person. I can't say I blame him. It's rather impersonal over the phone to hear any gory details. I can't ask you to sit in on that."

"I will have you know, Ron, that my husband was a police officer. I have heard my fair share of many such horrors from him. Besides that, I suffered through the added turmoil of watching him die a horrible death, lingering for months from a rare bone cancer and suffering through a pain that no one could ease. I promise you, I can and will be strong enough."

Sarah lifted her hand and placed it gently on Ron's hand, squeezing gently in support for his obvious consternation.

"Thank you," he said quietly. "I could use a friend just now."

A squad car pulled up outside the sidewalk cafe. Exiting and slamming the door, the occupant spotted Van Allen and made his way over to the table quickly. Sarah watched the tall, blond-haired man draw closer to them. As he drew closer, Sarah could read the worry behind those wire-rimmed, green-gray eyes.

A few of the other luncheon patrons looked up as the uniformed man passed by their tables. Exhibiting the same curiosity that affects passersby at a roadside accident, they continued to stare until they knew which table would end his journey.

The sheriff arrived at the side of their table. Ron Van Allen silently gestured that he sit down. Ian took a hesitant look at Sarah and then turned back to Van Allen for some reassurance.

"Ian," Ron began. "This is Sarah Caldwell. She has just become a new, supportive friend to me in the span of this afternoon and has committed herself to stay through our rather unpleasant conversation to provide moral support. For this, I thank her."

Ian then nodded politely in Sarah's direction.

"Ma'am," Ian replied, briefly touching his trooper's hat and drawing up a chair to sit down.

"Sarah," Ron added, "Ian Valin, our Grand Detour sheriff."

"Pleased to meet you," both said in unison with a slight smile of politeness towards the other.

"Ron, we believe that Rita may have been kidnapped."

"Who would do such a thing? Have you got any idea who might have taken her or where?"

"No, I'm sorry, Ron. I wish I had a better idea, but there was no note at all, and with Rita being an orphan…well, I have to assume that she was not taken for any kind of ransom."

"You're saying that you don't hold out much hope then," Ron said glumly.

"No, Ron," Ian said slowly. "The scenarios that the state troopers and myself have formulated really don't hold out a lot of hope based on the facts. I'm just hoping that she was, you know, possibly attacked and then dropped off. There is still a slight chance that we might still find her abandoned somewhere. We hope that the kidnapper perhaps just assaulted her and then turned her loose."

"You mean raped or something?"

"We feel that it could be a possible motive."

"Oh God," Ron moaned.

"The alternative scenarios that we have paint a much blacker picture, Ron. Unfortunately, I gave you the best choice first."

"Must you be so blunt?" Sarah demanded.

"Look, Ms. Caldwell," Ian replied tiredly. "I know both of these people very well. And they know me. I will not build up false hopes or tell them lies that will not happen. Ron must be prepared for the worst. I will do everything in my power to find Rita, but I will not sugar coat her disappearance. It makes everyone out to be a fool."

"I guess I understand. My husband felt the same way as you do. This is just my first time being on the receiving end; I've always heard about it in a third party kind of aspect. There is no good way to put it, is there?"

"No, Ms. Caldwell, there isn't. If you happen to find one, though, you let me know about it. I promise you that I don't like it any more than you do."

"I understand. And I'm sorry," Sarah said apologetically.

"What about lab results?" Van Allen interjected. "I know that you mentioned that you had called them in on this."

"Nothing conclusive as of now. Her car was still snug in the garage. They dusted the entire house for prints, but nothing is missing or disturbed, except Rita, of course. The only other thing disturbed, strangely enough, was a bowl of fish. There was also a single, green contact lens on the kitchen floor. It is as if she had vanished. There weren't any signs of a struggle. The lab rats hope to have something more for me by morning."

Van Allen bent over the table to rest his eyes onto his thumbs, as if in meditation.

"I'm headed up to Jack Elliot's right now," Ian said. "Maybe he can turn up something. Anyhow, I hope so because the county lab detectives couldn't turn up anything to substantiate a lead to follow without further trace evidence testing."

"Jack Elliot?" Sarah interjected.

"Ah, yes, ma'am," Ian replied. "Jack's got the best noses this side of the Mississippi."

"Noses?"

"Bloodhounds."

"Oh."

"She's my sister, you know," Van Allen mumbled quietly, unmoving.

"Rita McAllister is your sister?" Sarah asked.

"Your sister, Ron?" Ian said, surprised. "I never knew."

"Actually, my half sister," Van Allen added, sitting upright. "You see, my father had an affair early on in his marriage. Rita's mother put her in an orphanage so nothing would soil my father's reputation."

"How sad," Sarah said comfortingly.

"Rita's mother really did love him, you know. Not that my father ever deserved it. The poor woman died of a broken heart. I never knew her name. After my mother died, he had the decency to tell me about it so we could bring Rita here to the town's orphanage and give her some sort of normal life."

"Did she know?"

"Yes. After my father's death, I felt I owed it to her. So Rita would know that she was not alone in the world." Ron looked down, choking back his emotions. "We are closer than most full brothers and sisters ever are."

Ian pushed back his chair, got up from the table, and grasped Ron's shoulder.

"I want you to know that I'll do everything in my power to see this thing to a conclusion," Ian said.

"I just want you to find her. One way or another."

"Ma'am, it's been a pleasure," Ian said. "I just wish we could have met under happier circumstances."

"Me too," Sarah replied glumly.

As Ian turned and strode away to the waiting squad car, Sarah turned to Ron.

"You just sit here," Sarah said. "I'll get the check and bring the car around so you don't have to face anyone just now."

"Thank you."

Getting the check and paying it was easy. Getting away from Jack Darwin quickly was the difficult part. She hoped she hadn't been too rude when she had told him to mind his own business.

Jogging for the car, she wondered what kind of community she had gotten herself into. Damn, she thought. She could sure use Bruce now. Sarah would have given anything for his wonderful cop insight on this place. She hoped and prayed that Alex would arrive in town sooner than they had discussed. She knew that when Alex was on the road there would be no way to contact her, because when Alex was on the road, she did not *want* to be contacted.

Sarah drove over to the curb alongside the main door to The Blue Ram. She hadn't felt this alone before. Here she was in a town of strangers and already she was knee deep in a tragedy.

A week ago, a quick voice mail had told Alex that everything was in order for the equestrian center. Her cross-country drive had been uneventful, and now, on a dark, 4 AM overcast morning, her large truck and trailer pulled into the nearly empty parking lot of the Sleepy Hollow Riding Academy in Collinsville, Illinois. Alexandra Markum was pleased that the owner selling the horse had agreed to such an early morning tryout. More often than not, she was finding that having a large name in the horse world left her little anonymity when it came to looking for new horses.

Sleeping in the back seat of the extended cab and snoring lightly was her groom, Kendra Phillips. The blankets were drawn up around her in a tight little cocoon, and Alex simply did not have the heart to wake the kid up.

With a quick check of the monitor for the camera mounted inside the horse trailer, Alex could see that both horses were happily munching on hay. She smiled and silently wished that she could at times be a pampered horse in some nice person's barn. To be a lucky horse you received two, perhaps three, square meals a day, all-day pasture turnout where you could romp with your friends, and usually a forty-five-minute workout a day.

What a pleasure it must be to dodge the handicaps that people impose on one another! As a horse she would be spared the interaction that occurs when a stable owner has *the God* complex—Meaning when their tempers are lost over the least little things, their reasoning is usually selfish or irrational, and their fuses far too short. What, she wondered, drew these people into the horse world where patience was probably the most important tool they could possess? Being a horse, she could hide from these people as well as herself. Emitting a deep sigh, Alex turned off the engine and slipped out of the truck cab to enter the building.

A horse stable in the early morning hours is among one of the most peaceful places on earth. From the aroma assailing her nostrils, Alex could tell that the inhabitants were contentedly chomping on their sweet-smelling alfalfa hay. A few pleasant nickers greeted Alex as she entered quietly and closed the door.

"Hi," a disembodied voice said.

A blond-haired girl of about seventeen, complete with braces, rose up and looked through the bars of the first stall on the left.

"Wow, you really are Alexandra Markum! I thought that maybe you were one of my friends pulling my leg on the phone last night."

Alex paused. This was always an embarrassing spot for her. She felt totally inept when it came to expressing herself around the human race. If it were not for her gifted riding abilities, she would have never ventured away from her people on the reservation.

"I'm sorry. I put you on the spot didn't I?" the young girl asked as she emerged from the stall and placed the stall guard over the opening.

"You must be Chrissy," Alex said.

"I am. And this," Chrissy stated with pride, "is Silvia." Reaching out, she touched the delicate gray's face which now hung over the stall guard of the opened door.

"She's lovely," Alex remarked.

"I have her all brushed and ready to go for you, Ms. Markum."

"Call me Alex, please."

"Okay," Chrissy replied, smiling.

"Chrissy, would you take her out first and walk her down the aisle away from me and then jog her back?"

"Sure thing, Ms. Mark…er, um, sorry, Alex."

The pair walked down the aisle away from her, and Alex could tell that the mare's manner with the girl was more than pleasant. Just one look told her that the temperament the mare displayed was exactly what she had been looking for. Silvia jogged back quietly, if not a little on the lazy side.

"The indoor arena is right through there," Chrissy said, pointing through the large opening. "I flipped the light switches just a few minutes ago. They should be on by the time we get her saddled."

Chrissy handed Silvia's reins over to Alex. She didn't wish to hover over the famous rider and smother her. It was an honor to be able to say that an Olympic gold medalist had ridden her horse. She climbed the stairs to the clubhouse viewing room so Alex could have the privacy that she had requested last night on the telephone.

The woman swung easily into the saddle, and Chrissy found herself amazed at how well Silvia began to move under the expert rider's guidance. Tears welled into her eyes when Chrissy realized that more than likely this would be her last morning as Silvia's owner. Although Chrissy loved the little mare, her riding had improved enough that she was ready to move on to a horse that was less of a baby-sitter. In her heart, she knew there was no better owner her horse could go to.

Last night on the phone, the woman had told her that she was looking for a horse as a gift for her best friend. This friend did not have much in the way of riding skills and was in desperate need of a horse that seemed to fit Silvia's qualifications. A sad catch resounded in Chrissy's throat; she remembered that the woman had also assured her that if this was indeed the right horse, she would be pampered and kept by them for the rest of her natural life.

A hand reached out from the darkness behind her, and Chrissy swung around with a gasp when it touched her shoulders.

"Who's that?" Jan whispered.

"Jan, what are you doing here so early?" Chrissy questioned sternly.

"Hey, we were supposed to go on an early trail ride this morning remember? Does that fancy rig outside belong to this woman?"

"Yes."

"Chrissy, you are being awfully tight-lipped about this! Who is she?"

"Oh, Jan," Chrissy wailed. "You are going to spoil everything! That's Alexandra Markum out there."

"Oh, ha-ha," Jan snickered. "You had me going there for a minute. Very funny!"

"I am not kidding."

"No, you're not are you," Jan replied with a dawn of realization.

"Please, Jan, I need you to be quiet and stay out of sight," Chrissy pleaded. "She specifically requested to see Silvia this early so she would have complete privacy."

"Okay," Jan said.

The room was quiet again and both girls stood motionlessly behind the viewing room's darkened windows and watched the woman in the riding ring. Effortlessly, Alex balanced the horse and moved her around the ring gracefully.

"Hey, when did your horse learn to side pass?" Jan whined.

"She doesn't know how," Chrissy said.

"But she's doing it, and darn nicely I might say," Jan stammered.

"I can see that. I tried to get her to do that a million times and never got anywhere."

"Do you think she'd give me an autograph?" Jan asked.

"Jan!" Chrissy spat out under her breath. "Don't blow this. I think she really likes her and my parents aren't going to let me keep two horses for very much longer. Besides, she's really nice. The rumors about her have the facts all wrong. She's not the least bit snobbish. She really seems to be quite shy."

"Sorry," Jan muttered.

* * *

The figure in the ring brought the horse down to a walk and reached down to slightly loosen the girth holding the saddle in place. Silvia was allowed to walk out and stretch her nose as far to the ground as she wished in order to release any tension in her back. The rider leaned forward and patted the horse's neck affectionately. She was absolutely the perfect horse for Sarah. Alex only hoped that she would not wake Kendra when she loaded this horse in with the others.

Heading back towards Silvia's stall, Alex could see slight movement behind the darkened glass of the observation room. Even though she could detect a second person behind the darkened windows, Alex was very thankful that Chrissy had kept everything as quiet as she had originally promised. The last place that Alex had tried to slip into quietly had resulted in no less than twenty-five giggling teenage horse owners all clamoring for her autograph. She had been mortified.

After removing the equipment from the horse's back, Alex ran a trained hand over the animal to check for any unwanted physical reactions. There were none. She curried the horse lightly to rid her of the saddle marks and retrieved a peppermint candy from her pocket. The ears of the greedy animal perked up with the crinkling noise of the cellophane wrapper. This was another sign that the horse has been pampered by her owner. Silvia delicately took the candy from Alex's outstretched palm like the true lady that Alex believed her to be. Horses were such loving and gentle creatures by nature; Alex was often horrified as to the way in which many of her brothers and sisters were treated and tortured.

"You're quite the lady, aren't you?" Alex asked softly of the horse as she stroked the mare's glossy neck.

Without turning around, Alex sensed that Chrissy had resurfaced and was now standing behind her. In her pocket, Alex reached for the check that she had made out in case she'd taken a liking to the horse. When she turned around, Alex could tell from the look on her face that the girl was torn and fighting to hide tears.

"Chrissy," Alex smiled as she began, "you have done a really nice job with Silvia. She is just what I am looking for. I've brought along a check. Although it is short notice, I'd like to take her with me today."

The brimming tears that Chrissy had kept contained now spilled freely down her cheeks.

Walking past the horse, which was now standing in cross ties, Alex reached out and hugged the girl.

"I'll take good care of your baby, Chrissy. You're welcome to write or e-mail me about her anytime. I promise that I will answer every communication. Attached to the check is my card. On it you will find my e-mail address and my new address in Grand Detour. If you're going to be anywhere near that area, let me know and you can drop in and see her anytime."

"I'm sorry," Chrissy replied with a tearful sniff. "I've had her such a long time, and she has taught me so much. My parents will not let me keep both horses. I know you'll take good care of her."

"I promise."

"I'll help you load her up, Ms. Markum," Chrissy offered.

"Alex."

"Sorry. Alex."

The truck and trailer pulled down the driveway with three horses loaded inside. Alex smiled. It was nice to know that from time to time you can meet a person that could change your perspective. It's such a pity that the world could not be made up of more people like Chrissy.

"Silvia's gone already?" Jan questioned, coming out of the stables

"Yeah," sniffed Chrissy. "Here's the check and her card."

"Wait," Jan interjected quickly as she fingered the documents. "There's something else written on the back of that card. Holy cow, Chrissy! Do you know what this says?"

"No," Chrissy replied, snuffling.

"The note on the back of this says that you and your new horse are entitled to a free one-week stay at the Grand Detour Hotel equestrian retreat. It also says that you are to receive one week's worth of lessons. All for free!"

"Now who's pulling my leg?"

"Honest! It's right there. You can read it for yourself!"

Chrissy snatched the papers out of Jan's hand; it did indeed say that she was invited to be a guest any time she wished.

"Wow!"

* * *

Turning the large rig off the country road connecting to Interstate 55, Alex felt a sense of panic flow over her. The electric charge running through her spine normally signaled a warning of rough times ahead. Something was going to happen, and from the feeling, it was to be on a very large scale, too. Kendra stirred in the backseat of the cab; Alex cleared her mind and fought to shake off the bad feeling. Upsetting Kendra any further than the poor kid already was would lead to irreversible instability. Alex would never forgive herself if she were the inevitable cause of this child's collapse.

9

The lane leading up to the magnificent house was dark now. It was past eleven o'clock, and the headlights for the large truck and six-horse deluxe trailer lit up a small path. Fatigue had settled in on the driver, and she felt as though she had been on the road driving forever. It is really funny, she thought, how much longer a drive could be when you're hauling a large horse trailer.

She glanced over in the passenger seat to see the deep-sleeping form of her new groom. Alex hated to wake her, but it was a necessary evil.

Gently, Alex began to shake her lightly by the shoulder so she did not startle her. Sleepily, the young girl began to stir. She opened her eyes at the same time that a huge flash of lightning lit up the old hotel making it almost daylight.

"Nice timing, Alex," she snapped. "Were you just trying to scare me or hoping I'd go blind in the flash?"

"Now, Kendra, really," Alex teased. "You think I'm psychic enough to know just when and where that stuff is going to strike? You know, Grandfather is always saying that I have the *sight*. Perhaps he is right."

"Sure, now you're going to pull that ancient Grandfather Sitting Bull crap on me again."

"Actually, his name is Lightning Horse."

"Is? You mean you are suggesting to me that this fictitious person is even alive?"

"Of course. Why? Do you think that I am too old to have a living grandfather?"

"Trust me on this, Alex. You so do not want to hear my answer. By the way, what is Lightning Horse supposed to stand for?"

"It stands for swift, intelligent, and insightful."

"Do you have one of those corny names too?"

"Of course. However, humility prevents me from telling what it is or what it means. Besides, you couldn't pronounce it."

"Yeah, sure. Whatever, Alex."

"You know, one of these days, you're going to lose that chip on your shoulder, Kendra. You may even stop being a hunchback!"

"Ha-ha, Alex. Gee, that was witty!"

Lights suddenly came on in the front foyer of the building, and a figure came through the front door to race ahead to the stabling area. The closer they drew to the buildings, the more lights they could see turning on everywhere.

"God, who lives here? Frankenstein?" Kendra asked sarcastically.

"Now, Kendra," Alex warned. "You be nice to Sarah. She's my oldest and dearest friend. Not to mention one of my only friends. She's not likely to understand all your sarcasms like I do."

"I know, I know."

Alex opened her mouth to speak again, but before she could utter a sound Kendra had beaten her to it.

"And above all don't mention Bruce. Jeez, Alex, you'd think I was totally insensitive."

"Only when it comes to me and my ancestors I'm sure," Alex scolded.

"Alex, you know you made the whole thing up. I don't even think you have a drop of Indian blood in you. Besides, who ever heard of an Indian with green eyes!"

"Half, Kendra. I keep telling you that I'm only half. And it's *Native American*! Believe what you will. Nothing I can conjure up in sage wisdom will make you think otherwise."

"Alex, it's really too late in the evening for your sage wisdom."

"Okay, we'll just concentrate on getting the horses put away for the evening. Sage wisdom can wait until tomorrow afternoon," Alex replied, patting the younger girl's arm in a patronizing way.

"Is that before or after you put your computer together?"

"After."

"I knew it!"

"Kendra, in today's society, technology comes before sage wisdom; you must learn to roll with the punches."

"Alex,"

"Yes, Kendra?"

"Oh, never mind. How late do I get to sleep until?

"I'll let you know when I wake you up."

"Great," Kendra replied sarcastically.

With that, the big red truck and trailer rig turned into the circle drive in front of the stable entrance. Alex jumped out of the cab and ran to hug Sarah.

"What's new, kiddo?" Alex exclaimed.

"God, Alex, I don't even know where to begin," Sarah whined.

"Not you, too."

"Huh?"

"You're beginning to sound just like Kendra and you haven't even met her yet."

"Who," Sarah paused, "is a Kendra?"

"She's my new groom-in-training."

A very sleepy Kendra rolled out of the other side of the cab and stretched up into the dark sky.

"Kendra, Sarah. Sarah, Kendra," Alex said. "Now that you've been properly introduced, let's get the horses out."

"Alex. Horses?"

"Of course. You didn't think I'd come here empty-handed for you did you?" Lowering the ramp in the back of the trailer, Alex gently tugged on a silver tail, and the horse obediently backed down the trailer's ramp. "Silver's Lucky Lady, I'd like you to meet your new owner, Sarah Caldwell. Sarah, you can just call her Silvia."

"Oh, Alex, she's gorgeous."

"Uh-huh. Sarah, I promise you she looks even better in the daylight."

"Sarah?" Kendra asked.

"Yes?"

"Is she like this all the time? Is there some time during the day, or night for that matter, when she doesn't fly higher than a kite?"

"Alex," Sarah laughed, "is like the Unsinkable Molly Brown. Except that time you were riding that big bay in Virginia. You know that is the only time I've ever seen you get so angry."

"That isn't very funny, Sarah, especially after I just brought you a wonderful horse like Silvia!"

"Alex was angry?" Kendra asked incredulously.

"Forget it, Kendra," Alex replied.

"What happened? I want to hear all about it," Kendra begged.

"Another time maybe, Kendra," Sarah replied. "Old friends are very hard to come by right now."

"Don't you listen to her, Kendra. You will hear about it never! I know that you are anxious for any bit of gossip to turn against me, but I repeat: It will not happen!"

With a distinct pout, Kendra turned to unload another horse and enter the stable with him. She was unhappy that she could not learn one dark detail in Alex's spotless and shiny career.

"I hardly recognize him, Alex. Pev looks great—younger even."

"That's only because he's been chasing Silvia around the trailer for the last ten or so hours."

"No, Alex, I'm serious. He hasn't looked this good since you won the gold."

"I'm telling you, Sarah, nothing takes the starch out of the old man's stride like a pretty little filly. How many stalls did you get ready?"

"Just the one for Pev. I wasn't expecting Silvia."

"Well, I guess we'll just have to get two extras ready then."

"Two? You mean to tell me you brought another one, too?"

"Wait till you see her, Sarah!" Alex said with girlish excitement. "It's like Pev all over again, but I swear this one's got greater heart. Even I didn't think that would be possible. Unfortunately, she also seems to have more of a temper to go with that dedicated heart. I think, though, that the temper is something that she will outgrow given enough time."

"I don't think that's possible, Alex," Sarah said. "The heart part I mean."

"I didn't either, but just wait until you see her! Kendra, unload Terpsichore next and bed her down."

"I know, I know," Kendra groused. "No less than five bags of extra fluffy pine shavings. And I'll make sure that she has enough alfalfa hay that she never stops chewing all night."

"Good, Kendra, you're learning. I'll make you a first-class stable hand yet."

Giving Alex a dirty look, Kendra walked up the ramp into the trailer and emerged with a lead shank in her hand. As the huge, jet-black filly exited, prancing from the trailer, her head flew up in a regal stance, and she began to snort loudly, excitedly. Still fidgeting, she danced off beside Kendra into the stable.

"God, Alex, that could very well be the most beautiful horse that I have ever laid eyes on," Sarah gasped.

"Look closely. In eight years after she grows up, she's going to bring home the gold for me again. You can say you met this celebrity when she was a mere hot-headed yearling."

"Just a yearling, Alex? That filly is enormous now."

"I know she is," Alex said grinning. "I'm betting that she tops out at about 17'2 hands."

"I'm sure you'll tell me all about it tomorrow."

"You bet I will! That filly is the find of the century. I just have a feeling about her. A feeling of greatness. When you look into her eyes, you see a proud, eagle-like quality there. They will all be green with jealousy when they see her first time out."

"When you put your computer together tomorrow, make sure you e-mail that old scoundrel for me."

"What old scoundrel?" Kendra asked, returning outside to fetch buckets for the horses.

"What? You mean Alex hasn't quoted volumes of tribal lore about her grandfather, Lightning Horse?" Sarah questioned.

"Oh him. I thought you meant someone that was real," Kendra fired back, turning sharply to storm back into the barn.

"Alex, what was all that about?"

"Kendra is angry because she thinks I made up Lightning Horse."

"That's impossible. He is, after all, your grandfather."

"I'm having a hard time convincing her that I'm half Native American. Frankly, she doesn't believe me."

"But, Alex, it's in all the bio write-ups you get. I know you take after your father's side in looks, but, well, why would you make up something like L.H. anyway?"

"I'll let you in on a secret," Alex whispered behind one hand. "She thinks I'm senile."

"What?" Sarah exclaimed a little too loudly.

"Shhh. She's had a rough time and the chip on her shoulder is the size of Texas. If it helps take her mind off things, I let her think what she wants."

"Alex, you're too good."

"Well, I'm not going to be if I don't get some sleep soon. Have you got a room for Kendra too?"

"Absolutely. I knew you would bring someone with you. You always do. If you don't have a real working student, then you usually have some waif that's wandering around lost."

"This time I've got one that's both. Do me a favor though, Sarah, she's really a good kid at heart. Just don't pry. She'll open up in time. She's like my new horse. She needs time to grow. Look out, here she comes. I'll tell you all about it tomorrow."

"Find everything okay, Kendra?" Sarah asked.

"Anything else I'll find when I'm awake," Kendra replied.

"In that case, I'll show you where you'll stay. I've got a nice big room you can have all to yourself, Kendra."

"That will be nice," Kendra said. "At least I don't have to see Miss Perky first thing every morning."

Alex looked over at her and playfully scrunched up her nose at her. It was a classic Myrna Loy in *The Thin Man* type of look, and one of Alex's personal favorites.

With all the horses settled in, the tired trio then began to walk towards the front door of the house. All they heard before closing the door was one youthful whinny and the calming silence of munching hay.

"I've got another trailer coming late next week with ten to twelve more head," Alex said.

"So soon?" Sarah said.

"You bet. We've got to get this place up and running quickly and get some paying customers. Alfred and the boys will be here shortly to make sure that everything is running according to plan."

"Everything should run smoothly. I sent the last of your jump sketches to the lawyers' office and everything has been approved. Any new additions or future construction will have to be kept true to the period. The cross-country jumps all have that natural look, so we've had absolutely no objections there."

"Great. Alfred and the guys will need about twelve rooms for about two months while they are here building."

"Building what?" Kendra asked sleepily. "Alfred who?"

"All in good time, my dear," Alex said.

"Is that before or after the sage wisdom hour?" Kendra whined.

"After."

"Figures."

10

After showing her friends to their respective rooms, Sarah returned to her own room and flipped on the reading lamp by the side of her bed. Unable to unwind quickly from the late night arrival of Alex and Kendra, Sarah decided on reading a chapter from her newly purchased book. She lately had a taste for the flair of a good Victorian mystery. Right now, she was halfway through the book and dying to read a little more.

"Just one chapter tonight," Sarah said as she quickly threw off her jeans and navy blue sweatshirt in favor of a comfortable, oversized T-shirt. The nightshirt sported the picture of a cute, small black dog curled up on a pillow and dreaming of being a pirate.

Her normal routine of neatly turning down the sheets was followed by fluffing up two pillows for underneath her head, then Sarah comfortably snuggled underneath her covers and cracked open the book to her favorite bookmark, which depicted a row of cuddly Schipperke puppies all decked out in little party hats and all sporting silly little dog smiles. Sarah had only read a few pages when she was startled by what sounded like someone bumping heavily into furniture.

"Alex, is that you?" After a long, silent pause, Sarah called out again. "Kendra?"

Quickly sliding the bookmark back into place, Sarah jumped out of bed and walked at a fast pace toward the door. From what seemed like the opposite end of the hotel, she thought she could hear muffled sobs.

Cracking the door, Sarah strained to hear the sound again. Many minutes passed and she was just about to put the noise down to hearing things, when she heard the sounds again, and this time they came to her more loudly.

Stepping outside her room, Sarah ventured barefooted toward the room she had designated for Alex. Arriving at the door, she gently knocked and called out Alex's name again. When she received no answer, Sarah gently turned the handle and peered into the room. There was Alex, sound asleep on her bed. The familiar emerald green comforter was pulled up snugly under her chin and a computer cable could be seen clutched in her exposed hand.

Sarah tiptoed into the room to turn off the light that Alex had left blazing. Reaching for the cord, she looked down at a seventy-five percent completed job of hooking up a computer. She had always been amazed at Alex's energy. It astounded her how long her friend could continue and then just fall into a coma-like sleep, sometimes for just a few sparse hours. Sarah found it maddening that Alex could awaken completely refreshed and start all over again. Before leaving the room, Sarah tried to wrench the cable from the sleeping woman's hand, but met with no success.

Quickly, Sarah continued on down the hallway to Kendra's room. She hurried, thinking the girl might have hurt herself in the unfamiliar surroundings of the old house.

Again, Sarah gently knocked and called, "Kendra, are you okay?"

There was no answer. She tried the door and found that it, too, was unlocked. Sarah gingerly turned the handle. Although the door squeaked loudly, Sarah could see that Kendra was in a very deep sleep. Her covers were haphazardly thrown up around her. It was obvious from the tumbled appearance of the bed that Kendra had been comfortably snuggled up that way for some time.

Convincing herself that she was now truly imagining things, Sarah turned around to retreat to her own room when she heard the noises again. Now more loudly than ever, the loud sobbing seemed to fill the hallway in which she stood.

"What the…?" she exclaimed.

Sarah guessed that the intruder must be in the end suite. Intending to find out what that person was doing trespassing in her hotel, she sprinted down the hallway to investigate.

"Hello?" Sarah called cautiously while trying the door handle.

The door would not open. Throwing all of her weight against the stubborn door, it suddenly gave way and flew open with a loud bang, throwing Sarah off balance and causing her to fall into a heap on the floor.

"Wasn't that graceful?" Sarah said as she stood brushing the dust from her hands. She looked blankly into the empty room. The room was empty from people, that is, though not empty from cobwebs and old, dusty furniture.

Slowly, the cobwebs began to billow in a brisk, steadily building breeze. Sarah trembled, knowing that the breeze just could not be there. This was the last suite left on this floor that needed to be completely renovated. Sarah had by chance located the key for the door last week in an old trunk in the attic. Consequently, everything was still quite a mess.

There was a blinding light that suddenly engulfed the room. A transformation began to take place while Sarah stood frozen in fear. In the blink of an eye, everything was immaculately clean.

The empty bed frame, which had been stored up against the wall, was now put together, complete with mattress, linens, and a sea foam blue velveteen coverlet, trimmed in a rich mustard gold fringe. Tasteful, old-fashioned throw pillows, brimming with matching fringe, covered every inch of the pillow area of the bed. The faded red coverings of an ebonized Victorian platform rocker seemed to flourish with a renewed red brilliance. Beautiful, matching *Gone with the Wind* lights sat glowing eerily at a low setting on parlor tables situated on either side of the room.

Sarah's mind fought to justify what her eyes were seeing. It felt to Sarah as though she had stepped back in time. "Down the rabbit hole, Alice," she murmured. The hairs on her neck stood on end. Sarah uneasily came to the conclusion that she was viewing the room as it once had been.

The heavily brocaded gold curtains now billowed out strongly from a window that Sarah knew to be not only closed and locked, but painted shut, too.

The sad sobbing called out to her from the corner where the platform rocker stood. Turning towards the sound, Sarah gasped when she saw a cloud of mist envelop the chair. It never really took any particular kind of shape. It had to be a ghost.

The pitiful, tortured sound it made froze Sarah to the spot. An uncomfortable connection was made and she began to feel empathy for the entity. The windows shook in their tracks and then made a startling, slamming sound. The curtains began to slow their movement, and the sobbing diminished into a quiet whisper. Shortly, the sobbing had faded into nothingness, a memory. Sarah blinked, and the room had returned to the disrepair she knew it originally to be in. Feeling faint, Sarah struggled to find some power to get back to her own room.

In what seemed an eternity, Sarah stumbled back down the hallway. Her heart raced while she retreated to the safety of her own bed. She lay numb and could not even remember how she had gotten there.

"Could this have been a dream?" she whispered. Sarah called to mind the terrifying dream that had occurred that first day while waiting for Rita on the front porch. The day that Rita had disappeared.

Rising, she crossed back to her door and closed it, then returned to her bed. Suddenly it seemed odd to Sarah that neither Alex nor Kendra appeared to find out what all the noise was about. Could it be that neither one had even heard all that commotion? Sarah felt confused. Perhaps it had been a dream after all. She would ask Alex about it in the morning. Maybe she had been under considerably more strain than she thought or was willing to admit to herself.

Sarah once again found refuge under the covers, but remained restless. Her analytical mind tried to reason out what she had seen. It had been frightening, but why was it happening now? She had been all alone in the house for three weeks since the closing, waiting for Alex to arrive. Glancing at the clock, Sarah realized that morning was just two hours away. Perhaps if she could get some sleep things would seem more reasonable in the light of a new day. She reached out to turn the light off, but her hand began to shake uncontrollably and she found herself unable to flick the switch. Dream or not, her unconscious mind would not let her turn it off.

"Oh hell," she said. "I'll just sleep with the damn thing on."

* * *

With red-rimmed eyes, Sarah approached the stable doors at about eight-thirty in the morning. She could hear Alex cheerfully whistling away to her favorite collection of musical soundtracks. Right now something from the Star Wars collection was blasting away.

"How can you be so damn cheery in the morning?" Sarah scolded.

Alex turned away from the black horse she was brushing down to make a sharp retort and, instead, dropped the brush and her mouth simultaneously.

"You'll catch flies that way," Sarah said sarcastically.

"What happened to you, Sarah? You look awful!"

"Thanks. You'd look this way, too, if you had only about five minutes of sleep and had been scared out of your wits to boot."

"Scared? Scared of what?"

"Then you really didn't hear all that commotion last night?"

"What commotion?"

Sarah began to relate the story to Alex, but, while she did so, the black filly began to fidget impatiently in the crossties.

"Wait, Sarah. Let me put Terpsichore away, and we'll go sit down, and I'll make you a nice cup of your favorite hot tea."

Quickly, Alex put the impatient steed away in her stall. Terpsichore happily began to munch down a flake of green, sweet-smelling alfalfa while watching the two women walk out the front of the barn in the direction of the house.

"Now tell me again. You heard what?" Alex said, taking the whistling kettle away from the heat and pouring hot water into the waiting cups.

"Alex, it was the oddest thing. First, I heard sobbing. Checked on both you and Kendra. After systematically ruling out the two of you, I heard the sound continuing and went farther down the hall to investigate. At first, it was a very distant, muffled sort of sound. Then it got louder and louder, until I determined that it was coming from the unfinished suite at the end of the hall. I opened the door and saw what I expected—a room, one that has yet to be redecorated, chock full of thick, clinging cobwebs. By the way, I just remembered that you hate tea."

"I ran out of my last can of Coke last night about three hours from here," Alex said smiling. "But never mind about my drinking habits. Unless I trade it in for whiskey, I think I'll survive. Get on with it," Alex prodded impatiently.

"Anyway," Sarah continued, running her finger around the rim of her cup, "in a flash, or at least it seemed like a flash to me, the whole room transformed. I could swear that I was looking at a room that was from, well, hell, I don't know, a time vortex or something science-fictionish like that. Then the window made sounds like it was suddenly being pushed up by tremendous strength, and the curtains blew out strongly from the window frame, making it seem like I was experiencing an indoor hurricane."

"The sobbing increased," Sarah said as she continued her story. "I looked at the old rocker in the corner and there was some strange mist stuff floating around in that general area. The sobbing then got unbearably loud. Just when I thought I was going quite mad, the window slammed shut loudly enough that I swear I heard the walls shaking. I looked back into the room, and, in the blink of an eye, it had returned to the way it looks right now. Basically, in need of the redecorating fairy."

"Sarah," Alex replied with a small laugh. "If I didn't know you better I'd swear that you made this up on purpose just to pull my leg. Honestly, a time vortex? You'd think you were the sci-fi fanatic instead of me."

"Did Kendra say anything about maybe hearing something last night?"

"I don't know," Alex said. Just as she saw Sarah about to raise an objection, she also added, "Of course, Kendra is still asleep. I thought that I'd give her an easy first day."

"Then she probably didn't," Sarah replied, frowning. "If she'd heard what I'd heard, and seen what I'd seen, I guarantee that she would not still be sleeping. She'd be down here like I am right now—looking like hell and babbling like a ditsy blond."

"Have you experienced anything like this since you've moved in here?"

"No. Nothing at all. Although, I did have an odd dream the first day that I was here looking at the grounds."

"You had a dream in the daytime? Are you sure it wasn't a vision?"

"Yes. No. I don't know. Sort of."

"Oh please, Sarah, which is it? I might have psychic abilities, but even Nostradamus had his limitations."

"Well, that was the morning that I was waiting for the woman from the realty company to show up so I could go over the grounds in the daylight. I waited in the car at first because I didn't want to trespass here, but I got restless and figured who would care since no one has lived here in about a million years."

"Go on."

"I'm trying! Anyhow, during the course of my wait, I decided that I would like to curl up on the front porch in one of the wicker rockers to wait for her. While I was waiting, I had the oddest dream."

"Can you tell me about it?" Alex asked, noticing that her friend had gotten more noticeably agitated.

"I'll try. I must have dozed off. The next thing I knew I felt a hand on my shoulder, shaking me. I looked up at who I thought would be the realtor. Instead, it was this young woman wearing older clothes."

"Older clothes?"

"Vintage clothes. Anyhow, I was going to try and speak to her when," Sarah stopped and tears spilled over from her red-rimmed eyes.

"Can you go on?" Alex asked sympathetically.

"Give me a minute," Sarah said. "This was the really gross part. It was horrible at the time. To visualize it again is difficult."

There was an uncomfortable silence between the two for a few minutes; then Sarah began to relate the rest of her story.

"I finally pulled myself together and tried to speak with her when her entire appearance changed. Her body was ripped to shreds; cut away, right in front of me. It took place in a heartbeat. It was awful. The blood was everywhere. All over me. Staining my hands, my clothes. The entire porch was splattered in red; it was horrifying. The woman looked to me, I felt her desperation. Tears were spilling over from her eyes and staining her cheeks. Then, snap. She just faded from view along with all the blood. I felt I had imagined the entire thing. After she faded, I jolted awake and found myself still seated in the rocker."

"How awful for you."

"I had justified it along the parallel line of Bruce's illness. Alex, do you think I dreamed it?"

"I'm not sure…"

"Alex."

"I don't mean it the way you think. It's just, with all you've been through lately…"

"Alex, I'm sure now, after last night, that it has nothing to do with Bruce's death. I am not suffering from any posttraumatic, something or another, bullshit trauma. Everything else has been normal here for the entire time except for the disappearance that happened here a little over five weeks ago."

"Disappearance? What do you mean disappearance?" Alex exclaimed as she slammed the cup on the counter. "You didn't say anything about any disappearances while we've been talking over the past few weeks."

"I didn't think that meant anything at the time, Alex! The realtor that I had been waiting for never showed up. Her boss-slash-stepbrother ended up coming out and showing me the grounds. Her disappearance has been quite a mystery, because she just vanished without a trace."

Sarah spent the next fifteen minutes continuing to relate the complete story of Rita McAllister and Ron Van Allen to Alex. She remembered every detail about the woman's disappearance and how no one could figure out where she could have been taken.

"The sheriff and deputies have combed every home, barn, and shack in the area. Dogs were brought in to track, although there was some speculation that they were too late getting started with the dogs. The handlers complained that the trail had been allowed to get cold, but the man who owned them was in another county on a ransomed kidnapping. I tell you, Alex. It was really weird. If I hadn't met the woman myself I would swear that she had never existed."

There was a long silence between them, then suddenly a loud, piercing scream split the air, and both Alex and Sarah looked towards the back door of the old kitchen simultaneously. As if in slow motion, both got up to run, but Alex was faster and better rested. She easily beat Sarah to the door and across the yard to the stable area.

Arriving inside the open door of the barn within seconds of each other, both women found Kendra sitting on a bale of alfalfa outside one of the horse's stalls, shaking violently.

The horses, also visibly agitated, were screaming in their stalls. Terpsichore, the most sensitive of the three, was pounding away, kicking at the back of her stall with all her might.

"Sarah, grab that cooler hanging over there and wrap it around Kendra," Alex shouted to her friend over the turmoil.

Sarah quickly crossed the span of the floor and returned to wrap the frightened, unnerved girl in the red plaid wool cooler.

Meanwhile, Alex opened the door to Terpsichore's stall and was greeted by a terrified 1,200-pound baby. She worked with her, using Cherokee calming techniques, and was rewarded when the skittish animal began to return to normal. The only thing remaining of the animal's consternation was an occasional, excited snort.

"Kendra, what's wrong?" Sarah exclaimed. She grasped the girl by the hands and drew them apart, giving her the once over. "Are you all right? Have you hurt yourself somehow?"

Slowly and with what seemed to be a great effort Kendra shook her head from side to side. Her chin bobbed as she strained to suppress her tears of fright. Raising her hand towards the empty area where new stalls would be put in soon, she jerkily pointed in that direction.

"I s-sa-saw a man," she stammered.

"That's impossible," Sarah scoffed. "There aren't any men here yet."

"Could be a bum?" Alex said, turning to look at Sarah. "This place has been empty for quite a long time."

But before Sarah could answer her, Kendra cut in nervously.

"No," Kendra began. "You don't understand."

"What don't I understand, Kendra?" Alex asked. Turning again to Sarah, she added, "You better get a doctor up here right away, she looks like she may be going into shock."

Sarah turned away from them to sprint back to the house and call the doctor; she wondered what else could happen.

"It was an old man, Alex," Kendra sobbed.

"Some kind of vagrant or derelict you mean?"

"No, I-I-I mean that his age was old."

"Kendra, you must take a deep breath, because I cannot understand you. Can you do that for me now? I'm right here, and no one is going to harm you. I will not permit that. Now, try again to explain to me what you saw."

"I saw a man; he was about late thirties to early forties," Kendra managed to get out through her tears.

"Kendra, that's not very old; I'm thirty-five myself," Alex scolded.

"I don't mean that his age was old. I mean that he looked out of place."

"Out of place?"

"Because he was dressed funny."

"How do you mean *funny*, Kendra?"

"He had on really old clothes."

"Like tattered, torn, faded?" Alex asked. "How could you tell they were old?"

"No, nothing like that," Kendra replied. "It was like he was in costume."

"Costume? What kind of costume? Like a cowboy outfit?"

"Yes. No. I mean the clothes were, what's the word? Used? No, that's not it."

"Is vintage the word you want, Kendra?" Alex asked.

"Yes, vintage. I think that's the word I want. Even though he wasn't terribly ancient in age, it seemed that he was from a long time ago."

"Then what happened, Kendra?"

"His mouth moved like he was trying to tell me something, but I couldn't hear anything come out of him. He looked almost, well, frustrated, I guess, that he wasn't able to speak with me. Then he started some strange kind of hand gesturing."

"Can you show them to me?"

"No. I couldn't understand it either," Kendra sobbed.

"So, he ran off? Did he try to hurt you before he ran off?"

"Neither. He just looked sad. It was like he was disappointed with me or something like that. Then, he turned away from me. It was not until then that I realized that I could see right through him."

"Where did he go, Kendra?"

Pointing back to the empty space again, Kendra managed to summon whatever courage she had left and stated matter-of-factly, "Right through that solid barn wall."

11

The two women paced back and forth in anticipation through the hotel lobby. Quietly, they waited for the doctor to return after his examination of Kendra. The silence between them was beginning to be uncomfortable, but neither one knew quite where to start.

"She's going to be okay," Dr. Russell announced, descending the sweeping mahogany staircase. "I think that she's just had a nasty shock, but I've given her a sleeping pill, and that should help her sleep."

"Thank you for coming so promptly, Doctor," Alex said.

"It was really no trouble," he replied. "I usually just get the odd kid that falls out of a tree and brakes his arm. My Saturdays really are not very often busy. After all, this is a very small community."

"Well, thanks again," Sarah said. "We really do appreciate it."

"I would like to come back tomorrow and check in on her if I may?" Russell related.

"Of course, anytime at all," Sarah said. "Either Alex or myself will be here the entire day."

"Good. Then I'll see you tomorrow. Oh, before I forget," he added, turning to hand a small tube of pills to Alex, "if she seems to get upset again, or is having trouble getting to sleep, just give her one of these. The directions are on the label."

Alex replied with a tired looking smile. The doctor then turned and climbed the stairs up and out of the lobby and on to the front porch. The roaring of the bad muffler filled the air as the old Mercury pulled away from the hotel.

"Well, he could never sneak up on anyone, could he?" Alex laughed.

"No, I guess not," Sarah giggled. Then after a slight pause, "Alex, what's happening here? I've been here alone for the better part of three weeks. Nothing has even been remotely questionable, and then all of this happens in less than half a day."

"Are you forgetting your dream about the woman on the porch? You remember her—the one that exploded with blood and gore all over you and then disappeared."

There was a still silence.

"You're right. I had forgotten all about her. I'd already justified her right out of my mind." Again Sarah paused. "You haven't answered my question, Alex."

"I'm not sure, but I have an idea. I'd really like to ask my sage advisor what he thinks."

"Is your computer all set to go? You know it's really a hoot that your grandfather got into the Internet and e-mail thing."

"Yeah," Alex chuckled. "But it sure makes it handy to get hold of him and it definitely beats the heck out of smoke signals or beating drums."

As Alex began to mount the stairs, she turned and looked back at Sarah.

"Don't worry, kiddo, we'll figure it out. The important thing is to get this sorted out by the fall so that we can have our grand opening. Remember, I've already got a lot of paying clients lined up for those first few weeks."

"Hopefully, it won't be for a ghost hunt," Sarah muttered.

"Hey, cheer up! Anyhow, it has the novelty of never being tried doesn't it? While I'm busy could you keep an eye on Kendra for me?"

"Oh sure. Kendra. God, Alex! Shouldn't we phone her mother or something? That poor girl got scared out of her wits."

"Yes. Well, with all the excitement, I haven't been able to talk to you about that particular problem."

"What do you mean? What problem?"

"We can't exactly call her mother."

"What do you mean, *we can't*?"

"Well, that's one of the things that I wanted to talk to you about this morning while Kendra was still sleeping, but then we got a little sidetracked and we never finished."

"Okay, Alex, spill it. I've known you long enough to know when you don't really want to tell me something."

"You see, Kendra's parents both died two months ago in an auto wreck. I have arranged through the courts to take her on as my legal ward."

"God, the poor kid! She can't be much more than sixteen."

"She's just fifteen, Sarah. She's all alone in the world except for me. And now you and this place."

"I wondered why you've never mentioned her before. Where did she come from?"

"Last year Mrs. Phillips, that was Kendra's mother, called me. Then she wrote me. Then they showed up at the stables I was training at. Finally, they began to attend every show I went to whether I was riding, coaching, or judging. Frankly, they just about drove me crazy. Lila, that is, Mrs. Phillips, was sure that I could groom her daughter to become a great equestrian. They didn't have the finances to afford me, but thought that she could start at the bottom and begin by being my groom. One big problem I could see was that Kendra had, well, she'd frankly never been anywhere near horses. After my first experience with her, I bluntly told her mother that she showed no aptitude for horses. Based on the fact that Kendra had had no experience, I told Mrs. Phillips that it was out of the question."

"Well, then what happened?" Sarah asked.

"To be honest, I just ignored them for many months, hoping that they would go away after the proper amount of discouragement. Every time I turned around, there they were. Then, not long ago, there came a time when I looked up and all I saw was Kendra. There was no Mr. or Mrs. Phillips in sight. Angered, I finally spoke with Kendra. I wanted to know why her mother thought she could just drop a minor off at a stable and disappear. Kendra just looked at me and burst into tears. She said her mother and father had both died the previous week in a car accident, and that I was the only other person she knew."

"In town, you mean," Sarah said.

"No, period. I was the only other person she knew. Period. It seems the Phillips had just moved into the area for the sole purpose of locating me. She didn't have anywhere else to go. Hell, the kid hadn't eaten in three days. From what little the authorities have been able to tell me, there are no other living relatives anywhere."

"So, you basically felt obligated."

"And sad. Her parents gave up their entire lifestyle to track me down and convince me to make something out of their daughter. A girl that I understand had lots of trouble in school, fought with all the other children, and was generally a social misfit."

"Is that why the pink hair?"

"It's just for attention. You should have heard the heated discussion we had over the tongue stud."

"The tongue stud!"

"Thank heavens that's gone. Anyhow, all she's had for two months has been me riding her butt and those three nags out there. She has no one else to turn to. I'll be damned before I let her down."

"Alex."

"Yeah?"

"You're such a soft touch, Alex. I knew that there was a reason that we've been friends for so long."

12

Sarah was working back behind the old, huge mahogany check-in desk when suddenly she felt like someone was standing behind her. She nervously whirled around to find Kendra peering over her shoulder.

"Sorry," Kendra said. "I didn't mean to startle you."

"That's okay." Sarah exhaled nervously. She realized how relieved she felt that it was only Kendra. "How are you feeling? Are you all right?"

"I guess I feel all right, just kinda, you know, tired and a little thirsty. Must be the medicine."

"What can I get for you, Kendra?"

"I had a sudden urge for a large, cool glass of lemonade. Do you think you might possibly have some?"

"I'm sure that I can come up with something. I hope the instant kind is okay. I have not had much time yet to lay in a large number of supplies. Come on, let's go into the kitchen."

Sarah, after rummaging around in the refrigerator and cabinets, triumphantly held up a powdered can of drink mix.

"How about this?"

"Yeah, that will be fine," Kendra answered dreamily, still affected from the medication. "Where's Alex?"

"After this morning, she decided that a little ride would calm down her karma. At least, I think that is what she said."

"God," Kendra moaned. "If she isn't on a horse, she's on that computer of hers."

"Here you go—good, old-fashioned, instant!" Sarah said and smiled.

"Thanks. Oh, there's Alex." Kendra said, as she turned her head and glanced out of the large kitchen picture window.

"Go ahead and sit down. You've had a rough morning. Alex said that you deserved the day off."

"That's a surprise," Kendra said sarcastically. "I'd better at least help her feed the afternoon and evening meals, or there will be hell to pay."

Remembering the story that Alex had related earlier, Sarah believed it wiser to keep silent than to defend her friend. Sarah felt there was going to be a large learning curve when it came down to this new girl. Still, Alex had said to give her time.

Kendra sat quietly, drinking her lemonade and staring out the window; never taking her eyes off the figure astride outside. Kendra was studying Alex's every movement, no matter how slight, in the saddle. Sarah could tell that, although she would never admit it, the girl idolized Alex.

13

Alex could feel herself begin to relax. The horse's strides were large, consistent, and even. The rhythmic swaying sent Alex into a euphoric teaming with the animal. All the concerns of the day had always seemed better to her astride Peverell. He was her escape from the world, and best of all, from people. All problems faded away and the only thing around her was nature and being one with her best friend. The last bit of tension was leaving her brain, and her spiritual center had become whole.

There was a full moment of solitude, and then suddenly it struck her. The pain seared like lightning in her temples. It was excruciating. There were so many voices screaming out to her that it was overwhelming. The screams were agonizing. The expressed emotions were the likes of which Alex had never experienced before in her life. She dropped the reins like they were burning her hands.

Listing forward, Alex clutched her head in distress, emitting a small, painful gasp, and continued to bend forward from the waist. Alex then proceeded to pass out on the big horse's neck and flopped onto the ground like a lifeless rag doll. Peverell, confused by his rider's unusual movements, screeched to a halt, looking down over his fallen mistress, nudging her softly.

"Oh my god!" Kendra screamed. She slammed the lemonade glass down sideways, cracking the glass and sending it and the sticky lemonade all over the kitchen.

"What? What's the matter?" Sarah said breathlessly as she ran back into the kitchen from the front hall. There was no one in the kitchen when she got there. Sarah glanced around, but could not find Kendra in any corner of the room. All Sarah saw was the spilled lemonade dripping onto the floor. Her eyes suddenly averted to the window, and the scene before her made her blood turn cold. She saw Kendra running full tilt towards a horse and a crumpled figure on the ground. Alex. My God, she thought. What in the name of heaven or hell is next?

14

"Well, it's not very often that I return to the scene of the crime," Dr. Russell said with a smirk. "This has been an exciting day for you folks, hasn't it?"

"How is she, doctor?" Sarah asked. "Is she going to be all right?"

"She will be just fine," the doctor replied. "There is no apparent reason for the blackout, but, just in case, I have spoken with her about setting up some tests. Just to be safe, you know."

"Of course," Sarah said, "and I'll see to it personally that she goes and takes those tests too. Even if I have to break her arm to do it."

"Well, I've left her some medicine, and, if anything seems wrong, please give me a call. This time I'm also going to leave my car phone number too."

"Thank you again, doctor."

"Is she really okay?" asked a very small, frightened voice from the dark corner.

"Don't you worry, little lady," Dr. Russell said to Kendra. "She will be up and around in no time. Getting thrown from a horse always takes the wind out of your sails; I'm sure that her blackout is due to just a slight knock on the head. As for you, young lady, I think you should return to bed and get some rest yourself!"

The doctor turned his back and made for the door without turning around. If he had, he would have seen two comically speechless people with their mouths wide open, staring at each other in disbelief. A car door slammed, and the familiar sound of a bad muffler and backfire filled the still air around the Grand Detour Hotel.

"Thrown?" Sarah whispered.

"Off Pev?" Kendra added, equally stunned.

Quickly, the two ascended the stairs and knocked softly on Alex's door.

"Come in," sang a familiar, chipper voice.

As Sarah opened the door, the two were speechless to find Alex at the keyboard of her computer, typing away in a mad frenzy. Sarah and Kendra looked slowly at each other and then turned in an even, syncopated rhythm back towards Alex.

By this time, Alex had caught their comical movements out of the corner of her eye. She took the opportunity to freeze in a staged expression of fingers poised in the air, the typing ceased.

"Just what is wrong with you two?" Alex demanded. Her hands made fists and she drew them to attach to her waist.

"Dr. Russell said you were thrown off and then blacked out," both said in unison.

"Oh that," Alex blustered. She immediately waved her hand in a sort of dismissal and returned to typing in a frenzy.

"Just what do you mean by, *Oh that*," Sarah scolded.

"Well, at the time it seemed like a better alternative than telling him the truth, don't you think? Besides, he doesn't know anything about me and he certainly does not know that Peverell has never thrown a temper tantrum in his entire life."

"You can imagine my surprise," Kendra chimed in. "Since I saw the whole thing and I know that you passed out *before* you fell off."

"Yes, well there is that," Alex replied sheepishly, as she then straightened her voice uncomfortably. "Just let me finish writing this to Grandfather and then I will let you read it. Some things that have been happening have been bothering me in the last twenty-four hours and I want to make sure that I have the proper facts committed to memory. By the way, Kendra, how is Pev? I bet I shook the big baby up quite a bit."

"He is happy as a pig, and munching on his afternoon flakes of hay."

"Good, I always want a happy horse."

As Alex typed on in a mad, Machiavellian way, the other two looked on as though perhaps something had snapped in the equestrian.

"There, now I'm finished," Alex announced. "Come and read my theory. If you dare."

Silently the two bent over the large screen and read the e-mail that was indeed ready to be sent to Chief Lightning Horse. Alex could tell that both Sarah and Kendra had to stop and reread several sentences many times.

Finally, when she knew that they were finished, she waited for their reaction. It was not long in coming.

"What do you mean by this? Are you crazy?" Sarah questioned in bewilderment.

"Which part?"

"Damn it, Alex. The whole part!"

"I think that the spiritual activity that invades every nook and cranny of this house has finally found someone to release all their pent up frustration on. Frankly, I mean me."

"Alex, I don't think that this is very funny. Are you sure that your head is all right? It's not too late to call Dr. Russell back you know."

"I'm fine, and I don't find one bit of amusement in it myself. Do you think it is fun for at least a hundred voices to begin shrieking in agony on the inside of your head? In stereo, no less!"

"I thought that you always made up that mumbo jumbo about Lightning Horse saying you were a powerful psychic."

"Native American seer."

"Whatever," Sarah said crossly.

"Alex, you mean that you blacked out because of people shouting in your head?" Kendra asked slowly.

"Not exactly shouting, Kendra," Alex began sadly. "Screaming. Long. Loud. Terrible. A million screams, the likes of which no one should ever have to hear. Voices, which are sounding out about their agony from over the span of many years. It is a sound that I don't ever want to hear again. It is the sound my people call the death rattle. Of dying in torture and torment."

"Who was it?" Sarah asked. "Could you tell from what went on, or who it might have been?"

"There were so many of them, that I could not begin to untangle them all. I dare not even think about who they might or might not be. All I can tell you is that there was no one individual that stood out."

"This, then, is the reason that you blacked out?"

"I believe so, Kendra. Yes. I don't know when, but there has been much misery in this place and in this town. The door to the other world has been unlocked. I know this now for a fact. I can feel it now with almost every breath I take. I have unknowingly opened a terrible door that was left ajar. We will have to work very hard to untangle what has taken place here. Rest assured, I will not let down my defenses like that again. It was too easy for them to let themselves in. It was an experience that I would not like to repeat."

"Why would we have to untangle anything?" Sarah questioned. "The past is the past. Can't we just leave it there?"

"Unfortunately, no. Now that some restless spirits have broken through the hole in the wall, I believe to seek me out, the barrier between this world and theirs will become more and more fragile. The very essence, which separates them, will tear more and more with each passing incident. The past will invade the future, to stop this we will have to lay many spirits to rest."

"Why now, Alex? I was assured that this was a quiet town when I first began my search for a place like this."

"I believe that a lot of the reason could be my fault. My arrival has somehow triggered the beginning of the end here. The trapped souls have been chipping away at the delicate fabric that separates their world from ours. Events have become more prolonged, and, with the incident from this afternoon, well, all I can say is that I do not believe that we have much time."

"Much time for what, Alex?" Kendra asked, the fright coming through in her tone of voice.

"Time, I'm afraid, before, quite literally, all hell breaks loose."

Turning away from her friends, Alex hit the send key.

"All we can do now is wait. And hope that Grandfather has answers for me and hopefully help too."

15

The evening was perfect. Janey Stevenson had effectively sneaked out of her parent's home at 1221 Horne Court, thus flagrantly defying her father's grounding from earlier that afternoon. It was not a fair grounding anyway; at least not in Janey's eyes. She was enjoying a song on the radio, and it had really not been her fault that her fussy baby brother had wakened screaming because of the noise. She felt like she never had any fun. Besides, she had this date planned for over a week and she had no intention of breaking it, even for disapproving parents.

It's not fair. How could they understand about someone who is sixteen and in love, Janey thought.

Unfortunately, she had also chosen someone of whom her parents most emphatically did not approve; the undesirable boy's name was Billy Watson.

It had really been easier than she had thought, though. The minute both her parents and baby brother, Jimmy, had gone to sleep, she exited through her north bedroom window and silently crawled down the rose trellis. Only once did she slip and leave a strand of her stark blond hair behind.

Janey then headed towards the park in the center of the town square to meet her seventeen-year-old knight in shining armor. Her actions exhilarated and excited her, and she felt like her heart was on cloud nine. She grasped Billy's hand all the tighter as they walked to the late night movie house on the corner.

"What movie are we seeing?" she asked.

"It's a re-release of The Rock," Billy replied.

"Isn't that some wrestling guy?"

"No, goofy. The Rock. Alcatraz. Nicolas Cage. Sean Connery. Ringing any bells yet?"

"No, not really."

"Janey, where have you been? Under a rock?"

"Very funny. There's no spaceships or large creatures is there?"

"No. I know you hate those movies; this is purely an action flick."

"Oh."

Action was not Janey's idea of a great movie to see. Instead, she would much rather see one of the love stories that had recently come out, but Billy did not like romance pictures. Tonight, it did not matter. Tonight, she was with Billy and she would watch any movie. Well, almost any movie. Slasher/horror pictures were definitely out, and Billy had agreed that he would not inflict one of these on Janey. It was a mutual understanding between the two of them that Billy would see scary pictures with his friends and Janey would attend, as he called them, sappy love stories with hers. This left them the mutually agreed upon territory of comedies, action pictures, and the occasional western.

One movie, a shared large popcorn, and a beverage later, and the two young lovebirds were making plans for the following Saturday night and once again found themselves in the park and ready to part company.

"Come on, Janey," Billy said. "I really think that I should walk you home. I want to walk you home."

"You just can't," Janey whined back at him.

"It would be safer, and I would feel better about it if I did. Parents or no parents, Janey. They'll think even less of me if I don't see you home."

"I'll be fine," Janey insisted. "Home is just through those woods, and if we get caught, I won't be able to see you for months."

"Well," Billy began. "If you promise to ring the phone once when you get home so that I know you're okay."

"That's a much better deal," Janey said. "You'll see. What could possibly happen?"

After exchanging their goodnights, Janey noiselessly crept through a few backyards, taking a seldom-used shortcut home. There was a short patch of woods between her block and the next. It was dark, but she kept assuring herself that everything would be okay. Wasn't it funny, she thought, how very clever she had been to have pulled one over on her parents. Janey came to the base of a large, twisted dead oak on the trail. She hesitated briefly thinking that she had heard something. With a curious twist of the head, she peered around the trunk of the tree, thinking she had seen a large, rather unfriendly looking dog.

"I wish now that I had let Billy walk me home," she whispered.

A rustling noise from above startled her; sensing that something was above her, Janey instinctively crouched down. Experiencing shallow, rapid breathing, she forced herself to look upwards. Holding her breath, she prepared for the worst to befall her and relaxed a little when her eyes fell on what was probably the largest white owl she had ever seen. Janey exhaled with relief and turned her head back in the direction that she had originally intended to travel towards home.

When she turned, something heavy hit her on the head. It had hit her so hard that she blacked out immediately. She never even felt herself hit the ground.

* * *

Two hours had gone by since Janey and he had separated company in the park. Billy was pacing the floor and physically upset that Janey had not yet called. She had never before forgotten to call him and to top it off she would be in very big trouble if he called her home looking for her. When her parents had found out that she had flagrantly sneaked out of the house against their wishes, she would be punished. The fact that she had done this with someone that they so highly disapproved of would result, no doubt, in her being grounded forever.

Billy could never really understand why the Stevenson's had never liked him. He was a better-than-average student. He played on many of the sporting teams for Grand Detour High School. He had a good reputation. What he failed to realize was that it really did not matter to the Stevenson's which boy Janey dated; they would all rate the same. None of the young boys would be good enough for their daughter. He was just too young to understand about overprotective parents.

Now it was at the two and a half hour mark and Billy was frantic. He had decided, despite repercussions, to knock on his parent's door.

"Dad?" Billy called out quietly.

"Billy?" a craggy, sleepy voice said from behind a closed door.

A sleepy Jim Watson shuffled to the door and looked down into the face of a very anxious young man.

"What's the matter, son?"

"It's Janey, Dad."

"Is something wrong?"

"We went out tonight, to the movies. Its been hours and she promised me that she would call. She hasn't. I'm really worried. What do you think I should do?"

"I agree that you should be concerned. I think no matter what repercussions you fear from her parents, calling her home would be showing that you are responsible when it comes to Janey's well-being."

"I don't know what to say. We weren't supposed to be out. She was grounded."

Seeing the obvious worry in his son's face, Jim Watson said, "Well, we'll call them together. I'll talk parent to parent."

"Thanks, Dad," Billy said. He continued to pace impatiently behind his father while he began to dial.

The phone in the Stevenson household rang several times. Both Mr. and Mrs. Stevenson were both extremely deep sleepers. It is most likely that the call would have gone unnoticed if not for Jimmy's grating wail.

"Hello," Victor Stevenson mumbled.

"Mr. Stevenson?"

"Yes," he said, yawning sleepily. "Who's this?"

"This is Jim Watson, Victor."

"Jim Watson," Stevenson uttered, suddenly coming awake and grabbing the clock. "It's two-thirty in the morning! What on earth do you want?"

"I am calling to check up on Janey, Victor."

"At this time of night? She is home in bed, not running around at all hours of the night!"

"What I'm trying to explain to you is that she and Billy apparently ignored your rules and went out for a date tonight. She would not allow him to walk her home and she has not yet rung him to let him know that she made it home safely. My son is understandably concerned or he would not have awakened me at this hour either."

"That's impossible," Stevenson blustered. "She was grounded. She knows that she's not allowed to…" He looked over to his wife's side of the bed and noticed that she was no longer there.

"I assure you," Jim Watson continued, "That she was out at the movies with my son tonight."

"Victor," Barbara Stevenson said, reentering the room. "He's right. Janey's not in her room, and it looks like she's been gone all night! Her bed hasn't been slept in."

"I'm going to call the sheriff and would appreciate it if you and Billy could go through the facts with him also," Stevenson said.

"Anything to help. We'll both be right over."

The Stevenson's found themselves wide-awake. After hanging up from the Watson call, they were immediately dialing again. This time the call was getting placed to the sheriff. A sheriff who had already been sleeping poorly over the last five weeks and was about to find that the situations in town had only just begun.

* * *

A sharp, loud telephone ring broke the silence in Ian Valin's bedroom. Ian had just managed to fall asleep for about fifteen minutes, after tossing for hours. Sleepily, he reached over and turned on the light. His clock read 2:45 AM. He yawned, and reached for the receiver of the phone.

"Hello," he squeaked. Clearing his voice he tried again.

"Hello," he said again.

"This is the emergency desk; I have a call for you, Sheriff," the operator said.

"Go ahead and put it through," Ian said stifling a large yawn. "Hello."

Victor Stevenson gave Ian a brief, but detailed breakdown of the facts. At least what he knew them. Ian could hear Barbara Stevenson sobbing in the background and knew that he needed to get over there quickly. Assuring them that he would be right over, Ian put down the receiver and flung off the bedcovers. Stretching out his right hand he reached for the old, worn green chair sitting in the corner. It contained the previous day's clothing. Half dressed, with the cruiser keys hanging from his mouth, he made his way quickly into the night. Fervently hoping that Janey Stevenson would be much easier to find than Rita McAllister, Ian hurried toward the cruiser. It had been weeks, and there still was not one clue as to what had happened to her. Ian climbed into the car and turned the engine over; he had a bad feeling that somehow Rita had only been the beginning.

* * *

Aching all over and returning to consciousness, Janey's eyes began to flutter open. Her head was throbbing, and she could feel something warm and sticky on the right side of it. Her brain was trying valiantly to sort out a series of events, but was feeling disoriented and could not quite remember what had happened. Groggily, she tried to reach up and touch her head only to find herself tied tightly up. Her mind raced to try and come up with a solution as to where she was. The last thing she remembered was cutting home between blocks through Robinson Woods and having that stupid owl scare her. Billy. She had met Billy for a movie and she had been on her way home. This, however, was definitely not home. Her eyes focused on the orange flames of fire that were burning almost out of her visual range. Slowly, becoming more awake, Janey realized that she was tied quite tightly to a large slab of stone. In front of her was another large stone, and she could make out that there was something carved there, but because of her bleary eyes, she could only vaguely see and was unable to make out what the marks meant.

Janey's eyes focused more sharply; she could make out an oval circle within a circle with many little hash marks in the middle. A sharp gasp rose from her throat when a dark figure crept out from behind the large, free-standing, carved stone. His face was painted half red, half black and twisted with evil. He crept silently toward her with a shiny knife. Janey tried to scream, only to find that she could not. The only thing that came out of her throat was a strangled attempt at a cough.

He glided closer, and she could hear him chanting. It was not English or any other language that she had ever heard in school. Her heart was pounding so hard it threatened to break a rib. Though it was useless to struggle, she continued to fight the bindings that held her. Her thrashing about had succeeded only in the tightening of her restraints. Her breath now came in short gasps as she threatened to hyperventilate and black out from the terror. She was mesmerized by what may happen next and caught between being too frightened to look away and being too frightened to watch another second.

The chanting became louder now, more malevolent than before. His face—that horrible face—was now directly above her. She could smell his fetid breath. His arms slowly, dramatically drew forward. Her terror caught in her throat. Now she could see the wicked dagger poised over her heart. Her body began to tremble with the shock of knowing that the only alternative for her was death. In a quick motion, the shiny dagger plunged toward her.

Suddenly, there was a burning in her chest; she could look down and see the dagger sawing into her. Hysterical tears ran down her face. Unable to breath, she choked. Her eyes widened with terror and recognition. Suddenly Janey knew who was behind her terror. He drew the knife out of her and then stuck his hand inside. With a sickening grab he pulled out her heart and began to smear the blood that spurted from the organ onto his face.

His voice rang out into the night. His strange chanting, still indecipherable, echoed in the very corridors of hell.

16

Alex endured a hellacious night. The experiences from the previous day had caused great emotional upheaval. What little sleep she was able to maintain was ravaged with undecipherable, wild nightmares.

Other sleepless nights, in Alex's past, had always been cured by one thing. She got up to spend time with the one true calming influence that had been with her throughout her entire life. The horses. It was still very dark out, but she stumbled and groped her way to the barn door. Patting the unfamiliar door with her hands, she searched for the handle. The reward of the search was the door opening on hinges that badly needed to be oiled.

She was startled to find herself face to face with a man.

"Hello," Alex said.

The spectral man was dressed in a pristine, late-1800s suit. A gold watch fob of a horse dangled from the chain strung between his two vest pockets. He tried to mouth words. Words that Alex could not understand. This had to be the man that shocked Kendra yesterday. She did not fear him; almost the reverse was true. Along with that revelation came a large blast of depression. His eyes stared straight into hers and Alex, being unprepared, became overwhelmed with his feeling of sorrow as it poured into her soul.

He opened his mouth. His lips moved in unspoken words, but nothing audible came out.

"I'm sorry, I don't understand."

His hands were held out to her, pleading with her. Alex took a step forward, and the forlorn figure began to flash signs frantically with his hands. She recognized these as Native American signing, but did not comprehend their meaning. Alex struggled to understand him and felt a small bit of hope wash through him. This time he did not leave in defeat. For a few short seconds, their souls merged and she could feel that he was there to provide a warning. He was here to help them. Frustration, however, won out in the end, and he bent over shaking his head sadly. He turned and walked through the same wall in the exact manner as described earlier yesterday by Kendra.

Suddenly, Alex realized that she had been holding her breath. She inhaled deeply and reached out to flick on the lights.

"Wow!" she said tiredly.

Her equine children blinked sleepily at her. They gave her a look that seemed to say, *"Why did you do that Mom? It's too early."*

"Well, I wonder what that was all about," Alex said quietly to the horses.

Silently, she went about her morning chores and made a mental note to send her grandfather a detailed description of the encounter. She hoped to include the hand signals, if she could remember how to describe them accurately.

Alex exited through the back door with her first muck basket full of manure. She was naturally surprised to find yet another man behind her barn. This man, unlike the other, was quite real. He was tall, lean, and blond with wire-rimmed glasses. Judging from his tousled thick hair, Alex guessed that he'd had little or no sleep.

"Good morning," Alex offered.

"Um. Good morning," the man stammered. "I didn't expect to find anyone else up this early."

"Well, then I guess we're even. I didn't expect to find anyone behind my barn this morning either," Alex countered.

"Your barn?" came a confused reply. "I thought this place was owned by Sarah Caldwell."

"Half. The other half belongs to me," Alex said as she stepped forward and offered her hand. "I'm Alex, Alexandra Markum."

"Oh, that's right. Now that you mention it, I do remember her speaking of you before. Have that many weeks flown by already?"

"Hmm. Losing time can be a very scary thing, but I don't recall her talking to me about you before. I'm not sure who you are, but you look like you could use a cup of coffee or something. Would you step into my office?" Alex said, indicating the barn.

"Thanks, I think I could use the caffeine. I've been up since way before dawn and I'm in need of some legal stimulants at this point. By the way, I'm Ian. Ian Valin. The town sheriff."

"Thanks for the warning," Alex chuckled. "Now I know who not to speed in front of."

The two entered the barn, and Alex went over to a small stack of boxes and quickly unpacked the one marked coffee pot. After plugging it in she unwrapped a coffee mug decorated quite naturally with a cartoon horse design and waited for the offensive substance to perk.

"Won't you sit down? I have the more comfortable furniture out here," Alex said, indicating a sweet smelling bale of alfalfa hay.

"Don't mind if I do," Ian replied.

The tired man glanced around, taking in his new surroundings.

"Handsome horse this one," he added, jerking a thumb toward Peverell.

"Thanks, I'm sure he'd agree with you."

Alex handed him a cup of coffee and took a seat on a bale of hay facing his.

"You aren't having any of this?" he questioned.

"Can't stand the stuff myself, but don't worry. I don't put much arsenic in my private blend," Alex said as she wrinkled up her nose in disgust. She was amused to see him stop just as the cup was going to tip past his lips.

"Just kidding," she continued. "So what brings you to the back of my barn this morning, Sheriff? Do I have to worry about horse thieves?"

"I wish it were something as simple as that," Ian said, finally taking a sip of coffee. "Truth is, that there is a missing girl, and a group of people are spread out all over looking for her."

"Oh yes, Rita McAllister. Sarah told me the entire story in some detail just yesterday. Have there been any more leads to her disappearance?"

"No. And even more unfortunate is that the disappearance is not about Rita, although I wish it were," Ian said shaking his head sadly. "This is about someone else—a sixteen-year-old fool kid by the name of Janey Stevenson. She sneaked out of her parent's house late last night to meet up with her boyfriend. She had a date with him and hasn't been seen since. Everyone involved is worried sick, including myself. This is the second disappearance, and I'm sorry to say that we have no more clues for Janey than we did for Rita."

The man sounded somewhat defeated. Alex couldn't help feeling sorry for him.

"I, and a handful of people have been searching since about three o'clock this morning, but no one has found or seen any trace of this girl. I can't help but worry. It's a sheriff's nature to worry. Hopefully the hounds will find something later this morning.

"Hounds?"

"Bloodhounds. After Rita's disappearance, I was sorry that they hadn't been immediately available. The trail, I felt, was too cold by the time we could bring in the dogs. It would have been nice to, as they say, exhaust every possibility. Now that Jack Elliot is back in town we won't make the same mistake twice."

"Perhaps you could use a little help. I'd be glad to help search. After all, it would be quicker on horseback out here."

"Well, the help would be appreciated, but I don't think that I could ride anything as fancy as the two horses I see here."

"I would have to agree with you there, however, you don't have to. If you look over at the other side of the barn," Alex indicated with an outstretched finger. "You will see that there is a very charming little gray mare over there by the name of Silvia that is just crying to be your new best buddy. She's a nice little hunter type horse that could take care of a five-year-old."

"I don't know, I'm not much of a rider."

"Trust me, neither is Sarah, and that's who I bought her for. Only do me a favor and don't tell Sarah I said so. She would be crushed."

"Well, okay. I'll give it a try. It would be easier than trying to keep up with the hounds on foot."

"You just rest there for a few minutes while I quickly tack them up for us. No offense, but you look like you could use a small break."

"No offense taken," Ian smiled. "You're right, you know. Truth is, I'm just about ready to drop. That's the only reason I agreed to this at all. By the way, this is pretty good coffee, but if you don't mind my sheriff-like curiosity, why do you have a coffee pot if you don't drink the stuff yourself?"

"Oh, that's easy. In the wintertime, I dip the horses bits in it to warm them before I put them in their mouths."

A large smile hit her face as she turned her back and heard him spitting the coffee out of his mouth onto the floor of the barn.

"Alex," came a whisper from the doorframe. "Is everything okay?"

"Yes, Kendra," Alex whispered back playfully. "I'm just being interrogated by the local sheriff for allegedly beating my groom and the use of illegal coffee ingredients." Then in her normal voice she added, "Just what are you doing up anyway, young lady! You're supposed to be resting in bed."

"Oh, Alex," Kendra moaned in her normal voice. "After yesterday I was just worried about you and," she stopped short as she came in far enough to actually see that there was really another person in the barn.

Kendra froze and Alex could tell that the young girl would have a panic attack soon if she did not say something.

"Kendra, this is Sheriff Valin."

"Sheriff Valin, this is my ward and groom, Kendra Phillips."

"Go on, what happened yesterday," Ian asked curiously as he rolled his coffee cup back and forth in his hands.

"Um…well," Kendra stalled, obviously startled by the situation that she had stumbled into.

"I just didn't feel well yesterday. That's all. And dear, sweet Kendra was worried about me weren't you dear?" coached Alex, while nodding slightly.

"Well, yes. That is…where exactly are you going? Sarah will be worried you know."

"Sheriff Valin here needs a few extra hands, or rather, hooves to help look for a lost girl. I have volunteered my services. Since you are up you can spend the day going over the barn improvements with Sarah and Alfred."

"Alfred?"

"Yes, Kendra, Alfred and the rest of the crew will be here sometime this afternoon. They will be beginning at the break of dawn tomorrow to upgrade the barn and install the cross-country course that I mapped out. He will also be bringing with him the initial string of twelve horses that I handpicked for the resort. So I suggest that you hop to it. There are many things to do and stalls to ready. Until he arrives, you will have to remain close to the barn and keep an eye on Terpsichore."

"Just why is that? I'd like to take a shower you know."

"I'm sure that she can spare you for that long, but the other two horses are leaving shortly, and I do not want her upset by…other things. You know how important that horse is to me."

"Yes, Alex," Kendra replied in a dull monotone.

"Sheriff Valin."

"Ian, please."

"Very well, Ian. Would you mind if I talked to Kendra in private for just a few minutes."

"No, no, not at all. I'll just go outside for a minute." Under his breath he added, "Maybe the sun is up by now."

As he walked out the barn door, Kendra moved in towards Alex.

"Just what was that about?"

"I just had a few things that I wanted to speak with you about. Just take it easy and don't get so defensive."

"Okay," Kendra replied, moping.

"Now, first of all, I saw your vintage man this morning."

"You did?"

"Shhh! Quiet!"

"You did?" Kendra said much quieter this time.

"Yes. He was trying to tell me something. I tried but couldn't figure out what it was. He gave up, pulled a pouting face that I must say closely resembles yours at times and walked away from me in a dejected sort of state."

"Oh."

"What now?"

"I do not pout."

"Case closed."

"Hey!"

"Never mind. I need you and Sarah to monitor the computer to see if there is any mail from Grandfather. Kendra, things have been set in motion that are very important. I cannot explain it to you yet because I do not have all of the facts, nor do I understand all of their meanings at this point. Somehow all of this connects but I will need Grandfather's wisdom to sort it out. This is somewhat beyond my understanding."

"Alex, what is happening?"

"Perhaps when I return there will be time to tell the story. After all, the missing girl may only turn out to be a runaway, and have nothing to do with our situation here. I may know more by then. Besides, with the sheriff here it would be a poor time indeed to discuss evil spirits don't you think?"

"I guess so."

"You guess so? Kendra, when was the last time you saw a wanted poster depicting a ghost as the perpetrator?"

"You're right. It's just too early to think."

"Oh, and make sure that Sarah is present while you talk to Alfred about the plans. I want everything exactly the way I laid it out on the designs. The only person that has ever been able to read my chicken scratching is Sarah."

"Oh, Alex. I'm sure that I can handle it," Kendra replied stubbornly.

Alex sighed. "Just promise me, Kendra. I cannot be everywhere at once, and I can sense that going with the sheriff this morning may prove to be important. Besides, you should know by now that whining will get you absolutely nowhere!"

"Okay, Alex. Only, you will take care of yourself won't you? I'm…I'm frightened."

"Why, Kendra! I believe you really care what happens to your old slave driver! I know you're frightened, Kendra. That's why I want you to promise me that you will not leave this farm under any circumstances. No matter what. Above all else, do not go anywhere without me, Sarah, or even Alfred. Do you understand? You've already had a bad scare and you are not used to such things as these."

"And you are?"

"Kendra, I want you to promise."

"Okay, I promise, but I bet that you're not experienced either."

"Well, I wouldn't say that I've had any lengthy experiences either."

"Well then!"

"However, I am definitely more equipped to deal with these, well, these situations. My ancestors have at least had firsthand experience."

"But, Alex, you are not your ancestors. What happens if…"

"Kendra, not another word," Alex snapped as she tightened the girth on the last horse and began to lead both horses outside. "I have been made your legal guardian and because of that fact you must listen to me! It is the law. Case closed."

A dejected Kendra turned away from her with tears standing out in the young girl's eyes. The usual bantering of words back and forth with Alex was something that she had become accustomed to, but this was a new side of the horse trainer that she had never seen. She shuffled back into the deeper part of the stall area to console Terpsichore and to cry in private.

"Kendra, I'll talk to you when I return. I'm sorry if I hurt you, but I've got to go. I can't keep the sheriff waiting any longer."

"Bye, Alex," came the snuffled, dejected reply.

Kendra stayed back in the darker corner of the stall and listened to the horse's hooves ring out on the aisle floor as they were led outside. She cried, listening to the hoof beats fading in the distance. Terpsichore, sensing sadness as animals often do, faced the girl and tried to console her by putting her head down into Kendra's chest, nickering softly. Cautiously, the young girl reached out and hung on the horse's neck for both morale and physical support.

Alex and the sheriff were already to the horizon when Sarah entered the barn to find Kendra crying.

"Kendra, what's the matter and where is Alex? And the horses?"

After Kendra explained what had happened, she could see worry crossing Sarah's face.

"Sarah, what is wrong and why did Alex act that way. She has never snapped at me like that before," Kendra asked while fresh tears welled up in her eyes.

"Because, Kendra, our friend is hiding the fact that she is very frightened. If I know her as well as I think I do, she is very, very frightened. That alone worries me to death, because in her whole life Alex has never been scared or backed down from anything. Her fear is not a selfish fear for herself, Kendra, because that is just not Alex. She thinks of us as her extended family and I think that she is very worried about us all."

17

"Well, the suspense is killing me," Ian said.

"Suspense?" Alex replied absently.

"Why is that horse we left behind in the barn so important that she has to have a twenty-four-hour guard? Perhaps guard is not the word. More like baby-sitter," Ian said sarcastically.

"The answer is very simple. Horses are my life, if you wish, my livelihood. That particular horse, is the answer to a dream. Don't ask me how I know, but she will be a gold-medal winner in one of the upcoming Olympic games. Just give her a few years to grow up and get serious. I just can't take any chances that something stupid will happen to her."

"Oh sure," Ian said patronizingly.

"You know, Sheriff, I really don't care if you believe me or not. Equestrians are not exactly as popular as movie stars. Don't get me wrong, I love my anonymity. Terpsichore will give me a chance to win the second gold medal of my life. That is accomplishment enough for anyone."

"Uh-huh," he replied in a condescending tone.

"What time are we meeting with the hounds?" Alex said, abruptly changing subjects.

"In a half hour. I guess we should head out towards the park. That's the last location that a witness can place the missing girl."

* * *

Twenty minutes later, the pair arrived at a small, but well-maintained park. There was quite a crowd waiting for them when they arrived in the clearing. Curious onlookers, the handlers of the hounds, and volunteer posse members were all gathered together.

A few people began to giggle seeing their sheriff astride the small, delicate gray mare. Their only mental picture of him up until now was of Ian seated behind the wheel of a police cruiser. Nobody had ever seen him riding in, or for that matter, on, anything else. A light shade of scarlet was creeping into Ian's cheeks as he approached the crowd. He swore under his breath that he should have never listened to this woman.

She had seemed so normal at first. Initially, there were the goofy comments about the coffee pot's use. It had continued on from there, until she provided the colorful, future insight on the other horse in the barn. An Olympic rider in Grand Detour. Indeed. She obviously had a screw loose. He glanced over at her again; maybe, he hoped it was just a small screw. She was, after all, the prettiest woman he'd ever laid eyes on. With her raven hair and her dark green eyes, he had been quite taken with her the moment he'd seen her. Why, he thought to himself, were the pretty ones always nuts? With this thought, Ian let out an exasperated sigh.

"Did you say something, Ian?" Alex asked absently.

"No," he responded, shaking his head. "Not a single word."

The search was underway within mere seconds of their arrival. The hounds quickly pinpointed the spot in the trail where Janey had been clubbed in the head and carried off.

"What's the matter with the dogs?" Alex said, as she eyed the bloodhounds curiously.

"What do you mean?" Ian replied.

"They look like they are torn between tracking and refusing to track."

"Now how would you know something like that?" he scoffed.

"Forget it, Ian. Trust me, you wouldn't believe me anyway," Alex said with a sigh, then she nudged Peverell into high gear and charged him up and over the oncoming ridge.

"Crazy woman," Ian muttered under his breath.

Ian began to look closely at the dogs' behavior. He noticed that, indeed, the animals were behaving oddly.

"Jack," Ian called. "What's with the dogs?"

"I've never seen it before in all my life," the man in the hunting attire said. "It's as if they don't want to go, but are humoring me because it's their job."

"I'll be damned," Ian swore under his breath.

"What was that, Ian?" Jack asked.

"Never mind, Jack."

Obliging their sense of duty, the hounds rallied and took off in pursuit. The dogs displayed confusion. They were beginning to show signs of uncertainty. The handlers began to mumble amongst themselves as the dogs paced nervously, some emitting small timid whines here and there. Others retaliating with irritated snaps at each other. Unfamiliar smells were assailing their sensitive noses and their keen senses processed the information until the appropriate scent could be found. Suddenly, they began to sing as they picked up her scent again from the air. For a bloodhound, a trail this fresh was still easy enough to pick up out of the air, but everyone could tell that there was something wrong with this trail from the word go. The negative energy flowed from the dogs, traveled down the leashes, and transmitted the uncomfortable sensations to the handlers who were already very much on edge. Mile upon mile was traversed, and the handlers, following Jack Elliot's' lead, only stopped a few moments at a time to rest the dogs.

Ever diligent, the dogs moved on regardless of the soreness of their feet or the hesitation in their spirit. These were professional creatures, and, in the end, it all came down to one fact: the dogs knew their job.

Time passed. The posse tired and their numbers began to dwindle. Soon only a few handlers, Elliot, Ian, and Alex remained. They suddenly found that they were halfway to Nachusa when the dogs stopped and began to howl. An unearthly howl came from the top of the peak in rebuttal. Everyone, dogs included, froze in place.

"What the hell was that?" muttered one of the older handlers.

"That was no dog," Elliott stated matter-of-factly.

A small panic broke out between the men, and the group became very unsettled. Picking up on their human counterparts, the dogs were now thoroughly spooked and whining quietly. Suffering from the domino effect, both of the horses began to prance back and forth nervously, emitting excitable snorts to each other.

Peverell, whom Alex had raised from a newborn colt, had never reacted to anything like this in his life. Alex fought in the saddle, and it took every ounce of horsemanship that she possessed to get Peverell to continue up the peak overlooking the Rock River. Silvia, not wanting to be left alone, charged nervously up the peak after Peverell. She was determined not to be left behind despite the protests of her rider.

"I thought you said that this horse was a piece of cake," Ian retorted cynically.

"Under normal circumstances, she is. Any animal will be unpredictable while experiencing extreme fear. Anyone who tells you any differently is selling something," Alex replied tartly.

Tension was thick between them. As she neared the top, she saw, or thought she saw, the shadow of a large dog running behind a boulder. Then it had just disappeared. A quick snap told Alex without looking in his direction that Ian had just undone the safety of his gun.

Glancing behind her, Alex could see that neither the dog handlers nor Jack Elliot himself could encourage the bloodhounds to go any further. Their fear of something unknown had outweighed their natural born instinct to find the missing. In response to the urgings of the handlers, the older, more experienced dogs laid down whimpering as if on strike. The younger dogs tried to flee in the opposite direction, straining full force at their leashes. Alex could hear the confusion and shouting continually building as she and the sheriff rode out of hearing range.

Again, the woman equestrian began to experience trouble with Peverell. She tried to speak to him to alleviate both of their fears.

"Easy, boy," she cooed patting the big horse's muscular neck. "I need you more than ever big boy, just don't let me down now."

At the top of the peak, the two riders approached a long row of thick, densely populated evergreens. Hidden from view, Alex spotted the metaphysical hot spot of the area. In the shade of large, towering evergreens, she could see the stone altar and she stopped, staring. Her mouth was open in disbelief. Close behind her, Ian was quick to check her reaction, looking back and forth between the girl and the object of her fixation.

"What's that thing?" he asked. "Just what is it doing here?"

"It's an altar," Alex said quietly. "This is your town, Ian. Suppose you tell me: Just what the hell is this thing doing here?"

Ian thought that he heard a ring of fear in her voice, so he pressed her further.

"An altar? Just what kind of altar are you talking about?" he questioned.

"One for…" she hesitated uncomfortably, "for sacrifices."

"You want to tell me just how you would know something like that?" Ian shouted.

"I…"

"Yes?"

"That is, I am…"

"Yes?"

"You'll think that I'm crazy if I tell you," Alex said.

"I might begin to think that you could be guilty if you don't. I'm still waiting for your explanation!"

Wheeling an already nervous Peverell around to face him, Alex flashed Ian a look combined equally of fury and fear. Peverell's response to his mistress's wishes was quick and powerful. It had surprised Ian how skillfully and swiftly she had swung such an obviously powerful animal around in the blink of an eye. Ian stared into her deep, green eyes; he could see the tears of anger and pain forming. Ian could not get over how beautiful she looked at that moment. Her eyes looked like a storm at sea. Why had he said such things to her? Something was forcing him to strike out at her when he didn't want to. He found himself saying horrible things that he would never dream of saying to anyone. Inside, he felt ashamed at his outspokenness. His glance averted from her direct, burning gaze and then returned.

For a hypnotic moment they seemed linked, and he could feel an unexplainable power surge over him. It was an uncomfortable feeling, like small electric shocks all over his body. Ian had never experienced anything like this before, and, after a short period of being mesmerized, he blinked rapidly and shook his head to clear it, breaking the contact.

"What the hell was that?" he demanded.

The increasingly darkening sky, streaked with lightning bolts, announced the coming storm. The threat-filled blackened sky paled in comparison when he looked at her.

"I don't know how you could even think that of me," Alex said quietly. She had completely ignored his previous remark. Ian could tell she had no intention of explaining it either. The fury was there within her; a boiling point had been reached and she fought to control it. Ian could almost feel the energy reach out to slap him. He could tell that she was struggling to keep it from blazing through to the outside. For this, he decided to be grateful and change his approach for the present.

"Then tell me what you know, and how you know it," he said more gently.

"Just remember, Ian, you asked for this."

"I'm waiting."

"There has been much terror here. It has spanned the course of many years." Alex began as she stretched her hand out toward the altar. "I can feel that this is a place of horror. Torture. And sorrow. It is not however, alone in the world. Although this is the main sacrificial area, it is one of three in this area."

"How do you know that there are three?"

"What a silly question. There are always three. It is the universal symbolism—an unholy triad."

"Well, help me out here. Could you explain to me, please, just how you happen to know that this is part of a triad?"

"The three large boulders that surround the sacrificial stone symbolize the three main gods of this particular culture," she continued. "Your own history books will tell you that tribes such as the Aztecs often made sacrifices to many of their gods. Many died to pay homage to the gods of their time: the Sun God, Xochiquetzal, the God of Maize, Itzpapalotl, the Goddess Toci, Huitzilopochtli, and Quetzalcoatl, just to name a few.

"Let me get this straight," Ian countered. "You're telling me that we have Aztec worshipers running around here?"

"No. Not at all. The configurations are all wrong. The deaths do not fit with the pattern of slaughter and sacrifice that the Aztec high priests performed in the name of their gods. This is different, yet somehow the same."

"That makes a lot of sense!" Ian snapped.

"I'm sorry. It is the only impression that I can give you at this time. Perhaps I could learn more if I were to examine the altar more closely."

Sliding down from her horse, Alex slowly walked, leading Peverell, up to the altar itself. Her feet felt as though they were weighted down. With each step, she was barely able to thrust herself forward. Through the reins she held, the horse's nervousness remained clearly defined by his unwillingness to move forward.

It was within two feet of the altar that Alex could feel the violent push against her, and she found that she could go no further towards the altar. A dark presence began to invade her mind like a brush fire. It was out of fear that she backed up several feet, emitting a startled gasp.

"What was that all about?" Ian questioned.

"Please, give me a moment," Alex snapped. Mentally she fought off the lightheadedness that followed her attack. Her mind struggled within its own confines and she found herself breaking new barriers in levels of mind-calming techniques. Again she approached the area, this time knowing what waited for her. Holding out her hands, the stone began to glow before her in an eerie radiance. Alex was transfixed as the faces of many women over countless spans of time became unveiled to her. One after another their images flashed and Alex began to feel dizzy with the comprehension of the overwhelming number of souls reaching out to her. Each one conveyed a new terror. The flow of this seemed to go on for hours, but was, in reality, only seconds.

Ian looked on uncomfortably, feeling like he was being privy to a private ritual. The unknown was always a source of discomfort for unbelievers.

The last face appeared and burned its image into Alex's mind. The agony was fresh. The pain was so violent that Alex fell to her knees, sobbing loudly. Ian was beside her in an instant.

"What's wrong?" he asked, his tone more gentle than before.

"Get me out of here," she whispered.

He lifted her up to lie across the horse and saddle. Ian became alarmed when he noticed that she had passed out cold. From her eyes ran fresh tears. They were not tears of water, however, but tears of blood.

A hundred yards from the altar, Alex jolted awake, and, startling Ian, swung herself upright into the saddle like a gymnast.

"Are you all right?" he asked

"This girl that's missing. Janey. She is sixteen?" Alex asked, ignoring the personal reference about her well-being.

"Yes."

"She had shoulder-length, sandy brown hair, Freckles, brown eyes, and a cleft chin?"

"Yes. But, how could you...How could you know that? You've never even seen a picture of her yet."

"I know," Alex replied in a sad whisper.

"How do you mean that? And what was that blood about?" Ian remarked.

"She was killed. There on that altar. The altar began to glow, and many faces of tortured women passed before my eyes. Countless women have died here, Sheriff. The reason that I know about Janey is because I just relived her last moments. They were indescribably terrifying." Alex gasped and rubbed her arms to fight off an invisible chill.

Ian just stared at her like she was an escaped lunatic, complete with a straitjacket. His mind struggled with the information she had just delivered. How was it that Alex could describe Janey so well, unless of course she had something to do with it.

"Lady, you are crazy."

Alex dismounted and walked up to Ian who was still astride Silvia.

"Ian..."

"That's, *Sheriff*!"

"Fine, Sheriff. I know that what I am about to tell you is going to sound incredible. It is not an easy thing for me to talk about. All that I ask is that you hear me out. Will you agree?"

Silence.

"Will you agree?" Alex asked again.

"All right."

"I know you won't believe me, but I am a half-blooded Cherokee. My grandfather and all my ancestors before me have been powerful Native American seers and prophets. I have fought against this destiny, if you will, my entire life. The sight is not something that I want, but my grandfather has taught me that I am here for a purpose. I was put here to help people—all people, not just my own. No matter how many hours I hide with my animal companions, a disaster of epic proportions surfaces no matter where I go. Sheriff, I know how crazy this must all sound to you, but my grandfather says that I am like a spiritual magnet. Believe me, I do not want this *gift*, as he describes it. Every tortured soul literally grabs me right up, because I am sensitive to them. Just now I saw…I saw…I have never experienced anything more terrible than the horror that I have just relived." Spinning to face Ian, Alex added, "You have a terrible evil in this town—more terrible than I think even you can imagine."

Shaking his head in disbelief, Ian could not take in what he was hearing. He categorized Alex as a nearly hysterical, perhaps dangerously deranged, woman.

"I don't know who you are, lady, but you are one hundred percent crazy! You know, you really had me worrying about you for a minute there. I can see now that you were just play-acting. I don't believe in any of that malarkey.

"That is why you will fail," she replied.

"I want some answers right now on how you knew what that kid looks like. I want to know where she is. And I want to know right now. I also want to know where you were during the disappearance of Rita McAllister."

"I was not in town when Rita disappeared," Alex said coldly. "I have witnesses. Many of them can be found all across the country. People that you would respect. People of influence. People who would have no reason to lie. Their reputations are indisputable. I must say that I am not surprised that you do not believe. I've known many that do not. In your defense, I've spent an exhausting amount of time denying it myself. I, more than anyone, can understand this since I find the idea of it incredible, to say the least. I have denied the existence of it for many years; then things began to happen for which I could not account. I did not tell you so that I would be the recipient of any attention, for that is something that I least desire. The only reason that I told you is because you need to know what happened to that poor girl. Her family, her friends must come to peace with her passing. They will suffer terribly if you do nothing. Above all, you have to be made to understand that you and everyone you are sworn to protect in this town is in terrible danger. I sincerely believe that you are going to need all the help you can get. Whether you desire it or not."

Glancing back over her shoulder at the altar, Alex added, "This evil has been here so long that I'm not sure anyone can prevail."

"Well, now I've heard everything!" Ian replied hotly.

"Ian, you don't understand..."

"Sheriff Valin. And don't even think about leaving town. I'm sure that I'm not through with you. I'm either going to arrest your ass, or have you committed."

Anger, sadness, and depression coursed throughout Alex's body and soul. She swung up into the saddle as Peverell danced nervously around. The big horse reared slightly, and Alex pressed her strong legs into the dark horse's muscular sides, charging up in front of Silvia and grabbing the gray horse's reins in the process.

"What the...?" Ian exclaimed.

"Get off!" Alex demanded, her eyes ablaze with fury.

"What?"

"I said, get off! There is a vast difference between an unwilling unbeliever and someone who is just plain, insufferably stupid. I will never subject my horses to stupid people. Get off!"

Ian angrily complied, and watched Alex gallop off down the hill, ponying the gray horse behind her own.

Walking back to the edge of the steep hill, Ian could feel his fury growing. How could she be so unfair? Forget unfair. How could she be so crazy? Just what was he supposed to think when confronted with such outlandish fairy tales? His mind raced with lines of justification for the waiting posse below.

Even as he descended the hill, Ian could hear the snickers of the deputies.

"Hey, Ian, lost your horse?" one man laughed.

"Did Madam Spoo-oo-ky take it away?" came another catcall. This last comment broke the entire crowd of men into a fit of robust laughter.

Ian, too irritated to reply, stormed past the pack of men and dogs, heading back towards town with clenched fists.

All the way back to town his mind raced with ways to get her back for this humiliation he was being made to endure. Perhaps, he thought to himself, he wasn't such a good judge of character after all.

18

Glancing out the kitchen window, Sarah could see the outline of Alex and the horses appearing over the top of the farthest ridge. She felt a nudge at the base of her brain. That nudge was trying to tell her that there was something in the way her friend was holding herself. Something that was not quite right. The rider looked so rigid and unmoving in the saddle. Sarah knew instantly that there was a whirlwind of trouble ahead, and that it would be at her door in exactly five minutes or less.

"Kendra, I think that it would be a good idea for you to go surf the net for awhile."

"I can't."

"Why not?"

"I am forbidden to touch Alex's computer."

"Why would that be?" Sarah asked peeking out the window again.

"Because the last time I touched it before we arrived, I accidentally trashed a few files."

"A few files?" Sarah said absently.

"Okay, more than a few files. Somehow I managed to delete her entire operating system, and all of her files."

"Kendra, why don't you go upstairs and lay down for a while?" Sarah suggested.

"What? Sarah, I'm not tired!"

"Well, I think that this would be an excellent time for you to become so," Sarah said with encouragement. She looked again, trying to estimate how much time she had until Alex arrived

"Sarah, you haven't heard a word I've said," Kendra said chastisingly. "Are you trying to get rid of me?"

Rising up from her chair, Kendra crossed the room to join Sarah at the window. She frowned as she noticed the incoming dark and threatening sky. Then her eyes fell to the horizon and the quickly advancing figures beginning to emerge from the shadows of the nearest ridge.

"Is that Alex out there?"

"Yes, Kendra. I can see Silvia's shiny gray coat from here."

"Well. Hey, where's the sheriff? You know, the fellow that rode out of here with her."

"I suspect that right about now he is taking a very long walk," Sarah answered slowly.

"No kidding! She really dumped him out there somewhere?" Kendra exclaimed excitedly.

"Knowing Alex like I do, I would say that, well, whatever happened, he probably had it coming."

"Finally, something to tease her about."

"No!" Sarah retorted, a little too sharply.

Feeling dejected after having been snapped at twice in one day, Kendra slunk toward the stairs.

"Kendra." Sarah entered the front entryway calling after her. "I'm so sorry, Kendra. So much has happened and the tension here has become overwhelming. I didn't mean it. You would understand if you had been with Alex a little longer just how serious this could be. The way she is acting now is just not Alex."

"Don't tell me that now *you* are going to start in with that Native American seer stuff."

"I know that it sounds crazy, Kendra, but hanging around with Alex for so long, well I've seen many things that I wouldn't believe myself. You should meet her grandfather, he would make you believe in a heartbeat."

"Okay, so you want to get rid of me for some discussion with Alex. I get the picture. I'll go stare at the computer for a while. I might as well since I can't touch it."

"Oh my god, the computer!" Sarah exclaimed, slapping the palm of her hand to her forehead. "Kendra, I want you to break your computer restrictions and go upstairs to check for a return e-mail from Lightning Horse. Alex will hang me if a response has arrived and I didn't check."

* * *

"Stupid!" Alex screamed slamming her saddle roughly down on its appropriate rack. Peverell jerked his head up in alarm at the distress he could sense in his mistress's words. "How could I be so stupid?"

"Now what are you beating yourself up about?" said a taunting voice from the doorframe. "By the way, I can tell that you like him."

"Sarah, you have never been so wrong! I dislike him immensely. He's an *egotistical, brain dead, full-fledged, hot-tempered idiot*."

"That's really serious, Alex. I don't think in all the time I have known you that you have let a single person make you this angry and upset."

Rigidly, Alex crossed the stable floor and reentered Peverell's stall. She reached up and flung her arms around the large horse's neck, hanging there for several moments. In sympathy, the big gelding drew his head around Alex's back and returned the hug.

"I think that Pev is jealous, Alex."

"Sarah, please be serious for a moment. We are in very big trouble, and you've decided to run a dating service! I don't know if I can even explain it," said the muffled voice, still obscured by being buried in the thick neck of the equine.

"I don't think that it is a disaster for an Olympic rider to fall for a little hick town sheriff."

"Look, Sarah, I don't know what is going on here, but I don't think that you quite understand the enormity of the situation. If you did, I assure you that you would not be trying to play Cupid right now. No amount of joking around is going to help us either," Alex added, her voice full of misery.

Quietly, Sarah crossed over to the stall opening. She was very startled as Alex turned towards her; the face that she had come to know so well over the years looked like a stranger to her. In a few short hours Alex's face had become pinched with strain, her usual composure was gone. Her natural dark complexion had been replaced by paling skin. Her demeanor reeked of defeat. The severity of the situation was obvious by the look in her friend's haunted eyes. It was evident that her friend had been crying unwillingly for some time as well, but, what unnerved Sarah the most, were the small traces of dried blood on her friends cheeks. Sarah felt fear crawl up into her very soul and take root like a leech.

"Alex, my god, what is it? What's wrong?"

"Sarah, I have made a huge mistake."

"What could you have possibly done that would be so wrong."

"I told him what I saw. Or rather, what my second sight saw. Now he thinks *I'm* crazy. The worst part is, that he won't listen to what I told him."

"Why is that the worst part?"

"Because, if I'm right, and I think that I am, everyone in this town and surrounding area is at considerable risk. Many more people will die because of my lack of tactfulness. I was caught up in the horror of what I saw and was unable to stop myself in time from telling him…"

"About your gift."

"My gift," Alex hotly scoffed. "No, about my curse. Now, because of this afternoon's incident, I have put everyone's lives at an even greater peril.

"What did you see that could be so awful?" Sarah said. "I'm sure that he doesn't think as badly of you as you think."

"You weren't there. You couldn't possibly…Oh, never mind, Sarah. Just promise me that you will never, I mean never, let Kendra out of your sight. I want the two of you bound together so tightly that a circus barker would say that you two are actually Siamese twins."

"You know I wouldn't let anything happen to Kendra."

"It's not just Kendra that I am worried about. I do not want anything to happen to you either. As a matter of fact, I want Kendra to move into your suite tonight."

"Alex, tell me," Sarah pleaded.

"It…" Alex gasped. "Sarah, I have never encountered an evil like this before. Has Grandfather returned my e-mail yet? I think I'm going to need a lot of help."

"Alex," Sarah said almost inaudibly. "Tell me what we are fighting. I was married to a cop and I think I can deal with most everything that is evil."

"I don't think so. You are prepared for the normal evil that is known to man, rather, caused by man. This evil was not caused by a mere man. At least, not as we would define the term today. Nothing could prepare you for this. Here, sit down," Alex said lightly patting the hay bales which still remained on the floor from earlier that morning. "I need to tell you. Not because I want to, but because it is the right thing to do. You must learn about your opponent. Whoever, or whatever it is, it is very dangerous."

Sarah sat down gingerly and waited for Alex to compose herself, steeling herself for the most dreadful thing she could imagine. Unfortunately, no preparation could have made Sarah ready for what she was about to hear.

"It began well enough," Alex started. "We were riding in the direction of the next town. The dogs, after some coaxing, had the scent. I should have known then that things were going to go wrong. You could tell the dogs were torn between a dedication to duty and a sense of fear. I could feel it hanging in the air. Everyone could. They finally relented and traveled to the base of a small peak just outside of Nachusa. Then suddenly, they refused to go one more step towards this small peak."

"Bloodhounds refused to track?" Sarah stammered. "That is…Alex, that has never happened in all the years I've heard about tracking dogs from Bruce."

"Not only that, Sarah. Pev was acting so oddly that he almost did throw me. It took every bit of experience I had to stay on him. You have known that horse almost as long as I have, and you know how out of character that is for him. There was also this odd, heavy feeling to the air. I cannot describe it any other way than this. I have never experienced anything like it before. It was as if the air was weighted, pressurized in some way. It could even be some sort of explanation for why Ian jumped down my throat so viciously. The place reeked of an ancient wickedness. As we neared the top of the peak, I came face to face with a stone altar."

"An altar?"

"Yes. Then, as I gazed on it, it began to glow. It was an otherworldly glow. The worst part was that I was the only one who could see it."

"How could you tell that?"

"First of all, the horses. They, spiritual animals themselves, were completely unaffected by it. If not through sight, then surely their inborn sense of flight would have prevailed. When I mentioned it to the sheriff, he thought I was crazy. Faces of many women began to pass in front of me. Women from all ages. All walks of life. The constant stream of them was overwhelming. There were so many individuals that I lost count of how many there were. One thing was certain though—they were from all very different periods of time. Each of them was just like our apparitional friends that we are experiencing here at the hotel. I am sure that in some way they are tied with the spirits that walk this house. The last unfortunate one I experienced was the young girl who is presently presumed missing."

"Janey Stevenson?"

"Yes. Apparently I described her very well. Perhaps a little too well for our illustrious sheriff. Her memories, having just occurred, were, of course, the most…vivid," Alex shuddered.

She folded her chin tightly to her chest, and Sarah could feel that her friend was fighting back very strong emotions. Alex looked so very tired to her. Sarah had always thought of Alex as youthful, exuberant, and inexhaustible. She was never one to show her age. At this moment, Sarah could swear that Alex had aged ten years in ten minutes. Her spirit loomed dangerously close to destruction; everyone had their peak of limitations, and Sarah was afraid the Alex had reached that peak. When Sarah reached out to touch her shoulder, she was surprised when her friend almost jumped off the bale in fright.

"Sorry," Alex apologized, sniffing back the emotion that fought within her to get out. "Give me a minute; it has been a rough couple of hours."

"Take your time, Alex," Sarah said expressing concern.

After a long pause in meditation, Alex drew from her spirit within and tried to renew herself. There were no emotions evident from her; the only way that Sarah could tell if she was still alive was from the occasional steady breathing that she produced. The barn was quiet except for the contented munching of hay from the stalls. Sarah wanted to scream in frustration, shake her friend and have Alex come back to her the way she was when she arrived not that long ago—the way she had been consistently over the past twenty-five years of friendship. Hearing a sharp intake of breath, Sarah could tell that Alex was ready to continue.

"I don't know yet what force killed her, but whoever, or whatever, it was opened up this poor girls chest with a ceremonial dagger of some kind. The being was kind enough to give me a front row seat to view all the details."

"What do you mean?"

"I believe that this being is taunting me. Giving me small pieces of information at a time, like a cat playing with a mouse before he kills it. I was forced to watch the girl as the demon reached in its hand and pulled out her heart while she was still drawing her last breath. Her heart was still pumping blood as it was ripped forcibly from her body. The thing drew that heart towards itself and…" Alex hesitated, shaking, "wiped her blood across his face, but not before this demon tortured the living daylights out of her."

"Oh God!"

Abruptly, Sarah stood up and ran to the barn door, barely making it outside in time before vomiting. She was so consumed by the event that she did not hear Alex coming up behind her.

"I'm sorry that I have to tell you the whole thing, but you have to know what we are up against. Any omission would put you in even greater danger."

"Your vision, Alex. You called it a demon. Could you see who or what it was?"

"No. Whatever, or whoever, is behind this is very powerful. Its true image was kept hidden from me. There was no way that I could interpret it from the vision that I intercepted. All I can tell you is that the girl endured great fright all the way to the very end."

"And most of the faces you have seen."

"They are roughly between Kendra's age or ours. Sarah, I have given great thought to the Kendra issue on my ride back here to the estate. The decision has not been an easy one for me. I know in my heart that Kendra needs the support for her soul that I have been trying to give her, but I am afraid for her life if she stays. I believe that perhaps I should think about sending her away until, well, perhaps just sending her away. Lightning Horse and the tribe would take very good care of her. I think that maybe you should go as well, Sarah."

"I will not leave you here. Why can't we all go?"

"Wherever I now go, the dead and this demon will follow me. I would have no rest no matter how far I run; but you and Kendra—you would not have to face such a problem. I think it would be best if you both leave first thing tomorrow morning. I'll have Alfred drive you and the rig away with the horses."

"You don't expect to live through this, do you?" Sarah asked meekly.

"I won't lie to you, Sarah. I wish I knew."

"Then, I'm staying."

The two women quietly approached the house and both nearly jumped out of their skins as Kendra startled them when they entered the kitchen.

"You've got mail," she clamored.

19

"Why aren't you in the barn seeing to your chores?" Alex asked tiredly, trying her best to tease the girl with her limited energy supply.

"Terpsichore is fine. Honestly, she didn't miss you or the other horses while you were gone," Kendra shot back. "By the way, I'm sure you had a great laugh at my expense while I was away."

"What do you mean by that remark young lady?"

"You know very well what I mean! You specifically told me to get Sarah when I spoke to Alfred. Sneak that you are! You knew that I would go and try to speak to him alone. What you didn't tell me is that Alfred doesn't speak any English!"

"Kendra," Alex began with an exasperated sigh, "I have had about the worst day that I've ever experienced in my life and it is only half over. In fact, it has been so wonderful that I just can't wait to see what happens next. So please tell me, in English, just exactly what are you talking about? I am far too tired for our usual bantering of words. I'm even too tired to go over the meaning of sage wisdom for today."

"That," Kendra replied with dramatic annoyance, "is what I have been trying to explain to you in some detail. I tried to go over the plans first with Alfred myself. I found out after just mere seconds of trying to converse with him that he only speaks this weird Cherokee gibberish."

Alex looked at Sarah, who just gave her one of those innocent deer in the headlight looks and then added to the picture by shrugging her shoulders. A smile lit Alex's face. It was a tired smile, but nonetheless a smile. The first one she had experienced in many hours. Alex had almost forgotten how it felt to laugh. She chuckled; it felt good, even if it only lasted for a few moments.

"Leave it to Alfred," Alex choked out in between suppressed giggles.

"What is so funny?" Kendra demanded.

"The joke is on you, Kendra," Sarah snickered.

"Kendra," Alex replied in between giggles, as she grabbed Sarah's shoulder for support. Alfred Fox speaks just as well as either Sarah or I! Sometimes even better. I'm afraid that Alfred was having a bit of fun with you. I truly meant what I said to you earlier. Alfred and I both write like pigs, in fact, his English written words do resemble Cherokee."

Laughing, the three of them opened the kitchen door and walked down the corridor toward the main staircase. Alex was so anxious to get to the message that was waiting for her that she did not look above them until Sarah screamed out loud and pointed upwards.

Alex became immediately transfixed at the sight. There, in a spectral, translucent form was a man, hanging by his neck over the highly polished oak check-in desk. Though dead, the form seemed to be very animated. His face reflected sadness, and his hands kept flashing a set of symbols to the onlookers. All three women stood motionless, frozen in time, and all three were unable to tear their gaze from the apparition. This newest specter continued to fade away in a similar fashion to the ghost that Sarah had first encountered on the front porch. At first, the transformation was not so terrible to watch, but it was not long before the dimensions of the face melted into frozen muscles and bulging eyes. It finally deteriorated down to a frightening, skeletal form, sporting an obvious broken neck.

When the specter began to decompose before their eyes, Kendra turned to Alex for comfort. The older woman shielded her from the frightening display playing out directly above their heads. As quickly as he had appeared, the ghost faded from sight. Anyone else who heard their story would try to make them believe that he had been nothing more than a product of their imagination all along.

"The hand motions!" Alex exclaimed.

"What about them?" Sarah asked.

"They are the same."

"The same as what, Alex?"

"Those are the same hand motions that the man in the barn flashed at me. I wish I knew what those meant!"

"What man in the barn?" Sarah asked.

"I knew there was something about today I left out," Alex replied snapping her fingers in a forgetful fashion.

"Okay, Alex. Give. If I know you half as well as I think I do, you have left out the most important fact of the day," Sarah scolded.

"Come on now, Sarah. Even you have to admit that it has been a busy day. Please allow me the smallest margin of error for forgetting this one little thing. On the scheme of things, this occurrence was relatively unimportant. That is, comparatively speaking. However, at the same time, now that I think of it, the significance could be extremely important."

"Oh, for God's sake, Alex. Would you please just make up your mind!" Sarah said.

"Never mind the bantering, you two, who, or what, was that?" Kendra whispered, finally finding her voice. "And, is he gone yet?"

"Yes, Kendra the spirit is gone. He is a restless spirit, and he seemed to want to tell us something, too," Alex replied. Her voice floated as if she were in a dreamlike trance.

Ascending the stairs, Sarah finally began to speak, "He seemed so sad."

"Well, if I were dead, I'd be sad, too!" Kendra shot back.

"That is not what she meant, Kendra," Alex retorted. "He has obviously failed at some mission in his life and now, in death, he's trying to warn us of the danger that permeates this place. It would all be so easy if we could just be smart enough to figure out what he is trying to say to us. The poor man has become just another tortured soul that in some strange way is chained to the legacy of this house. What we have to do is figure out what and why."

"How about the library?" Sarah asked.

"There's a library in this old house?" Alex questioned.

"No, but there's simply an ancient one in town. They are sure to have some records of the community."

"An excellent suggestion," Alex replied. "Tomorrow, we shall all go there and try to find some shred of evidence that could have started all of this. I only wish that I knew where to begin. Better yet, what century to look in."

As they came to the head of the stairs, the trio turned left to go down the hallway towards Alex's room. Lingering behind the other two, Alex took one more look over her shoulder where the latest ghost had been. Shaking her head, she turned back towards her friends and followed them into the room.

No sooner had Alex entered the room, when it began. The loud sobbing began to emanate from down the hallway. Alex looked immediately at Sarah, and could tell from the look on her face, that it was a sound her friend recognized.

"Remember the first night, when you two arrived with the horses?" Sarah whispered.

"Yes."

"This was the sobbing I heard that night also. I thought at first that one of you might be in trouble or having a bad dream."

The trio peered out of the doorway and down the hallway to the suite found at the very end. Timidly, the three women crept down the hallway towards the sound of the sobbing. Alex led the way down the hallway first, Kendra second, and Sarah bringing up the rear.

As they drew near, a strange, bright glow could be seen from under the closed door. Alex jumped forward and threw the door open. She expected to find the scene behind the door to resemble the strange theatrics Sarah had described the other night. Instead, not only wasn't anything strange going on, there was nothing going on at all. Everything was in order. That is, it was in order as far as a room in sad need of the redecorating fairy. There was no cleaned up room, but there were plenty of cobwebs. No billowing curtains. No pillows with fringe. Nothing. Most of all, there was nothing the slightest bit supernatural going on. It was the most normal looking room that Alex had seen in the entire hotel.

"The ghosts are coming more frequently. Alex, isn't that a bad sign?" Kendra whispered. "Are they trying to hurt us?"

"No, Kendra, these poor souls are not trying to hurt us," Alex replied. "The truth is, even though you are frightened of them, I believe they are trying to help us. To warn us, if you wish. But, they are getting discouraged with us not comprehending them. I believe that the appearances are becoming more frequent because our lack of understanding is frustrating them. They are beginning to become bolder in their appearances. I believe they hope that this will better enable us to figure out what they are trying to tell us."

"And the sobbing ghost?"

"Is a tortured soul. Unhappy with whatever took place in the past. Perhaps in time the sobbing ghost will also take some kind of visual form."

"How far in the past?" Kendra asked.

"I wish I knew," Alex replied. "Fashions in the past were never my strongest suit."

"Fashions of the present aren't either," Sarah added.

Alex feigned a hurt look and then glanced down at her clothing.

"I guess that I do look a little rumpled at that."

"Oh, don't mind me, Alex, you look fine. That is if filthy, dirty breeches are in high fashion, along with those mud spattered riding boots you've tromped through the hotel in."

"Oops!"

"Never mind the oops, Alexandra Markum. Just you wait until I stick you with the carpet cleaning bill for this place."

"Okay, okay," Alex said holding her hands out in front of her and shaking them vigorously. "From now on I'll take my boots off before I get to the house. You know, things have been a little busy here. Now, on to more important things, I better read my mail."

The three women turned and retreated back down the hallway to their own set of rooms.

"Sarah, while I read this, I would like you to attend to that other thing we discussed in the barn," Alex said.

"Okay," Sarah replied.

"What thing is that?" Kendra asked

"I'll let you know what the letter contains after I read it," Alex continued, completely ignoring Kendra. Turning into her room, Alex left her two companions together in the hallway.

"Alex would like you to pack up your stuff and move into…" Sarah began.

"What? Oh no. I cannot take more mornings of Miss Perky! I had to share with her all the way here and I just can't…"

"Kendra," Sarah interrupted sternly. "She wants you to bunk with me, so you can just cut the dramatics."

"Well, that's slightly different, in a much better way. Why?"

"I will not kid you, she thinks that we will be safer together."

"Can I ask you a question?"

"I think you just did."

"Sarah, you're being just like Alex," Kendra whined.

"Okay," Sarah said. "I'm sorry. What do you want to know?"

"Are you a morning person?"

"Only if morning starts at ten. Even that's after at least two cups of coffee."

"That is all that I wanted to hear, roomy."

The two entered the doorframe to Kendra's room and began to grab up handfuls of stuff to take into Sarah's room. They were too busy to notice the astonished look on Alex's face as they passed by her open door; if they had, they might have noticed that it was quickly replaced by a scowl.

20

Ian had been miserable all evening. The rest of the day had turned up no clues whatsoever on Janey Stevenson's whereabouts. It was as if she had disappeared right off the face of the earth. Another victim, and it had happened just like Rita. To make matters much worse, he had involved a civilian—that insufferable Markum woman. Admittedly, it had been his idea and it had seemed sound enough at the time. He had quickly regretted his decision after the turn of events.

Ian was a descendant from a long line of policeman, and no one from the old school of thought went in for this psychic mumbo jumbo that she had been spouting. She had made him look ridiculous in front of his town. It was okay for her, because after all, she could pack her bags and leave anytime she wanted. He was tied to this place just as surely as if he had a ball and chain around his ankle. The Valins had made a commitment of protection to the town, and all had carried a secret pact amongst themselves to clear the name of the man who came to America and started it all for them, Ian's great-grandfather, Graham Valin. This chore had been passed on from generation to generation—to exonerate the family name.

He sighed. It was just his luck to fall for a beautiful lunatic. After contemplating the afternoon, he knew that the real reason he had lashed out at her was that he found her disturbingly attractive. How dare someone that he felt such an interest in be so blatantly insane. Damn, how could that Markum woman be so excruciatingly irritating? He had known the moment he had insinuated that she could be implicated, it had felt all wrong. Becoming increasingly ashamed of his brashness, Ian wished that he could have taken it all back.

After all, maybe she was just a little nuts, like that fellow that kept claiming that he was a Russian prince. Everyone just humored him and no one ever got hurt over it. Perhaps she was just someone with an overactive imagination. Now, with his pointing, accusatory finger, he had also made her extremely angry. In front of all his police friends, too. My, he had been busy hadn't he? Ian was sure that by the next morning his folly would be spread all over town. Not that the present situation wasn't bad enough, but as rumors spread they gained in fantastic untruths, especially in this town. By morning, not only would they say he had made such a fool of himself over some crazy woman, but they will probably say that he was dressed in a pink tutu to boot. He groaned and slumped over on his desk, head in hands. So engrossed was he in the day's events that Ian hardly heard Ron Van Allen come through his front door.

"Why hello, Sigmund," Ron said.

"Not you, too," Ian groaned.

"Why not me, too?" Ron asked. "What better friend do you have to tell you what an ass you made out of yourself today."

"Well, you're right there. I should have my head examined for ever listening to that woman in the first place."

"Wrong. I think you should have your head examined for *not* listening to her in the second place."

"What? Ron, how could you possibly…? You were not there; you couldn't possibly begin to know what took place out there!"

"I think this small town life has gotten to you, Ian Valin. How dare you shoot down another person and their theories just because their ideas differ slightly from your own? I expected better from you; after all, you went to Berkeley. Didn't they teach you to have an open mind there?"

"Slightly! Have you got any idea, any idea at all, what that nut said to me out there? Carrying on with her trances and visions. I have never heard such a bunch of bull!"

"I think that I know exactly how those ideals and theories would play out in your narrow little mind, Ian Valin. However, I have done my homework and you have not."

"Just what exactly do you mean by that crack?" Ian said sharply.

"Simply this," Ron replied as he took his arm out from behind his back and produced a rolled up magazine.

"A magazine? What are you going to do, hit me across the nose with it?"

"Don't tempt me. Say, actually, that is not such a bad idea!"

"Do you honestly want me to change all my scruples based on the insides of a magazine?"

"Not just any magazine."

"I suppose not," Ian sneered. "It's probably one of those crazy UFO magazines which features flying saucers, creatures from other worlds, and the MIB who are placed here on earth to solve every problem. I suppose that they are headed my way next?"

"Oh no," Ron said shaking his head slowly. "This magazine has even worse filth in it. Why I'm shocked to even suggest that you should look at the cover of this trashy periodical."

Ian stretched out his hand and angrily took the rolled up periodical from his friend. As he unrolled it, his eyes caught the title, and, without looking up, he could hear Ron exploding into a peal of hysterical laughter.

The magazine was one of the many law enforcement magazines that Ian himself subscribed to. Right there, in full color, Ian could see a picture of a woman. The woman. The woman that he had been riding with all afternoon. She was pictured astride the exact same horse that she had ridden today. He knew instantly that it was Alex. He had committed every line in her face to memory. In an accompanying picture on the cover, he could see something else that greatly disturbed him. The person in the picture was a woman in a professional riding habit, complete with the tail-coat and top hat. She was hugging an all-too-familiar horse that had a gold medal hanging on the front of its chest. It did no good for Ian to try and deny the facts to himself; the woman on the front cover was indeed Alexandra Markum. The headline below the picture indicated that she was on the cover of the magazine because she had been helping the Wyoming State Police search for a missing girl.

"I hope you enjoy the article," Ron purred. "Oh, and you might want to take a peek at what name is printed on the subscription label."

"I..." Ian began. Then, dumbfounded, he broke off in silence. "Ron, this magazine has my name on it! Where did you...?"

"Do you remember the church rummage sale last month? You donated numerous stacks of things, and among them were a few law enforcement magazines. Quite a coincidence that you got rid of this one isn't it? Perhaps you should read these magazines before you throw them out. After all, you wouldn't want me blabbing all over town that you are wasting the taxpayer's money! Well, good night. I wouldn't want to keep you from any important reading that you might, or should, have to do. Or any apologizing for that matter."

With that, Ron turned on his heels and marched swiftly out the door and into the night. The know-it-all grin on his face would burn in Ian's memory for a very long time to come.

Motionless, Ian stood there gazing at the cover. He couldn't believe his own eyes. If it hadn't been for his name on the cover, he would've sworn that Van Allen had mocked-up this magazine as a joke. He walked slowly back over to his chair and began to read. When he finished, he read it again. And then again.

When he awoke the next morning after a fitful night of sleep, Ian found himself still sitting in that chair, feet propped up on the desktop, clutching the magazine tightly in his hands.

21

Alex's dreams were getting worse. She could vividly see a woman with fair skin and flaming red hair cleaning a room in the hotel. She could even hear the woman happily humming what sounded like a Celtic tune. Suddenly, Alex found herself being the woman. It was her legs that walked down the staircase and out into the hotel gardens. No matter how she tried to break free she found that she was trapped into following the woman's footsteps. At first, her breathing came rapidly and Alex fought to break free from the vision. Finding that tactic useless, she tried to slow her breathing and relax, willing herself to melt into the vision.

Walking over a wooden footbridge, she noticed a pond full of exotic goldfish. The night sky was alive with beauty. Twinkling stars framed a beautiful orange harvest moon that lit her way to the garden gazebo.

Entering the gazebo, she took a seat and waited. A large stray dog crept close to her in the nearby bushes.

"Stephen," Alex called out trancelike, with an obvious Irish lilt to her voice.

She could feel the panic building as the woman sat there alone. Abruptly, a hand clamped viciously over her mouth so she was unable to cry out. Alex could feel the wet tears as they rolled down her cheeks. She screamed into the man's hand and turned to look over her left shoulder. There she saw an eight-inch, shiny blade poised above her. It glowed with the orange light of the moon. Alex watched in a frozen horror as the knife plunged down into her chest. The stroke of the blade seemed to take an eternity. Tears pooled in her eyes and she screamed, though it came out in her slumber as a mere whimper.

In the next few seconds, she found herself floating above the scene as in an out-of-body experience. She saw the woman on the floor in the gazebo, barely alive, trying to say something with only a red bubble appearing at her lips. Then she was gone.

Time fast-forwarded. A solemn group of three men approached the gazebo.

"Ian," she whispered.

But it was not Ian. The clothes were all wrong. This was another time, another man. The men began to speak, and she could clearly hear their conversation.

"Her name is Daphne. Daphne Breckinridge," said the first man. He was dressed expensively. Alex sensed that he was a man of importance but she could see him only from the back. "We are looking for her husband. We have so far been unable to find him."

"Unable to find him?" the man who looked like Ian exclaimed. "With his wife slaughtered, he is missing? Officer Grant, take another man with you and find Mr. Breckinridge."

"Oh no, not Stephen," stammered the first man. "A more gentle man I have never seen. He could not possibly..."

"I am not going to assume he is guilty, but he must be found," said the Ian look-alike.

"I understand," murmured the first man, and then he walked away, turning his face into the shadows. Alex had been unable to catch a glimpse of his face.

The only man left at the dead girl's side was the man that resembled Ian. He gave a deep sigh as he looked over the scene for any clues. Taking out a notepad, he began to make observations of the crime scene. Kneeling by the girl's body he began to study something that had apparently fallen down the cracks and lodged underneath the gazebo. He stood and brushed the dust off his trousers. Then he stepped down the tree stairs to meet the quickly approaching officer.

"Inspector," Officer Grant said, returning to the gazebo area to check in. "We have combed the grounds and have been unable to locate Stephen Breckinridge."

"I do not require you to search for Mr. Breckinridge any further, Officer Grant," the Inspector said.

"You've found him then, sir?" the officer asked.

The Inspector motioned to the officer to follow him up onto the platform of the gazebo, where he pointed to the floor directly beneath the body of Daphne. Upon closer investigation the startled officer gasped and jumped back as he found himself looking unexpectedly into the eyes of a dead man.

Alex gasped, and sat bolt upright. The last thing that she saw was through the dead man's eyes, then abruptly the vision ended. Upset, she quietly cried herself to sleep.

* * *

It was a beautiful morning, and Alex could almost have swept away the bad memories of the previous day if not for one thing. The same apparition that met her in the barn yesterday morning, met her first thing this morning. His demeanor was sad, and his transparent hands were again flashing their secret message. The hands seemed more aggressive this time; their delivery screamed of desperate urgency. It was the same message that the ghost in the hallway had been trying in vain to get across to her. After what had just seemed a few moments, the apparition apparently gave up and turned dejectedly into the same wall as before.

"I wish I knew what you were trying to tell me," Alex said.

Turning, she saw that Alfred was standing behind her in the doorframe. He looked as white as a sheet, and Alex wondered what more could possibly happen.

"Mornin', Alex," he mumbled quietly.

"Good morning, Alfred," she replied. "By the way, Alfred, that was a dirty trick you pulled on Kendra yesterday."

"Me?" He indicated himself innocently.

"Yes, you! You know exactly what I mean, too. Don't you even try to act innocent with me," Alex said, shaking her finger at him in a menacing way. "Incidentally, all the horses you brought with you look to be in great shape! But, I don't remember buying that little black and white piebald in the end stall."

"I picked him out myself," Alfred said smiling. "I thought you might like him, for you-know-who."

"Is that the horse you picked out for Kendra? Alfred, I see that I must let you pick out horses more often," Alex said.

"Then you like him?" Alfred said proudly.

"Yes, I like him very much, and I'm quite sure that Kendra will also."

Alfred's grin, however, was short lived and faded rapidly from his face.

"Miss Alex, there is a problem."

"Oh really?" Alex replied. "Nothing serious I hope?"

"I'm afraid so."

"Please tell me that we have lost a shipment of fence posts or something like that."

"I wish I could, Alex. The news is much worse."

"What might that be?"

"Come, I will show you."

The two walked away from the barn and towards the pond. Alex's mind raced to figure out what would make Alfred so uncharacteristically serious. The last thing she needed right now was another disaster. Although Alfred was completely unaware of the placement of the long-torn-down gazebo, visions from the previous night's sleep ran through Alex's brain, telling her that this was where it had been. She got a cold chill as they approached the area.

"You see, Alex. We were beginning to dig so that we could lay the foundation for the water complex. You know how we must secure the base in all the corners so that the bank will last."

"Yes, I know. Go on."

"Well, after we broke ground and got to about three feet deep, we found some things in the ground."

"What kind of things, Alfred?"

"I think that you should see for yourself.

"You say that like I am not going to like what I see."

"I know that you won't. I certainly don't like it. No one ever likes to find bad omens. As a seer, you will understand. As we uncovered this, a white owl sang in the trees, and we all saw a large wolf or dog skulking in the nearby trees."

"That is bad. Alfred, why didn't you come and get me right away?"

"I was busy with the work crew. Mass panic broke out. It was pure chaos at first. I think that you should know that the men and their families have already gone. I will be including myself in the list of the missing just as soon as we are done here this afternoon."

"What do you mean?" Alex yelled, as she stopped and put her hands on her hips. "Alfred, we have known each other for our entire lives. We have had this deal for almost as long. If we were not cousins, I would clobber you for what you just said."

"The men are afraid, Alex. I'm sorry to say that so am I. You should be, too."

"Afraid. Afraid of what?"

"Come, you will see better over here," Alfred said guiding her towards the pit.

Alex gazed down into the pit. She was totally unprepared for what she saw. Skeletons. A mass grave of skeletons.

"Ye gods!" she exclaimed, catching her breath.

"You see, Alex. No amount of loyalty can make those men stay here. I don't think that even you can blame them. Many of them still follow the old traditions, believe in the old ways. When the dead are moved to hallowed ground, then maybe they can be persuaded to return. You know our beliefs as well as I do."

"I understand, Alfred. I'll do what I can, as quickly as I can. Only, please don't go far. Ancient beliefs or not, I might need some quick, last-minute help."

"You know that you can count on me, Alex," Alfred said as he swallowed uncomfortably. "Everyone else will be staying a few towns away. I will try to stay in town. You have the cell phone number. Just call me, and I will return. Oh…I almost forgot."

"With this staring you in the face," Alex said sarcastically, "how could you possibly forget to tell me anything?"

"This," Alfred said as he dug his hand in the pocket of his jeans. "This talisman was buried in the pit with these bodies."

As he began to hand it over, Alex suddenly snatched her outstretched hand away as if she had been bitten viciously by a rattlesnake. Alfred again tried to hand it to her, and Alex again had the same reaction, only this time Alfred had brought the talisman just a little closer than before.

The power that emitted from the talisman surged at the seer, pushing her away with a vicious slap. Alex had never in her life experienced the power that totally encompassed her. It felt as though every ounce of energy was being drained from her body and soul. It was a few mere seconds until the exposure had its final effect. Alfred looked on in amazement. He had never before seen Alex have one of her trances. It was something that the elders of the tribe had always spoken of, but he had never witnessed it. In any event, he wasn't quick enough to catch her as she passed out. Using a fireman's carry, Alfred moved Alex away from the rim of the pit and back towards the barn area.

Minutes later, after Alfred was able to awaken her, Alex seemed disoriented; her world was still spinning. She mumbled something inaudible and then snapped to a full-awake status.

"What did I just say?" Alex asked frantically.

"Darned if I know," Alfred replied. "That was the craziest dialect that I've ever heard. It sounded something like 'twah' something or another with some additional mumbo jumbo thrown in for good measure."

"Is that all you remember?"

"Yes, Alex. I'm sorry."

"Damn," she swore under her breath.

"I wish I had been listening more closely. I was terribly afraid for you."

"That's okay, Alfred. Let me see the talisman again."

As Alfred brought it forward, Alex involuntarily leaned away from it. "Just hold it for a minute and let me look at the carvings," she said.

Alfred turned the talisman over in his hands so that Alex could see the marks.

"These symbols, do they mean anything to you?" she asked.

"Not to me, but honestly I don't like the feeling that the stone gives me."

"Apparently, neither do I. I am finding it difficult just being this close to it. Yet, somehow it reminds me of something familiar. Bring it up to the house and give it to Sarah. I'm afraid that we will have to call the sheriff's office about this other matter," Alex said gesturing in the direction of the pit of bones.

Alex breathed a tired sigh, and the pair headed off in the direction of the house. What was going to turn up next? Every time Alex thought things had hit absolute rock bottom, something else turned up to prove her wrong. She walked inside the kitchen door; Sarah turned to look at her friend. One glance at Alex conveyed an entire message.

"Oh no! Now what?" Sarah groaned.

"There, um…Well, um, Sarah it seems that we have a slight landfill problem here on the property."

"Landfill problem?"

"Well. Sort of. Sarah," Alex said, pausing uncomfortably, "I don't suppose that I could get you to call the sheriff out here could I? After all, he and I didn't end on exactly the most congenial note when we were last together."

"Do you think that involving Ian is really necessary?"

"I'm afraid that we have no choice," Alex replied as she glanced at Alfred who was now approaching the refrigerator.

"Alex, give. And right now. I don't like the look on your face!"

"I guarantee that you are going to like it even less in a minute."

"Alex!"

"You better tell her, Alex," Alfred said from across the room.

"Okay, okay. Alfred, give Sarah the talisman."

Alfred stepped forward and gladly gave the pendant to Sarah. He could feel relief wash over him as he handed the amulet off to someone else. Apparently, from the way he saw her handle it, the amulet did not bother her in the least.

"Where did you find this?" Sarah asked. "It's very odd looking, but surely this small amulet is not the source of the problem."

"It was found where Alfred and the crew were digging for the water jump complex."

"Well, its definitely ugly, but I do not see why we would need the sheriff out for this small trinket."

"This was not the only thing in the pit, Sarah."

"Oh? Oh!" she exclaimed in realization. "Please, Alex don't tell me…"

"Yes, I'm afraid that we have our own private little graveyard right here in River City."

"God, what in heaven's name is next? I'll call him right away. Oh, Alex," Sarah continued, holding up the amulet, "what do you want me to do with this thing?"

"Keep it. Hide it. I can't seem to get near it."

"That's an understatement," Alfred added. "She fainted dead away when I tried to hand that thing to her."

"Tattletale."

"Are you all right?" Sarah asked, concerned for her friend.

"For the moment. Somehow though, I sense that it is an important piece to our puzzle. I can't quite place it, but I know that I've seen that pattern somewhere before. I'm going out on Pev for a while. I've got an idea of sorts. I'd like to check it out."

"I thought we were going to the library today?" Kendra said, as she interrupted the conversation while standing in the kitchen doorframe.

"Kiddo, I forgot one thing yesterday," Alex said.

"Only one? Well, run up the flag. Imagine that, Sarah—Alex forgot something."

"Apparently so did you," Alex replied.

"What might that be?"

"Today is Sunday, and if I'm not mistaken, in a small town like this…"

"The library would be closed today," Kendra finished in a monotone.

"Right, but out in the barn you will find your daily chores waiting for you. You need to get to them as soon as you can."

"Alex, it's Sunday. I'm tired! Jeez, this place is enough to drive anyone nuts."

"That might be. However, work is good for the soul. Besides, there's something new that has been added to the barn, and I want you to look at it."

"Okay," Kendra replied moaning. "You've probably got some new automatic watering system that you want me to learn the mechanics of."

"Alfred," Alex began, with a wink. "I would like you to take Kendra out to the barn and go through the new procedure with her that we spoke of earlier."

"Okay, boss," Alfred said. "Anything you say."

"Oh," Alex whispered. "Keep her away from you know what."

"Sure thing, boss."

With that Kendra turned and moodily shuffled out the door after the retreating form of Alfred, upset about the exclusion of whispers.

"Did Alfred bring one?" Sarah asked.

Alex lifted her finger to her lips and hushed her while nodding.

"He's just the cutest little thing, too! But Kendra is going to hate his name."

"Why? What is it?"

"The halter plate says 'Geronimo'."

"Oh, I see your point. Well, now for the happy phone call. Only I have no idea how I'll get the sheriff out here. Have you got any ideas? You made such a lasting impression and all," Sarah said trying to antagonize Alex.

"Tell him that it's me that has died and you discovered me buried in the pit. He should be here in a record time of two seconds to gloat over the body," Alex replied.

"That is not the slightest bit funny, Alexandra Markum!"

"It wasn't meant to be."

"Alex!" Sarah scolded.

"Sorry. It is the best possible solution to his problems that I could think of. It would make him ecstatic."

"Alex, do you think that it's wise to go out alone with all that has been going on lately?"

"No, it probably isn't wise. Frankly, it's probably pretty stupid. For the most part Grandfather's e-mail was unable to help much. He shocked me because he had some silly notion of coming here to help me. He said he needed to see these things in order to judge them correctly."

"And?"

"And, I said that I would send him a Polaroid! Really, Sarah, you think that I am going to let him come here? He thinks that I'm in over my head and that I need him. I told him to stay put for the present and that I was handling things just fine."

"But, Alex, what if you can't?" Sarah said, biting her lip. "Maybe he's right; maybe you do need someone else. Perhaps not Lightning Horse himself, but maybe someone else?"

"You know what his answer would be to that, don't you?"

"Yes," Sarah replied with a deep sigh. "We couldn't make him stay away, could we?"

"Not even, if you'll excuse the expression, with wild horses. I told him that he could help me most by being the one safe place I would have to send the rest of my family. That is why we need more information. I will contact him again just as soon as we have some kind of clue of what to tell him."

"You're going to that altar place again, aren't you?"

"Sarah, are you gaining the sight as well?"

"No, just all those years of being married to a cop. Remember the old saying that they always return to the scene of the crime?"

"But, Sarah, I'm not guilty of anything."

"I don't know about that. I think that you qualify for the most bull-headed award."

"Maybe I'm a close runner up to the sheriff."

"Okay, I'll concede to that. I never meant to imply that I was talking about you being guilty anyway! You be careful out there. Maybe you would like to take Bruce's gun?"

"A gun? Me?" Alex said incredulously. "Sarah, who do you think I am anyhow? I wouldn't know what to do with one of those. I'd probably shoot myself in the foot with the damn thing. I'll take my bows and arrows instead!"

"Then maybe I should come with you. I used to do all right on a practice range."

"If you did, then no one would be here with Kendra except Alfred, temporarily."

"What do you mean, temporarily?"

"There is some other news that I haven't broken to you yet."

"Is this where the other shoe drops?"

"It is. The work crew has already left. Alfred himself will not stay past this afternoon. They were all very frightened at the occurrences today. Besides the pit itself, they spotted a white owl in the daytime and a large wolf-type dog. Who could blame them?"

"Alex, I'm sorry. I know those are additional bad omens that your people believe in."

"Kendra is still in a very delicate state. She could turn quite unstable if left alone. Especially given the circumstances in this town. I know that you don't think so, but there are many times that she's right on the edge. Kendra has learned to hide it very well and while she may appear to have a hide of a rhinoceros, it really more closely resembles a fragile eggshell. She often has experienced bad dreams about her parents. You will need to keep that in mind, now that you two are sharing rooms. Her nightmares seem to have subsided here, but it was not that long ago that she had very violent nightmares. She blames herself, in her own way, for their deaths. She has often wished, through her tears, to join them. I can't let that happen, she has much to give, given time."

"But, Alex…"

"Don't *but Alex* me, because who, besides you, could dazzle our own town, dunderheaded sheriff. Someone will have to lead him to the bodies in the pit. You'll have to explain to him several times why we just happened to be digging there. I hope that you can do so without conjuring up any pictures of me poised in the dark of the night with a shovel in my hand. Last, but certainly not least, you will have to explain that they are dead and all of that. Plus, you will have to account for my whereabouts during the last, oh, say, one hundred and fifty years. You might even have to describe what a dead body looks like. He might even try and fall into the pit. Perhaps you should stay and give him a shove."

"Alexandra Markum!" Sarah exclaimed. "You stop right there! I think that you are being unfair to Sheriff Valin."

"Unfair! Say whose side are you on anyhow? I thought that I was your oldest and dearest friend. Just where do you think you get off telling me that I'm unfair."

"Because, I am your oldest and dearest friend. As you well know, only your oldest and dearest friend could possibly tell you that you are wrong about him. It just so happens that I think that you are as bullheaded as he is!"

"Don't hold anything back, Sarah. Tell me what you really think."

"You two will be the best couple since Bonnie and Clyde."

"If we live. Remember what happened to Bonnie and Clyde."

"Alex. Did you have to bring that up? Be reasonable, I know you like him."

"And just how do you know that?"

"Look at yourself, Alex. I've never seen you so angry with anyone in your life. Not even that guy with the bay…"

"Let's not go into that old story again. That was five show seasons ago, and I was but a young, naive child."

"All I'm saying is that sometimes your *sense* is a little off center when it comes to men. Give Sheriff Valin a chance, Alex. He's just got a little to learn. Women like you don't come along every day you know."

"My friend! I just have to remember not to turn my back on you."

"I would like to do something different tomorrow night; something to get us all out of the house for a little while. Hopefully, it is something that will give us all a little, well-deserved break," Sarah said.

"Name it. This spook central is getting a little nerve racking, even for me."

"I think that the three of us should go out tomorrow and put our heads together with any facts we might find at the library. The change of scenery may clear our heads and give us a clear perspective. We will have a good old-fashioned, you'll pardon the pun, powwow. We should all three try to attack this from a different angle and compare notes. Perhaps we can come up with something that will help us. Maybe even speak to some locals."

"Just where would you expect to get this accomplished at?"

"This place called The Blue Ram. I'll call Mr. Van Allen also. See if he would like to join us. He's lived here all his life; maybe he can give us some insight on town history."

"Okay. As long as it's *just,* Mr. Van Allen we are inviting," Alex exclaimed shooting Sarah a warning glance.

"Trust me."

"Sarah, I'm always terrified when you say that."

22

"Alfred," Alex called out entering the barn.

"Yes, Miss Alex."

"Alfred, I need some help. I know how you feel about the situation at hand, and that this would be extremely difficult for you, but I desperately need you to stay until tonight."

Alfred froze with his lips slightly parted. Alex could feel the tension in him while he decided between tradition and loyalty. She heaved a sigh of relief when loyalty won out in her favor.

"I need someone to introduce Kendra to Geronimo properly. She will need riding instruction; do not let her make you believe otherwise."

"Okay, boss!"

"Oh, and Alfred…"

"Yes, Alex?"

"Watch. Watch everything. Take care of yourself, Kendra, and Sarah. Let me know about anything that happens here. This time, if someone says something strange, listen closely to it all right?"

"Gotcha, boss!"

* * *

The phone rang out with alarming clarity, causing Ian to jolt severely and bolt out of his comfortable office chair. The sun beat through the window, but Ian didn't feel the least bit sunny. His bleary demeanor proved detrimental to his understanding of the woman on the other end.

"Could you please repeat that?" he said slowly. Then he listened again while the person repeated their end of the conversation. "Okay, I'll be right out."

Well, these two women were friends after all, he thought. It would only stand to reason that one would be almost as loony as the other.

Halfheartedly, he once again angrily glared at the picture on the front cover of his magazine. He hung up the receiver.

"Just who are you, lady?" he said, snatching up the magazine and shaking it as someone would a naughty child. "And why are you trying to ruin my life?"

* * *

Perhaps this man *was* as dense as Alex had suggested, thought Sarah as she hung up the phone. He'd sounded like he'd been up all night tying one on. How many times should you have to tell the sheriff of the town that there were bodies buried on the property before he thinks that something might be wrong?

* * *

Ian picked up the phone receiver and dialed.

"Cherokee police department," came the voice over the receiver.

"Yes, would Captain Parker be in?" Ian asked.

Ian was disappointed to find that Captain Parker was out. He became even more discouraged when he learned that the police cadet on the phone had not been on the force around the time the Alexandra Markum article was published. The cadet assured Ian that directly upon Captain Parker's return Ian would get a call from him. In not too gentle a fashion, Ian returned the receiver to the phone cradle and looked up in time to see Ron Van Allen entering his office.

"Now isn't that just like a criminal? Returning to the scene of the crime are you, Ron?" Ian asked.

"Just wanted to get a glimpse of our beloved town sheriff eating crow."

"And just what makes you think that I would be doing that?" Ian snapped.

"I figured by now you'd have read that article that I left for you about six or seven times."

"Ten, actually."

"Well, better yet. I would bet by now that you have also tried calling the Cherokee police station in Wyoming to confirm the article."

"Ron, your deductive reasoning astounds me. He wasn't in."

"Who wasn't?"

"The captain of the Cherokee police department."

"Oh, so, I have been right on track. It's too bad that I didn't allow for that possibility. I should have added two hours more to my waiting time so that I could have the pleasure of telling you that I told you so."

"Ron, you missed your calling."

"And what, pray tell, was that?"

"You are truly wasting your time at that real estate office. With your power of deductions you should really be…"

"Careful now, Ian. Be nice," Ron said, shaking his index finger back and forth.

"What I was going to say, is that you belong in the U.S. Marshal's office. I mean, how could you miss?"

"How long will it take?"

"How long will it take for what? To join the U.S. Marshal's office?"

"For you to apologize to Alexandra Markum."

"Well, who says that I'm going to?"

"I do, and if you're nice to me, I'll tell you where she will be tomorrow night so that you can do just that."

"Ron, I really don't care."

"Of course you do. Now, tomorrow night, all three of them will be meeting with yours truly to discuss the historical events of Grand Detour."

"For what purpose might I ask?"

"They think that somehow there is an event or multiple events from the past that has conjured up our present troubles."

"Just what do they think this could be?"

"I don't really know, but I will be finding out tomorrow night at The Blue Ram."

"Our town's own den of iniquity? That Blue Ram?"

"Yes, and if you have any sense at all, you'll join us there."

"I'm already going to have my fill of Ms. Markum this evening, thank you."

"Why is that?" Ron asked with genuine surprise.

"Ms. Caldwell just called me not so long ago and told me that the workers that arrived yesterday were beginning construction on one of those cross-country fences that riders always break their necks on."

"That is extremely commendable, Ian."

"And just what might that be?"

"I sense a note of concern in your voice, Ian."

"Nonsense! If they want to take unnecessary risks with their lives, that's their problem. Anyway, while they were digging this pit, they seemed to have uncovered quite a nice pile of skeletons in the process."

Ron's character went from chipper to sullen in the flash of an eye. His complexion took on an ashen tone, and immediately Ian knew what was racing through Ron's mind.

"Sorry, Ron, I wasn't thinking. From what they told me this is more like an ancient burial ground. The description of the bones makes them at least one hundred years old."

Ian could hear the man take an audible sigh of relief, and was thankful that the news had not been crushing.

"You know, Ron, I won't rest until I find Rita."

"I know you won't," Ron said as he breathed quietly. "Neither will I."

Grabbing his coat with his free hand, Ian tossed the now mangled magazine back onto the pile of papers on his desk. The two men went out the door together.

23

The sun was high in the sky by the time Alex could swing a leg over her trusted steed. The smell of the day was fresh and clean and it filled her lungs with freedom. It was an exhilarating feeling to be out there alone; just a girl and her horse was such a relaxing frame of mind to be in. And the best part was there were no men with bad attitudes anywhere in sight. The newly mowed smell of grass drifted into her nostrils, and she rode up over the rise between her property and the next. Who would have thought that such a beautiful place could hold such a dark past. It was not until her brain registered where she was going that a scowl uncontrollably overtook her face. There was something that nagged at her from the back of her memory. She remembered, yet she did not; there was something about that altar area, and she was determined to find out what that something was.

* * *

Reaching the top of the peak, Alex found herself face to face with the troublesome altar. Bright sunlight beamed down upon her, and Alex could hear the chirping of the nearby songbirds. The scary occurrences from yesterday were momentarily forgotten, and she drew closer to the stone. Alex could still feel the malevolent vibrations emitting from it. The Janey Stevenson incident had been far too fresh yesterday. The spiritual power blasting from it had almost been too much for Alex to stand. The air definitely had a different feel to it today. Even with the many appearances of the tortured, Alex found that she was not in as much distress as the previous day. Drawing closer, Alex noticed the upright stone behind the altar. She could make out two oblong circles, one inside the other. The numerous cross marks had some significance, of that she was certain. Crossing over to her horse, Alex produced a notepad and pencil from her cantle bag and began to draw the figures represented in stone. Here, at last, was a shred of evidence to send to her grandfather. The markings on this stone were identical to the markings on that evil pendant. Of course she would not know that for sure until she had returned to match the patterns, but there was almost no doubt in her mind.

Returning pad and paper to the pouch, Alex swung up onto the horse.

The backside of the rise was somewhere that she had not yet ventured. The golden sun fell upon them, warming them as they rode. Alex and Peverell descended deeper into the valley and continued to the next rise. A disturbing feeling began to wash over them both. It was one that she had felt before, when she had experienced her vision of Janey Stevenson. Although Alex was sweating slightly from the sun, she found herself battling with odd, unmanageable chills.

An unusual sound came to her from miles away. No, not miles away, it was actually spanning a greater bridge than mere miles. The sounds were crossing the barriers of time; their memories had been freed from their frozen place in history. They grew in volume, reaching out to her. It was a sound her ears had never before heard except in the context of the tales of old: the crying out of war whoops. The sound of them made her blood freeze.

The horizon blurred slightly, and, before she knew what was happening, she found herself heading deep into another vision. Alex prepared her mind as best she could in the short time given to her and turned to face the onslaught.

The vision overtook her, and the sun was blotted out by the dark night. Though the stars were all out, in the distance, large, black, angry clouds could be seen rolling in on the horizon. She could see many quickly approaching riders. These riders were on roughly built, bulky horses, a pack of mustangs no doubt. Broomtails, they had been called in years gone by; but it was the riders that caused Alex the greatest amount of anxiety. The riders drew nearer and she could make out their frightening faces. They were painted half black and half red, just as the singular face had appeared in the vision with Janey Stevenson. Their image was disturbing to her.

Alex's eyes fell upon the last rider in the chain; this figure atop the horse was no Native American. Behind the last rider was ponied a fair-haired woman. She was in an uncomplimentary position over the saddle and was quite obviously tied there. The group made their way past Alex's position on the ridge top. They were headed toward an upright rectangle frame that had not been there just seconds ago when Alex had looked. It astounded her that these things continually appeared and disappeared with such rapidity.

Alex continued to look on in amazement as the woman was then roughly pulled from the horse's back and tied spread-eagle onto the frame. It was obvious that the poor being was terrified. She screamed in vain, hoping against all hope that someone would hear her out here in the middle of the wilderness. Alex felt so helpless as she watched the scene play out in front of her.

But this was in the past, years before Alex's parents, grandparents, or even her great-grandparents had been born. There was nothing that she could do to save a woman that had been dead for years. She had slipped into a sideways pocket of time and was being forced to watch a rerun of a torture scene. Alex had to remember not to let it get to her. It was an unfair battle. Alex found that she had no advantage or tools with which to fight the image. She kept trying to meditate. Repeating to herself in her mind that it was only a rerun of sorts, played solely for her benefit. It took every calming technique she had to keep herself from screaming aloud. Her main clue again was Peverell. He did not react in any way to the scene playing out before them. He calmly munched on some grass stalks and clover that she had allowed him to have.

The woman screamed; her captors struggled with her and forced her to swallow something.

The men then traveled forward to make a circle, while chanting to their god. The words were foreign to Alex; to her ears it just sounded like gibberish. Though she was certain that the language was not Cherokee, it very definitely was a Native American tongue. The black sky gave way to an eerie red sky and the first morning star. It rose, and three previously chosen men of the group approached the woman. By now the drug had begun to wear off, and the woman was becoming more aware by the second of what was going on around her. The captive woman froze, pop-eyed at the trio advancing on her.

A sudden and indescribable connection was opened between the two women of past and present, just like last night's vision, only today Alex was wide awake. She could feel that the woman was struggling in vain to free herself, and in desperation tried to scream through the gag, which had been placed in her mouth to guarantee her silence. Suddenly, Alex found that she could see through the woman's eyes, and the two merged, becoming one. Without warning, Alex found that it was she that now stood before the hideously painted faces. The features were evil and twisted, and she could feel her heart pound as they advanced upon her and the other woman. Astonishment sparked in her gaze as she felt herself caught up in the other woman's circumstances. Alex struggled to free herself. During her struggles she looked up towards the ridge and saw only Peverell. Her own figure was not there astride him where she knew she must be.

Confused, Alex snapped back to the terror in front of her. She continued to watch the chosen three produce a lit torch, an arrow, and a large glistening dagger.

The man with the torch approached first and set fire to the horrified young woman's clothing; only it was Alex that could feel the heat of the flames. He began the most unearthly chanting that Alex had ever heard; her breathing became more rapid as her eyes momentarily rolled back into her head.

An uncomfortable searing feeling pulsed through her body and brain. The second man approached, chanting as well, and, drawing his bow, he sent an arrow cascading through the woman's side, just under the arms. There was a sharp thrust in Alex's body as she felt the arrow slide through her. The pain was excruciating. Then, with a sudden flash, the pain was gone, and she was back in her own body, astride Peverell. Again, she had become the onlooker.

The woman's body was being burned alive slowly, and streams of blood dripped from her carefully inflicted wounds. None of this, however, would be enough to kill her. This was a ritual that had been perfected to extend the victim's suffering past the limits of normal endurance. The third man stepped forward. He approached the previous two men at the base of the frame. He joined in the ritual, chanting and brandishing his contribution of torture. He approached the helpless figure stealthily with his glistening, eight-inch dagger. He began to stab into her chest, and Alex could feel herself relive the last few moments of life in terror as this woman from the past had experienced it.

Blessedly, this poor woman of the past, held below in the frame, had blacked out. She never knew the complete terror she had yet to undergo. As the beast finished carving up her chest, he viciously dug his fist into it and ripped out her heart, rubbing the blood over his face. His gaze was terrifying, filled with exuberance over the fresh kill. The evil of the moment swelled up and overflowed the boundaries of the past, and Alex could swear that she felt it reach out for her, brushing her soul. She gasped in absolute fear of its touch, the touch of death.

Alex jumped, startled by more sudden activity in the vision. She saw that all of the other men besides the chosen three had picked up their bows and began to shoot arrows into the body. After the arrows, the torch-bearer stepped forward and began to pull all the arrows out of the body except for the original one. This man reached up and took a handful of blood from the woman's open cavity, smearing it on his face as well.

More activity now brewed as Alex saw the Native American women coming forward. Their faces, also painted in the half black and half red, were filled with hatred. The sticks and spears they held were used to strike the dead woman's body in a new, sick and twisted version of an Native American counting coup. The fire continued to burn and scorched the body until it finally consumed it all together. All the people, both men and woman, began chanting, but Alex could not quite make out their words. It seemed like they were purposefully garbling their speech to keep their meanings from her. The evil had reached out and dangled a carrot in front of her nose. The evil threatened to drag her further into its world. Closer and closer so that it might destroy her.

The nightmare was over, and it was again daylight in the modern day. Confused, Alex looked around for a clue and then glanced at her watch. The torturous episode that seemed to last forever, had in reality taken a mere minute or two for Alex to relive. That memorable span of time would be ingrained in her psyche forever. Alex would never again look at the world in exactly the same way. Gazing past her watch, she stared out at the horizon, blaming her vivid imagination on the fact that she could still smell burning material and flesh. Alex was shocked when she looked herself over and saw that her clothing was burnt and smoke was coming from them. Feeling wetness at her side, Alex investigated; when she drew her hand back, she was shocked to find it full of blood. Scanning her surroundings, Alex looked for evidence of the horrifying vision. There was no indication left of the entire ceremony, save her singed clothes and fallen spirit. Her eyes had deceived her. Alex shivered at the realization that so many others had met their death in this similar, horrible fashion. She wept for them—for the terror they had to endure, for the restlessness of their souls in torment. This was truly the meaning of hell.

Alex turned Peverell towards the east. The vision had been confusing, but there was no more she could do here. There were many mysterious pieces in her mind, but so far, they had not fallen into place. From the way she shook, Alex knew that another vision episode like this was something that she could not endure again. It unnerved her when she tried to guess if her tormentor knew that information.

* * *

Approaching the final bend in the river before passing the altar hill on her way home, Alex could hear quiet sobbing. Pressing her leg into Peverell's strong, muscled body, she asked the horse for a quicker pace. Rounding another corner, the horse suddenly came to an abrupt and unasked for halt. Alex found herself looking at a figure sitting on a large rock by the river. The woman was obviously distressed as she softly cried to herself with her face buried in her hands. The only thing Alex could make out at first was the fine, strawberry-blond hair and the manicured nails. Dismounting, she took the opportunity to try and come closer to the figure. Alex noticed that this new woman also had clothes that looked torn and singed.

"Can I help you somehow?" Alex asked.

The figure continued to sob. "She cannot buy that house. I have to warn her."

"Are you hurt?" Alex asked. This time reaching out to comfort the woman, Alex was startled when her hand passed right through her. It was quite a surprise considering the mystery woman had appeared quite solid to Alex's eye.

Acting like Alex was not there, the figure began to cry out hysterically and then scream violently at attackers that were not visible to anyone but her. She bolted from them and was caught by invisible arms. Like a voodoo doll, her legs and arms were invisibly tied away from her in the spread-eagle fashion of the woman tied to the wooden frame. She uttered an unearthly scream and her image exploded in flames. Peverell surprised Alex by rearing and then running backwards. He sought to get away from the figure, and Alex clenched the reins tightly. She fought to stay on her feet and moved quickly so as not to be dragged behind the powerful animal. His reaction to this vision was violent, so unlike his total lack of interest in the previous episode. This mystery woman had obviously passed on recently. Therefore, her impression on this world was still a fairly strong one. Alex was convinced that this could be the reasoning for Peverell's violent reaction.

Alex, regaining control over Peverell, turned back to look towards the area where she had seen the figure in flames. Her manner of dress was unlike the vision of the woman before. Dressed very modern and stylish, she had not looked transparent. She had appeared more solid, just like the Stevenson girl. Her apparition was too solid to have it explained any other way. So then, who was she? It only took Alex a minute to fully realize who it must have been.

Remounting a prancing Peverell, Alex started off towards home.

24

Alfred smiled while he watched Kendra ride around the edge of the arena on the black and white piebald. The two had taken to each other in an instant, and he knew that it would only be a matter of days before they were inseparable.

He could tell from the way she rode that Kendra had not had much experience on a horse before. Still, he had to admit that there was an abundance of natural talent. He could see why Alex had taken such a special interest in the girl. It had been no small wonder that Alex had requested an *extraordinary* horse for her.

Alfred called out to the girl as the horse began to drift off the rail. "That looks very nice, Kendra, now put more pressure in the left calf and make that lazy broomtail carry his own weight,"

"He is not a broomtail!" Kendra wailed indignantly.

"You don't even know what that means!"

"It doesn't matter," she replied. "But, it doesn't sound very complimentary!"

"Well, you are right there. Whether Geronimo is or isn't a broomtail, the fact remains that he is still hanging on your left rein."

"He is not!"

"Kendra," Alfred began, "do you want lessons from me or would you prefer them from Alex? I test rode that horse myself and I know exactly what he does and does not do by himself."

"Alfred," she whined.

"Just do it and do not argue!"

The girl applied the requested pressure of her leg and immediately felt the difference in the left rein.

"Cool!"

"Just remember this the next time that I tell you to do something."

"Yes, Alfred."

Out of the corner of his eye, Alfred saw the police cruiser barreling up the driveway towards the house and barn area.

"Kendra, that's enough for one day. Put Geronimo up just like Alex has taught you. When I come in to check on the both of you, I want to see my face in his coat."

"You will!" Kendra assured him happily.

A smile came to Alfred's face, and he turned to watch the pair bonding. Kendra was using a circular method on Geronimo's face that he knew had been taught to her by Alex. There had been many times that he had watched Alex tame the worst renegade horse with that particular calming technique. For Geronimo's part though, he was simply enjoying the comforting massage.

Alfred walked off to meet the sheriff. He turned once again and was pleased at what he saw. Kendra loosened the girth around the horse's belly to enable the heart line of the horse to expand comfortably after the workout. The back buckle of the girth flopped, and the front buckle remained on the first hole. Telltale marks of Alexandra's touches ran all over this girl. A small amount of pressure remained on the horse's back due to the presence of the saddle. This enabled the animal to relieve the weight of the saddle and rider a little at a time. The stirrups were then run up to the top of the leathers so they were not swinging loose where they might catch on something and excite the horse. She then continued on to the horse's head and completely undid the buckle for the noseband and flash attachment on the bridle. The saddle pad would remain on for a short while after the removal of the saddle so the slightly sweaty back of the horse would not have even the remotest possibility of catching a chill.

His heart was filled with joy for the girl. Alex had told him all about Kendra's past, and it was a pleasure to watch the black and white horse follow his new owner into the barn like a happy, thousand-pound puppy.

"I will be back shortly to show you how to make a special bran mash for him," Alfred called to the back of a departing Kendra.

She merely smiled, waved, and disappeared into the barn.

* * *

Ian was leaning against the cruiser, waiting, as the other man approached.

"Alfred," he said, extending his hand.

"Ian." Returning the gesture, Ian extended his hand.

"Oh," Alfred said with a smile. "So, you are the one."

"The one?" Ian replied making a slight grimace.

"You know which one," Alfred expressed with a laugh. "Anyhow, you are a very small crew for such a large problem."

"Oh, that," Ian replied. "Well, there is a large crew of county workers on their way here with vehicles to take care of the, um, the problem. They will take the remains to the coroner's office where they will process them and make out their various reports. I will then expedite the removal of the remains to sanctified ground for the final burial and will close the file based on their report and mine."

"Hmm," Alfred said. "Sounds like loads of laughs to me."

Ian was about to respond when both turned toward the sound of the kitchen door opening and closing. Sarah Caldwell approached the pair of men quickly.

"Alfred," she said, "they looked wonderful together. I was watching from the kitchen window and I think Kendra was in heaven."

"She and the horse both, Miss Sarah. She will learn quickly from him, you wait and see."

Ian rolled his eyes up at the last few remarks. Professional horse people! Were they all crazy? At this point, Ian cleared his throat loudly. It was done on purpose, and everyone present knew it.

"Ah, Sheriff Valin. How nice to see you again," Sarah said accommodatingly." I see that you have already met Alex's cousin."

"Cousin?"

"Alfred. He is Alex's cousin."

"He didn't tell me that, Ms. Caldwell," Ian said after a long pause. "Is Ms. Markum here as well?"

"No, Ian. I'm afraid that you will have to apologize to her sometime later."

"Who said anything about apologizing?" he replied scornfully as his brows came together in a scowl.

"Well, if you don't, you should, you know. She had every right to drop you off in the middle of the forest after what you did."

"I'm not here to discuss this," he said hotly. "As I recall, you called me here about another kind of problem altogether."

"It's just your stubborn pride you know."

"And just what would you know about such things?"

"I was married to a New York City cop. It might surprise you to know that you, and my Bruce, could have been twins when it comes to being stubborn."

The three found themselves trapped in an uncomfortable silence, which Sarah broke by turning to speak to Alfred.

"Alfred, I am going to talk to Kendra in the stable. I'll keep her busy, so that she doesn't get too curious about the happenings out here. Why don't you show the sheriff here our little problem. Sheriff, I would appreciate it if you said nothing to Kendra if you see her. We haven't told her yet about the, you know, the reason for your visit. Alex thinks that it might upset her too much."

"I will most certainly abide by your wishes on this account," Ian replied.

Sarah set off for the barn, and the two men simultaneously headed off in the direction of the pond, which was set off in a corner, away from both the main hotel and the barn area.

* * *

"Well, what do you think, Kendra?" Sarah asked as she entered the barn door way.

"He's wonderful. He's fabulous," Kendra said enthusiastically. "Is he really mine, or was Alfred kidding me?"

"He's really yours, Kendra. He is a gift from Alex, Alfred, and myself."

"Oh, thank you!" Kendra exclaimed grabbing Sarah in a meaningful hug. "By the way, where's Alex?"

"She, um, she rode out on an errand, Kendra."

"Oh," Kendra said, as her face fell in disappointment. "I was hoping that she would watch me ride him for the first time."

It was obvious to Sarah that Kendra was bitterly disappointed that Alex had not been there. For all the words that they bantered back and forth, Kendra really did want Alex's acceptance and love. It had been just like Alex had said all along. Kendra had been saying all those things trying to get the attention that her soul cried out for. Sarah reached out and gave the saddened girl a supportive hug.

"Kendra, I'm sure that Alex would like nothing better than to share in your happiness; she just couldn't be here."

Embarrassed by her showing of emotion, Kendra broke away sniffing and bent over to grab up one of the many brushes. Wiping her tears on her sleeve, she silently turned to the little black-and-white's coat and began to brush briskly.

* * *

"Has Miss Alex returned yet?" Alfred asked entering the barn with the sheriff in tow.

"No, Alfred, she hasn't. I have to say that I did not like the look of determination she had on her face when she left."

"Neither did I."

"Where exactly did Miss Markum get off to?" Ian asked.

"Actually, she wasn't going to tell me at first," Sarah replied. "Somehow, I guessed that she was going to return to that altar place that you two rode out to yesterday."

Sarah grew uneasy as she saw the sheriff's lips pull into a grim, straight line. She could tell that he was struggling not to lose his composure.

"She went where?" he exclaimed. "Doesn't she realize how dangerous it could be to ride up there by herself?"

"If I were not so worried about her myself, Sheriff," Sarah said, "I would tease you about how much it sounds like you almost care."

"Well, on a personal level, and for the record, I don't. However, on a professional one, I do. Anything could happen to her out there alone."

"Anything?" Sarah said with panic rising in her voice.

"No, not that. I mean almost anything." The sudden picture that Ian conjured up in his mind terrified him. The last thing he wanted was to have Alex go missing like the other women. He struggled to keep the growing concern from his face. He suddenly knew that he wanted more from her than just a picture on one of his dated magazines. He wanted to care for her, but recent incidents seemed to make that impossible.

"Well, I think the point now is rather academic," Kendra interjected approaching the company of the three adults.

"Why is that?" Sarah asked.

"Because I can see the silhouette of her and Peverell against the setting sun on the ridge. She's really moving, too. Just look at that horse gallop!"

Ian and Sarah followed Kendra's pointed finger towards the quickly approaching figure of Alex and Peverell. Sarah pretended not to notice as the sheriff tried nonchalantly to rush toward the large barn door opening, which framed the oncoming horse and rider. Kendra grabbed a cooler, lead, and halter for the big horse and hurried outside to greet her mentor.

"What was that you said, I didn't quite hear you?" Sarah asked.

"I said *Thank God*. Okay!"

25

It had felt good for both woman and horse alike to break loose and gallop. There was nothing that broke up a good case of the tensions like a quick, flat-out run. Alex drew near the barn area and she could make out the figure of Kendra quickly advancing in her direction. She signaled the big horse to slow down to a canter and then to a long, striding walk. With his head in a lowered position, Alex could feel Peverell relax his spine as she drew alongside Kendra.

"Where have you been, Alex?" Kendra said, disappointment showing in her voice.

"Did you like him?" Alex asked flashing the best smile she could muster.

"I rode him, and he is just wonderful! Even Alfred says that I did a great job!" Then Kendra added after a long pause, "Gee, Alex, what happened to your clothes?"

"Oh, nothing important. I think I just carelessly pulled some old clothes out of the trunks," Alex answered. "Just take care of the big guy here. Walk him out, hose him down, and graze him for me, would you?"

"I know the routine by now, Alex."

"Good, then you won't mind taking him out behind the barn. I think I saw some tasty looking clover out there this morning."

"Okay."

"And, Kendra?"

"Yeah?"

"Take Alfred with you, okay? Have him graze Terpsichore while you're at it."

"Alex, you know I can take care of them both," Kendra whined.

"No buts, please, Kendra. Understand that it has nothing to do with what you can or cannot handle as far as the horses are concerned. Things have just been way too unpredictable to suit me and I want someone with you at all times."

"Okay."

Gathering up the reins, Kendra undid every buckle just like she had done earlier on Geronimo. With that done, she whisked Peverell into the barn so she could rinse him off in the heated wash rack. After that, she would find Alfred so they could graze the horses together.

Alex entered the barn. She looked surprised to see the sheriff still present at the hotel grounds.

"Sheriff," she said.

"Alex, are you all right?" Sarah asked, coming towards her.

"Of course I am," Alex replied.

"What were you thinking, going out there alone?" Ian demanded.

"If I remember the county lines properly, sheriff," Alex retorted hotly, "I did not leave the designated area of suspicion. Or did I?"

"Okay. Okay. I had that coming. That and more most likely. If I recall, the last time you visited that place you passed out, and I had to drag you away from that huge rock up there."

"Alex, you didn't tell me that," Sarah interjected with a worried expression.

"It wasn't that important," Alex replied.

"You know, you take all!" Ian shouted. "I know that was not an act you pulled last time. You were out cold. I've seen many people trying to fake it; you really had no control over the situation. The blood leaking from your eyes was real. I saw it myself. There were no gimmicks, and there was no way you could have simulated that either. Now you want your friends and family to not worry about you when you take off for the same area again."

"Tell me, sheriff, which category do you fall into?" Alex replied snidely.

"Knock it off, both of you!" Sarah exclaimed at the top of her voice. "There are more important things going on here than you two having a power struggle over heaven knows what."

"You're right, Sarah," Alex replied, sighing deeply and resting the bridge of her nose between her thumb and index finger. "I'm sorry, I just have very little patience left right now."

"*You* have a small amount of patience left?" Ian exclaimed. "I like that. You move in here, and suddenly the town turns upside down. You embarrass me in front of all my working associates and friends. You worry everyone half to death by running off to an area that has proven to be at the very least hazardous to you. And, by the way, what happened to your clothes? You smell like you smoked an entire pack of Camel cigarettes in the last five minutes and put them out on your clothes."

"Alex, your clothes do look rather singed," Sarah added.

"Its nothing; merely old worn clothes that I put on by accident. Please pay it no mind." Alex was careful to keep her arms at her sides to cover the bloodstains.

"Fine, I won't," Ian snarled suspiciously. "I'll be going now. You be sure and let me know if you find anything else around here, like the truth."

"Sure, sheriff," Sarah said as she hustled Alex towards the house in an angry silence.

The squad car spun its wheels angrily in the gravel and then stopped at the end to meet the oncoming vans, which were sent to collect the remains in the pit. Sarah grabbed Alex by her arm and swung her around to face her.

"Just what exactly did he mean when he said blood was leaking from your eyes, Alexandra Markum?" Sarah demanded, then gasped "There's blood on your shirt!"

"It is nothing to worry about," Alex replied, tiredly.

"Nothing to…Markum, have you lost your mind? This blood is fresh and it looks like its yours!"

"I'll tell you, Sarah, whatever happened just happened. It didn't hurt, and, furthermore, no one saw anything like that but him," Alex lied as she jerked her thumb in the direction of the driveway.

"Just like the events that made this mess of your clothes. I bet it didn't hurt, either!"

Alex ignored the statement.

"Look, Alex, I covered for you. You better be telling me the truth."

"I am."

"And there was no passing out this time?"

"No, but I had another vision."

"Oh no, not the Stevenson girl again."

"No, this poor girl was from much further back in the past. Her manner of dress was odd. I was on a hillside, viewing her entire attack. Suddenly I became one with her. I could feel her pain. Her fear."

"You said that there wasn't any pain!"

"Well, there wasn't much."

"Right. That's why blood is all over your shirt. Why did you hide that from Ian?"

"Do you want to hear the rest of this or not?"

"Okay, but we are going to revisit this really soon!"

"Fine. Anyhow, the tribe that attacked her was, to say the least, frightening."

"The tribe?"

"Yes, there was an Native American tribe that brought this poor, drugged woman out into a deserted area near the altar and tied her upright into a frame. I will not go through all the gruesome details with you, however, I can tell you that it was a horrifying ritual to go through even though I knew in my mind that it could not harm me."

"Did they more or less burn her at the stake?"

"Yes, why do you ask?"

"Is that why your clothes are singed?"

"I suppose so."

"Then how do you know that they couldn't hurt you?"

"You're right; I don't," Alex said slowly, and she froze with the dawning of realization. Her eyes grew wide with a newfound respect of fear, and she continued slowly, "They let me live."

"What do you mean they *let* you live?"

"They had one purpose. They want to taunt me before they kill me."

"Alex, don't say things like that!"

"It's true. Tomorrow, you and Kendra are leaving, even if I have to make Alfred drag you from this place. You must go and stay with Grandfather. He will protect you and cleanse any bad spirits that may follow."

"Alex, I will not leave here. We have already had this discussion once."

"We'll speak of it later."

"No, *we* will speak of it right this minute."

"Sarah. Please. You must do this for me."

"I said I wouldn't leave you and I meant it. Let Alfred take Kendra away. I stand with you."

"I need to rest right now. I'll discuss this with you when I've had some needed sleep," Alex said as the two women entered the back door leading into the kitchen. "I'm suddenly so very tired."

"I shouldn't wonder!"

Sarah crossed to the bay window to watch the grim procession of vehicles coming up their driveway.

"Did you instruct Alfred to keep Kendra away from the pit?"

"Yes, Alex, I did. You won't keep this from her long, you know," Sarah added. "She's a smart kid and she'll figure it out sooner or later."

"As long as it's later and she's away from here. I don't really care anymore. She must go, Sarah, and now, this very minute, wouldn't be soon enough." Alex turned to leave the room and said quietly, "I'll be upstairs in my room if you need me."

"Get some rest," Sarah said with worry. "You look like you deserve it."

"Oh, Sarah?"

"Yes, Alex?"

"Did you say that we were meeting with Ron Van Allen tomorrow night?"

"Yes, I did."

"That is going to be a difficult meeting for me, as well as Ron."

"Why is that?"

"Because, I forgot to tell you the other encounter I had today."

"You had an experience that has to do with Ron?"

"Yes. I'm afraid that I'll have to tell him that Rita is dead."

"Oh, no! Are you sure?"

"She had the same strawberry-blond hair that he has. She's about thirty-two years old. Peach nail polish."

"Yes, that sounds like her all right," Sarah said sadly.

"I'm really very sorry. Now, if you'll excuse me, I'm very tired."

Sarah watched sadly as her friend dragged herself up the stairs in a totally uncharacteristic manner. She was so shocked by all that she had just heard that she did not notice that Kendra had been hiding in the shadows during the conversation between herself and Alex.

* * *

Two hours later, Sarah quietly cracked open the door to Alex's suite. She stuck her head inside and was disappointed to find her friend seated at her computer with a pair of glasses enhancing the strain that shone in her eyes.

"Just what are you doing!" Sarah exclaimed as she opened the door fully and placed her hand firmly on her right hip. "You are supposed to be resting!"

"Writing up the days details for Grandfather. I now have more pieces to the puzzle. I'm unsure of what they mean, but perhaps he can shed some light on the matter."

"Alex, you can't continue at this rate," Sarah said sharply.

"Oh that. Well, I tried to close my eyes, and this afternoon kept roaring back into my mind. I guess I need a little more time before sleep can cleanse my mind."

"Alex."

"Yes," she replied glancing up from her work.

~~Sarah could see the lines of type reflecting in the pane of Alex's glasses.~~

"I still can't believe that Rita is dead!"

"That is the only person I can deduce it to be unless someone else is missing from town recently besides her and Janey."

"No. The description is correct. She's the only other one presently missing."

"I'm not sure I like the way you said that."

"Neither do I. Don't you wish we had never come here?"

"Do I wish I could take the move back? Yes, I do. Do I think it would change much? Yes."

"How could you say that, Alex?"

"Because somehow I think we unknowingly started all of this. The first victim was Rita, and she was showing you this property."

"So maybe the evil didn't want us to own this house?"

"No. I think the exact opposite is true. I think it wanted us here very badly. However, I think something has turned the tide against us. We have found more here than this entity wanted us to. I believe that Rita may have wanted to change your mind about buying this property."

"Did she tell you that this afternoon?"

"Yeah, kind of."

"Dinner will be ready soon," Sarah said changing the subject.

"I'm not hungry, Sarah," Alex answered quietly.

"I'll check in with you when it's ready," Sarah replied, ignoring the scowl that Alex directed at her.

Alex then rose and walked over to her bed. She tumbled in, singed clothes and all, falling asleep almost instantly. Sarah quietly backed out of the room, closing the door behind her.

"Good night," Sarah whispered.

26

Morning came too soon for the weary equestrian. The bright, cheery sun veered into the horizon, and Alex struggled to wake up. It was a feeling so utterly unlike any that Alex was used to. In her entire life, she dutifully practiced being up early, and enjoyed the quietness of the morning hours. She enjoyed puttering in the stables before anyone else would come and join her.

Propping herself up on one elbow, Alex wrinkled her nose in distaste as the scent of the charred clothing assailed her nostrils. The previous day's memories came flooding back to her and a streak of depression entered her usual carefree morning mood. She raised her other hand and gently massaged her forehead, covering her right eye in the process. There was no doubt in her mind. Yesterday had definitely been the worst day in her life. The prospect of facing what would come today did not lighten her mood in the least. Uttering a deep sigh, Alex forced herself to rise and amble toward the shower. At least she might feel human if she could get this wretched smell off of her.

The warm water flowed over her head and she could feel the knots of tension release in her back. She dressed quickly and headed out towards a morning with her horse children.

Stepping outside, Alex glanced up into the sky and saw dark clouds quickly moving in the direction of the hotel.

"Wonderful," she muttered.

A storm certainly would not lift her deteriorating mood. On the other hand, if it was going to be an awful day she would not have to feel guilty about not exercising the horses. The new indoor ring had not even been started yet, so, unless she wanted to get soaked, there really was no alternative. Crossing the complex between the house and barn, Alex opened the door and was not surprised when her transparent, morning barn man greeted her in his customary way. Once again, the ghost rapidly flashed his hand signals and became cross and disgusted with her when she did not immediately understand.

After feeding the horses, Alex crossed back across the compound and reentered using the kitchen door. She turned to grasp the door handle, but didn't see the entry of another person behind her. Alex jumped, startled when she turned and caught the figure out of the corner of her eye.

"Sorry, Alex," Alfred apologized. "I didn't mean to startle you."

"Alfred, you nearly scared me half to death! What are you doing here? I thought you said that you wouldn't stay past evening. That was yesterday."

"I know that's what I said. We are, however, blood relations, and I felt that whether it was the correct decision or not I should stand with you."

"Alfred, Sarah shamed you into staying, didn't she?"

"Well, yes. Now that you mention it, she did."

"Why did you let her get away with that?"

"Because, Alex. I'm ashamed to say it, but she was right. I need to look past the old ways. After all, I'm younger than you! I should be able to take the changes much easier than you."

"Thanks, Alfred," Alex said sarcastically. "I think."

"Since I am staying, I will watch the horses today. I know that you, Sarah, and Kendra will be doing some research in town. You'll feel more comfortable knowing that someone is here."

"That's a very nice gesture on your part, Alfred. I will bring it up to the tribe elders, that is if I ever see any of them again."

"Alex, don't talk like that!" scolded a voice from the darkened hallway.

"You're up pretty early today, Sarah," Alex said.

"It must be the upcoming storm. I found that I couldn't sleep."

"Yes, well," Alex began, "it seems to have had that effect on everyone except Kendra. Is she still sleeping?"

"Yes, but fitfully so. Good morning, Alfred."

"Good morning, Miss Sarah."

"No hard feelings?"

"No," Alfred replied smiling. "You just got to me on one of my sentimental days."

"How late was the removal crew here?" Alex asked.

"Oh, they were here well into the late evening hours, but they said that they removed everything," Alfred replied.

"And Kendra? Were you able to keep her from them?"

"I conned her into a long trail ride on the other side of the property. When we returned, it was very dark and she could not have seen anything," he continued.

"Hmm. That's good. I hope we can keep it that way," Alex said.

"He didn't return to the house?" Sarah inquired.

"What are you talking about?" asked Alex.

"The sheriff. He didn't return to the house at any time last evening."

"Well, who cares about that?" Alex replied with annoyance.

"You do."

"I do not!"

"You do. You're just too stubborn to admit it."

"Sarah, when will you learn that there is just too much going on here for you to keep daydreaming up a relationship between myself and the sheriff."

"Alex, I know you better than that."

"No, you do not!" Alex scoffed. "And you," she pointed to Alfred, "wipe that silly smirk off of your face right this minute."

"I was just thinking," Alfred said.

"About what?" Alex snapped sarcastically.

"That Sarah is right."

"Don't be ridiculous," she snorted.

"Thou doth protest too much," Sarah chanted.

"I...You two are the biggest idiots I have ever seen," Alex said in exasperation.

"Just what do you mean by that remark, Alexandra," Sarah exclaimed with a feigned hurt tone to her voice.

"I do not understand how the two of you can entertain such fantastic ideas considering the fact that by tomorrow, one or all of us could possibly end up being quite dead."

"It's just our way of taking our minds off that very fact," Sarah said. "Besides, it's kinda of fun to watch you get all defensive on us and blush."

Alfred just snickered. Alex shook her head and walked out of the door into the next room. She knew that there was no point in trying to win against those two. It had been foolish to try.

*   *   *

Dark, malevolent eyes peered out from the darkness of the cellar. Those burning, piercing eyes emanated from a face painted half red and half black. There was fury in his features of stone. The private cache of sacrifices to his god had been penetrated, violated, and carted away. The very symbol of his reigning power was now in the hands of the enemy. The entity began to plot the final fall of its foes. Originally, the plans had been to make the women of the Grand Detour Hotel an example that evil could indeed last forever. Instead, it had backfired. One of them possessed the sight. It had been fun at first to taunt her with the vicious visions. On occasion, when she had been caught off guard it had made the evil being stronger to involve her in its past escapades. She had proven stronger than he had believed possible and her failure to crumble had frustrated him.

After all, being a mere mortal had been taken from him many years ago. Now, he would be considered a god. He intended to be treated so and would do anything to make this seer bow down to him. The fun was just beginning for her; he would see to that. A gleam glowed in his evil eyes and he plotted to drag her in even further, until it would be too late, until she found herself unable to turn back from the very brink of hell. An evil grimace blossomed, and he felt himself aroused at the prospect of a more worthy opponent. It had been so long since he had met anyone who could challenge his existence. She would not succeed, though. He could promise her that. She would perish, like all the others who had come before her.

In the end, he would strike at the thing closest to the woman's heart. By doing so, he would be able to defeat her so totally that the final triumph would be easy for him. Who knows, perhaps the gods would grant him the power to corrupt her into his bride. It would destroy the seer's mind. Her will. Her very soul. The thought pleased him, and he withdrew into the darkest recesses of the cellar to pay homage to his god. The being that had brought him his ultimate power. Soon it would again be time to make the sacrifice to the Morning Star, and this time he was sure that the next few days would be Alex's last few on this earth.

27

The library wasn't very busy. The three women crossed the front door threshold and immediately disappeared into the stacks. Try as she might, Kendra had a tendency to get easily distracted, and Alex had to drag her from the fiction section on several different occasions. While Sarah browsed through the nine hundred section of the Dewey decimal system looking for books on local history, Alex fingered each and every file folder in the local history drawer of the central files.

Both of the older women scribbled furiously in their notebooks when they viewed materials that could not be checked out because of their historical value. They jotted down anything that might have any pertinent value to the conversation that they would have later that evening. Armloads of materials that could be checked out were gathered together at a study desk so Sarah and Alex could glance at them before deciding whether to review them or not.

Checking the back of the file drawer, Alex found a folder that had slipped in towards the back of the drawer and somehow fallen behind the normal line of sight. When she opened it, she found that it contained the entire history of the first owners of their hotel. The first clipping she began to read was the story about the tragic deaths of Thomas and Mildred Conrad. It unnerved Alex to read about it. Here were two extremely successful business people and they had been violently killed.

The story continued by saying that the attack had taken place in broad daylight, just outside of town. The newspaper was quick to point towards the fact that murder had never taken place in the town of Grand Detour before this. There was something significant about their murders; she could feel it.

Alex looked at the first of the old-fashioned photos in the back of the folder. Flipping the photo over, she discovered that the name handwritten on the back was Mildred Conrad. When she caught sight of the next photo in the folder, her blood turned to ice and she could feel the goose bumps on her arms. She recognized this man. Stiffly, she stood up and, as if in a daze, walked over to where Sarah was sitting.

Sarah looked up over her reading glasses as she began to watch Alex approach. She could tell that there was something in her friend's uneasy gait that suggested a clue had been unearthed. Alex drew close to her side, and Sarah gazed at the picture that Alex laid on the table in front of her.

"Who is that?" Sarah whispered.

"It says on the back of the photo that it is Thomas Conrad."

"The man who built our hotel?"

"Yes. He is also the man who greets me in the stable every morning. The one flashing the hand signals at me."

"What?" Sarah exclaimed quietly. Her voice intonation was loud enough to collect a stern look from the old, wrinkled librarian behind the counter.

"I'm telling you, Sarah; this is the man."

"Are you sure?"

"I'm sure, but if you want I could probably have Kendra verify it. She, after all, was the first to encounter him."

"Can you check that folder out?"

"No, why?"

"Because, I want Ron Van Allen to take a look at that picture."

"Well, since I am probably going to die anyhow, I'm sure that a few infractions of library laws are not going to travel with me to my next life."

"Alex, stop!" Sarah cried out, watching Alex stuff a few paper items into her purse.

"Sorry. Private property now. You find anything yet?"

"No, but I've been reading about some of the financial histories of the town. Did you know at one time this community was extremely wealthy?"

"Really? Well, you sure can't tell that now. Keep looking because it is almost closing time and I want to get every drop of information out of here that we can."

"Alex, we can always come back tomorrow."

"I have an unexplainable feeling that says that we cannot. We better do this all in one swoop. I don't think that we'll get another chance."

"Where's Kendra?"

"I don't know; I thought she was with you."

"There she is," Sarah said with a sigh, pointing towards the fiction section.

"Again? I tell you, Sarah, this girl sometimes cannot tell the difference between fantasy and reality."

"Alex, go easy on her. She's only a kid, you know."

"Yeah, I know. I want to see her grow up and become an old woman, too. That is, if I don't strangle her myself first."

"Now I know that you are getting back a little bit of your old self," Sarah said laughing quietly. "I haven't heard you threaten Kendra in at least three days."

"Sometimes old habits are the hardest to break."

"Alex?"

"Yes?"

"It has been awful quiet today. Do you think that things might just dissipate now?"

"No, and if you'll excuse the expression, I think that we are experiencing the proverbial calm before the storm."

"I hope you are wrong."

"So do I; anyhow, I think we should get back to work."

Closing time at the library neared, and the three gathered up their materials and headed to check out.

"I hardly think that Agatha Christie novel is going to help us any with our research, Kendra," Alex said.

"Oh, lighten up," the girl quipped back. "I need to read something for fun and she is my all-time favorite."

"Ssh!" Sarah exclaimed, turning quickly from the pair. "This is a library!" She forced a sweet smile towards the sour-looking woman behind the counter.

Alex could hear the key turn in the lock behind them and they just missed getting the door slammed into their backsides by inches.

"You don't think we stayed too long?" Alex asked.

"No, but in this small of a town they are probably used to locking up a half an hour before actual closing," Sarah replied. "By the way, do you still have all the contents of that file folder you showed me earlier. You really didn't take those did you?"

"I have to confess, Sarah," Alex replied. "I stuffed it, and a few others in my purse. If I'm still here in a week, I'll return them."

"Why, where are we going?" Kendra asked.

"You, Alfred, and the horses are going on a trip tomorrow."

"Aren't you and Sarah coming?"

"We have a few things to attend to here and then we will follow along behind."

"Why do I have to go?" Kendra asked suspiciously.

"Because, I need you to go and look after my grandfather. The last time I spoke with him I was concerned about the state of his health and I need you to go and see to him until I am able to join you."

"You wouldn't be trying to get rid of me or anything would you?"

"Of course not! How could you say such a thing! Sarah will come for you, while I tend to details here," Alex said indignantly.

"Just checking," Kendra answered sullenly.

"We will both be coming for you," Sarah added.

Alex shot Sarah an unconvinced look.

"Both of us," Sarah repeated firmly, as if to assure herself as well.

28

Pulling up in front of The Blue Ram, the trio found that they were a little early. Ron Van Allen was not due yet so they had some time to kill. A young girl with long, red hair began to show them to a table in a dark corner, when Alex piped up and said that she preferred to sit outside. The hostess glanced up and frowned as she looked at the darkening sky.

"It looks as though it might rain," she said, trying to persuade them to stay inside.

"Thanks," Alex replied. "We'll take our chances."

The hostess turned away from them, rolled her eyes up in youthful disgust, and led them outside. Having shown them to their seats, the young red-haired girl walked back inside. Alex turned toward Sarah and shrugged her shoulders.

"Sorry, I just could not bear to think of sitting inside that dingy place," Alex said. "Whatever made you pick this place, Sarah?"

"To be honest, it's the only place that I know of in town. Ron brought me here that first day. The day that Rita never showed up," Sarah replied.

"I think it's neat!" Kendra exclaimed.

"You would!" Alex countered.

"It looks like a set for an old horror movie."

"Kendra, please knock it off!" Alex sighed. "We do have work to do, you know. That was our whole purpose for this little sightseeing trip."

"Okay, Alex," Kendra replied glumly. "I was only trying to have a little fun." Under her breath she added, "But I'm sure that you wouldn't have the slightest idea about what that is!"

Alex shot Kendra a sour look that made the young girl realize that the last comment had indeed been heard. Kendra felt guilty. That last comment had hurt Alex far more than she had originally intended. Suddenly, it was not quite so much fun to shoot the quips back and she lowered her eyes and bit her lower lip, avoiding glancing up at Alex completely.

The two older women at the table reached into their bags and drew out their notes from the entire day spent sifting through the town history.

"I don't know what you two found out," Sarah began. "But I feel that this little town has had more than its fair share of misery."

"I would have to agree with you on that," Alex said.

Ron Van Allen was approaching their table. Sarah noticed that he looked much more tired than he had on their last meeting. The dark circles under his eyes indicated to her that he had been suffering since Rita's disappearance. When he arrived at the table, Sarah, the only one of them who officially knew him, smiled and rose to greet him.

"Ron, thank heavens you're early. It's so nice of you to meet us here," she said.

"Nice of you to invite me," he replied. "It's better to have something to occupy your time while you are waiting for any kind of news."

"Ron, this is Alex," Sarah said.

"This is certainly a pleasure," he replied. "I've had the opportunity to read quite a bit about you both as professional horsewoman and…"

"Probably a voodoo queen on horseback," Alex said laughing. "I've seen some of those tabloid-style articles. It depends entirely on whether you read the supermarket version or the accounts written by real journalists. I've heard quite a bit about you, also."

Alex grasped his outstretched hand. In shaking his hand, Alex could feel the warmth of Ron's humanity. She could detect a good-natured sense of humor, and his deep nagging commitment to find his sister. It hurt her to know that she would have to be the one to tell him about the unfortunate demise of Rita. The toll that her disappearance had taken on him was immensely apparent.

"Really, I am quite a believer. I have read every legitimate article about you. The way you helped to save that boy in Wyoming last year was truly remarkable."

Alex was silent. This kind of thing always made her uncomfortable. It never got any easier for her to deal with statements like this. After all, what could you really say?

"I've made you uneasy," Ron said apologetically. "For that, I am sorry."

A smile of relief flooded Alex's face.

"And this is Kendra. She is Alex's ward," Sarah said.

"Kendra, also a very great pleasure," Ron said as he again extended his hand towards the young girl."

A quiet hello was all that Kendra managed to muster.

"My, she is very quiet," Ron commented. "Is she always this shy?"

"No," Alex replied smiling. "You just managed to catch her in a rare quiet mood."

Kendra allowed her eyes to avert to the floor and didn't reply, surprising both women with her lack of response.

"Well," Sarah giggled after a slightly uncomfortable pause, "won't you sit down and join us?" She indicated the only other empty chair at the table, and then knowingly shot a sarcastic glance towards Alex, raising one eyebrow in a form of silent expression.

Alex instantly knew what Sarah had meant by the unspoken gesture. All of the chairs had been filled, and there was no sign of the sheriff anywhere. The problem was that Alex herself couldn't be sure if she was relieved or disappointed.

A slight woman with close-cropped, salt-and-pepper hair approached their table.

"Good evening," she said. "My name is Cheryl and I'll be your server tonight. Looks like rain. Are you sure you folks wouldn't like to move on inside?"

"We're fine," Alex answered quickly.

"How about some appetizers while we decide?" Ron asked.

"Excellent," Kendra said as she spoke up.

"See," Alex said. "There is the real Kendra we all know and love."

Kendra blushed.

"No, that's a great start," Sarah said with enthusiasm. "Let's get the loaded potato skins, buffalo chicken wings, and…"

"Fried zucchini," Kendra added.

"Fried zucchini," Sarah said as she nodded to the waitress. They quickly ordered drinks, and the waitress left them to get to work.

"Looks like the two of you have stacks of notes," Ron said.

"At one time this was quite a booming little community," Sarah replied.

"That took place a long time ago in our history," Ron stated. "It was considered to be the beginning of our end, if you'll pardon the pun."

"It's a shame about the dairy suddenly choosing another town," Kendra interjected.

"Yes, that was a more hopeful time in our near recent past," Ron concurred.

"But that was not the beginning of your problems, was it?" Alex asked.

"No, they go further back in time," Ron said. "Back in 1881, this town was a bustling community. At one time we were actually a popular vacation spot for the rich and rapacious. During this era, your hotel was the jewel in the crown of this town. Everything centered on it."

"The original owners, Thomas and Mildred Conrad, were quite the innkeepers I understand," Sarah said.

"Oh, indeed," Ron replied in agreement. "In fact, Thomas Conrad himself designed the huge wraparound, double-decker porch that you see there today. It was said that he was very particular. And his wife, Mildred, was just as meticulous with her touches in the hotel. She had picked every piece of furniture, wallpaper, adornments, and chintzes. Her taste was noted for being exceptional, especially in the kitchen. At least, so I've been told."

"This is a picture we found of Thomas Conrad," Alex said as she slid the picture across the table to Ron.

"I believe it is," Ron replied. "There aren't too many photos of Mildred and Thomas. And there were none to be found of their young son, Jonathan, either."

"Really? That's a little odd," Sarah said.

"From what I've read, things started getting a little chaotic early on," Alex said. "The Conrads were brutally murdered. Apparently by highwaymen."

"That's true," Ron replied. "Their son, though, he wouldn't let their murders drop. See, there were some bad feelings in this town. It all boiled down to greed. The townsfolk back then really believed that the Conrads were not doing all they could to help out the community. Jonathan Conrad believed that some town vigilantes got carried away when they plotted to murder his parents. He set out to ruin the town and he managed to do just that."

"How exactly did he do that?" Kendra asked.

"He used many methods," Ron said. "He fashioned boutiques at the hotel that outshined anything in town. Put them all out of business, he did. If folks were angry before, he opened up a hornet's nest when he declared war on their livelihood."

"After that is when it started, wasn't it, Ron?" Alex asked.

"What started?"

"All the disappearances."

"Oh, there weren't all that many that I recall. There were a few my father told me about around 1940 or so. I don't recall hearing about many disappearances from back then," Ron said.

"I think, Ron," Alex began slowly. "That you will find that the problems go way back to just after the Conrad's time."

Cautiously, Alex again reached inside of her wallet and pulled out an old piece of newspaper. Carefully, she unfolded the clipping and set it in front of Ron so that he could see it.

"I found this newspaper item wedged far back in the corner of the file cabinet that contained these photographs and a slim collection of facts about the Conrads and their untimely demise. Since you say that you are a believer, Ron, then I must tell you that one of the ghosts that I see on a daily basis in my barn is Thomas Conrad."

"That's amazing! Really?" Ron exclaimed.

"I gather," Alex continued, "that as patriarch of the family and the unproclaimed founder of this town, his spirit continues to be the most restless. He carries with him a strong obligation, and it is that obligation that continually forces him to cross over into the present world."

"Fascinating," Ron said as he breathed heavily.

"This newspaper article," Alex said as she continued, "was about a girl. A girl named Samantha Harding. She was dragged into an alley, and basically dismembered, torn to pieces. The street cleaner that found her, George Fisher, was originally blamed, but then locked up in an institution after he lost his mind from the incident."

"Ah, Alex, food's here," Sarah interjected. Alex knew at Sarah's tone to shut up while the woman was anywhere near the table.

"Are you ready to order anything else?" the waitress questioned.

Guilt expressed on every face, everyone realized that no one had looked at the menus.

"Four hamburgers," Ron blurted out. "Well done. Fries. Thanks."

The waitress walked away and Sarah looked at Ron. He replied, "Well, you didn't want her hanging around the table did you?"

"Do we have an official badge for Ron so he can join the group?" Alex said. "Now, where were we? Oh yeah, Samantha Harding and her murder."

"I don't remember that story," Ron admitted.

"According to the clippings that I found, her murder was one year to the day of the Conrad's murder."

"Wow," Ron said as he looked over the clipping. "Well, Ian would know all about this stuff. I'm surprised that you didn't ask him to meet us here too."

"What do you mean, the sheriff would know more?" Alex asked suspiciously.

"Well, it says right here that the investigation was headed by Inspector Graham Valin. That was Ian's ancestor. He's descended from a long line of policemen in this area."

"Ian's ancestor?" Alex asked.

"Yeah. He disappeared in disgrace, leaving behind his wife and son. No one ever knew where he went."

"Really," Alex said with an air of sarcasm. She quickly remembered the dream vision she had with Ian's twin in it.

Sarah shot her a look of warning from across the table.

"Ron, did you hear about the pit we found on the grounds?" Sarah asked.

"Hear about it," he replied. "There isn't anyone in town who hasn't heard about it."

"Then we've had at least a hundred women or more who have gone missing," Alex concluded. "But what happened between then and now. What happened to Jonathan Conrad for example?"

"Rumor has it," Ron said. "That Jonathan Conrad became a bitter old man as the years went on. After the Depression, a large milk company was offering to make Grand Detour their main city of operation. Apparently, negotiations were underway between the town and the board of directors for the dairy. The only thing the town had to do was put up the money for the railroad spur."

"And?" Sarah asked.

"And, since only one man had money, they decided to approach him about lending the money to the town."

"Obviously, Conrad refused them," Sarah said.

"Not exactly," Ron said.

"How not exactly?" Alex asked.

"Well, when they went to him, they felt they had an offer that he could not refuse. They certainly were disappointed when they got there to see him."

"Because he kicked their butts off the property?" Kendra questioned.

"No, because he was dead."

"Dead?" Alex and Sarah said in unison.

"Not just dead, but apparently he had committed suicide many years before. The committee statement said that the hotel had become an eyesore. Conrad had turned into a recluse in his final years. When they opened the hotel doors they saw that the huge chandeliers were filled with cobwebs the size of hammocks. Dust and dirt hung like a giant cloud in the air. That's when they noticed him."

"Noticed him?" Kendra gulped.

"Yes. Swinging from the chandelier over the desk and the staircase was a skeleton. It had been hung by the neck. It was said that he was nothing but bones and a decayed smoking jacket was hanging in tatters off of him.

"Is that who we saw?" Kendra said.

"Apparently," Alex replied.

"Maybe he is also trying to tell us what happened?" Sarah suggested.

"It is a possibility. I wish that I could have found a photo of him in the archives," Alex lamented. "It seems that none were ever taken, or, if any were, all were lost."

"I have a photograph myself to show you," Sarah interjected. She stuck her hand down into her purse and slowly, dramatically began to bring out an old tintype photo along with a newspaper clipping.

"Didn't you just yell at me this afternoon for *borrowing* library materials?" Alex said, razzing her.

"Yes, I believe I did. However, after careful consideration, I decided that the idea had some merit and I decided to follow your wonderful example." Dramatically, Sarah turned the photo over to unveil the subject. Alex had to force herself to exhale in order to breathe. She found herself staring at a disturbingly familiar face.

"That looks just like…" Ron said.

"That's right," Sarah exclaimed proudly, again having the topper over her friend. "It looks just like Ian."

"Let me see that," Alex snapped as she swiped the clipping and photo out of her friend's hand.

"Wait, I haven't even had a chance to read that yet!" Sarah protested.

"Well, it seems that our sheriff has also been lending a helping hand to protect the loss of information in this town," Ron said quietly.

"Maybe he had a good reason."

Everyone stared at Kendra.

"After all, it is his ancestor," she continued, "Maybe he's just a private person. Family pride and all that kind of stuff."

"Or family skeletons," Alex muttered.

"You know," Ron said pointing his index finger slightly toward the sky and shaking it as if in deep thought, "young lady, you are probably right. I've known Ian all my life, and he is a very private kind of person."

"Maybe," Alex said quietly.

"Anyhow, getting back to our research," Sarah said.

"Yes, well," Alex continued. "Many of the signals I am getting from this place suggest a sacrificial rite, but I cannot explain the culture. They are a tribe of Native Americans; my last vision proved that conclusively. Inexplicably, there is also a white man tangled up in this somehow."

"I don't understand," Ron said.

"I have had visions from years that encircle the Conrad's demise," Alex said as she continued, then paused. "Ron, I can't go any further without telling you what happened to me the other day. There is no good way to tell you this, but I have seen your sister."

"You've found Rita?"

"Your sister, Ron, is gone from this world. I experienced her spirit along the river in the large bend on the way to Nachusa. According to the newspaper clippings, it's the same bend where the Conrads were first killed all those years ago. From the way I described her to Sarah, she has confirmed her identity. I am truly sorry."

Alex leaned forward and gently grasped the man's shoulder. Quiet tears welled up in his eyes, and it became obvious to Alex through her contact with him, that he was in some danger as she felt a buildup in the man's system. Empathically, Alex sent as much comforting energy as she could muster under her own weariness to try and combat his stress. Kendra and Sarah looked on, speechless, as a faint golden glowing emanated from between Alex's hand and Ron's shoulder.

"Have you ever seen her do that before?" Kendra whispered in as quiet a voice as she could muster.

"No, I haven't," Sarah whispered back in awe.

"There is no need to whisper," Alex said, startling the pair of them. "The danger has passed, and there was no danger of breaking my concentration in the first place."

"What was that?" Sarah asked.

"Yeah, and why is he so still like?" Kendra asked.

"Ron, for lack of better words, is in a healing trance right now. What I gave to him was a forced psychic healing. Some cultures refer to it as Reiki or energy healing. Only my mother and I have ever achieved it amongst our people."

"Why?"

"Why, Kendra? I'll tell you why. Ron has been traveling slowly down the road towards a vicious heart attack from the stress of his missing sister. When I wake him from this trancelike state, he will remember the information about his sister's death, but he will find himself now physically strong enough to deal with it.

Turning toward Ron, Alex again laid her hand on his shoulder. Her other hand waved slightly in front of his eyes. "Now, Ron, you will awaken. The memories of our conversation will stay in your mind. You will find yourself with renewed strength, free from all mental and bodily stress.

Then he awoke. "I am so sorry, Ron. There was no other way to break the news to you. Sheriff Valin would never have believed me if I had told him about Rita. If you are a true believer as you claim to be, then I know that you will understand how hard it was for me to reveal this to you in such a way. I hope in time you will be able to forgive me, but you deserve to know the truth."

"What happened?" he gasped. "A dark veil dropped over me and suddenly, I wasn't here anymore. I could see a bright light and standing in that bright light was Rita." Tears of affection rolled down his cheeks as his mind came to terms with the fact that his sister was gone from him. "She smiled at me, then turned and walked away. What does that mean?"

"Your strong desire to find her was pulling her back to this earthbound place. Her spirit will now find closure with your acceptance of her passing. I wish I could change what has happened here. I hope to stop it before more are made to suffer."

"What exactly do you mean by that?" he asked.

"The being that has done this to her, and many other innocent victims like her, is still out there. Doing what he likes to do best, terrify and kill. I have to find out who or what it is and put a stop to it."

"Do you have any idea where her…"

"No, Ron. I do not know the whereabouts of her remains. That information is unknown to me, but her soul is what needed the closure. Remember that is the important part, the peace, if you will."

Looking down at the ground and rubbing his hands together in thought, slowly, Ron began to speak again. "I heard a story about Janey Stevenson on the way over here," Ron said. "They said that you could see her being killed. Is that true?"

"Yes."

"Ssh!" Sarah hissed.

"What is it, Sarah?" asked Alex.

Sarah did not have time to reply. Coming through the glass door area was the owner of The Blue Ram, Jack Darwin, along with the their waitress carrying hamburgers. She set the plates down and cleared out quickly.

"Welcome guests!" he announced. "Miss Caldwell, you are as good as your word."

"Who is that?" Alex mouthed to Sarah inaudibly from behind her hand.

"What word would that be, Mr. Darwin?" Sarah asked innocently.

"Why, to bring this lovely and talented woman into my establishment so that I might meet her," Darwin cooed.

"Jack Darwin," Sarah said as she extended her hand palm upwards towards him. Moving across the span between them she continued. "Alexandra Markum."

"What a rare treat to have you here," Darwin said as he grasped Alex's hand and kissed the back of it before she could utter an objection.

A small gasp of surprise emanated from Alex. The stranger's forwardness had caught her completely off guard, as she was more attuned to the company of animals rather than people.

"I am sorry," Darwin said innocently. "I have offended you and for that I will forever be sorry. And of course, Mr. Van Allen. Such a pleasure to have you here again so soon with such lovely companions."

"That's…that's okay," Alex stammered in a breathy voice. When she heard herself, she did not even recognize her own voice. Her nerves were all on edge at once. She felt like an eagle was fluttering around in her stomach. Who was this man anyhow?

"I shall return to speak with you another time," Darwin continued. "Again, please forgive me for startling you." With that, he turned and strode back through the door he had just come through.

"Don't make it too soon," Ron muttered under his breath.

"I don't believe it," Kendra said in a teasing way. "I always kinda thought you were sweet on Ian, but this new guy just left you crimson and speechless!"

"It's not that way with either of them, Kendra," Alex snapped. "And, yes, Ron, to answer your question, the vision was exactly that way, but it was only Janey. The vision containing Rita had none of those particular gruesome qualities," Alex lied.

Sarah gave Alex a questioning sidelong glance, knowing that her friend was lying. Alex parried by giving a glance to Sarah that said *not now*.

Ron rose and excused himself, insisting that he had to make a phone call.

Sarah watched him leave, and Alex could tell that her friend was falling for the handsome and extremely charming strawberry-blond man.

"He is a nice man, Sarah," Alex said, smiling knowingly at her friend.

"Sorry," Sarah stammered. "It's just that I've been so alone for some time, and he is such a friendly, nice man."

"There is no need to make excuses, my friend," Alex said comfortingly. "Bruce would not want you to stay alone forever. Remember that."

"You like him?" Sarah asked.

"I like him," Alex replied.

"Cut the mush!" Kendra exclaimed in a disgusted tone. "Alex, could he have died tonight?"

"Not necessarily tonight, Kendra. It could have happened anytime.

"But Alex, you lied to him," Sarah said.

"Would you have preferred that I put the poor man over the edge? To know what I saw will not make him deal with her passing any better. He is a caring man, with deep convictions. From what you've told me of him, Sarah, he will always feel guilty for his fathers' indiscretion. You would do well to remember that always. He is a man who can be easily hurt."

"Can we go home now?" Kendra whined.

"Yes, we can all go home after you finish your burger. And on our way home, Miss Sarah, you can explain to me who this Jack Darwin is and why you felt it was necessary that we ate here."

"Honestly, Alex, I'd forgotten all about him. If I'd remembered, I would have chosen another place."

"I don't think she's too upset, if you ask me," Kendra said. "I think someone should break it to Ian that he's got more than a little competition."

Less than one minute in the back seat of the truck cab, Kendra fell fast asleep. Alex called her name several times before she was certain that she had fallen asleep.

"Sarah, that article and picture that you showed us in the restaurant."

"Yes. What about it?"

"Did you read that article that I took from the file?"

"Well, no not really. Just skimmed it and with the picture I thought it would be a real hoot to show you."

"That's not what I mean, Sarah."

"Oh?"

"If you had taken time to read that article, you would have seen that the main focus of the article was written by this Graham Valin's immediate superior."

"And? That means exactly what to us?"

"He indicated in that article that he felt Graham Valin was responsible for the disappearances."

"What?"

"You read it for yourself when we get home. If that is the case, then Ian has more than a little private history to keep quiet. He may be covering up the solution to all those murders."

"There is something else, isn't there?"

"You know me too well, my friend."

"Tell me."

"Remember when I said that there were Native Americans involved, but the rituals that are taking place are actually under the direction of a white man?"

"Yes, I remember you saying something like that."

"Stretch your imagination into the unknown for a moment. We know that this is an ancient evil. A being that spans time as you and I know it, whether that means it is one being or a reincarnation of the same being. We know from the article that Graham Valin disappeared without a trace and that his superior laid all of the murders on him."

"Alex, you're wrong."

"Think about it, Sarah. We also know for a fact that Ian is a dead ringer for Graham Valin. How can we be sure that he is what you think he is, instead of what I am beginning to suspect he might be?"

"I think that I'm too tired for that last statement, but if you are saying what I think you are saying, then I think that you are mistaken."

"Are you sure about that? What better place to hide a hideous evil than in a law enforcement office?"

"Well, yes. No. God, Alex. I don't know what to think anymore!"

"Neither do I, but we must double our caution. If it is him, then we must guard against the knowledge of that picture and article at all costs."

"It won't be easy, will it?"

"No it won't. But, look on the bright side."

"There's a bright side to this?"

"Sure, now you get to brush up on your magnificent acting ability."

Silence filled the truck cab as Sarah leaned back into her seat. No one spoke again until they reached home unless that is, anyone counted the soft snoring of Kendra coming from the back seat.

29

The figure was seated at a desk, alone in the dark. A hand reached out and pulled on the chain of the standard issue desk lamp that every sheriff's office contained. A dim glow surrounding the occupant of the chair and he was clutching the now well-worn magazine in one hand and hanging up the telephone receiver with the other. The article was genuine. There could be no doubt of that now. A long conversation with the Wyoming sheriff had confirmed what Ian had wanted to believe but could not because of his close-mindedness to the supernatural. Alex's *talents,* for lack of a better word, were now authenticated. The facts spoke for themselves.

Captain Parker had related to Ian that he had once been in a situation similar to the one Ian now found himself in. The mental acceptance of the paranormal was always difficult, especially for an officer of the law. Ian's mind had struggled to accept all that he heard. He stared in complete concentration at the picture of the woman and horse displayed on the front cover.

So engrossed was he that, when the door opened and someone entered, he didn't even hear them. The figure set a small travel bag down just inside the door and advanced toward the light, which beaconed out in the darkened room.

"I can't believe that I treated her like this when it's all true," Ian said.

"Hi-wo:-ni-a u-ne:-g ya'-n'-s-si'," a voice spoke from the shadows.

Ian leaped up from his chair and drew his gun in the direction of the voice. "Who are you? How did you get in here?"

"Please," said the calming voice, now speaking in a recognizable language. The owner of the disembodied voice stepped from the shadows. "Put away your weapon; I am unarmed."

The person was an older man with shiny silver hair drawn neatly back into a long pigtail, plaited down his back. The face was well-worn and showed an inner wisdom that Ian respected instantly. Ian also detected an undeniable trace of puckish humor.

"Who are you?" Ian said putting his weapon away. "And just what the devil was that gibberish you were spouting?"

"The gibberish you speak of is Tsa-la-gi."

"Huh?"

"Tsa-la-gi is the Cherokee language."

"And the previous statement that I could never possibly pronounce was what?"

"The du-yu-du Ka-no-he-s-gi, the truth declarer of our people."

"Look, I'm sorry, but it's late. I'm tired, and, quite frankly, extremely cranky," Ian said shaking his head.

"She is known to you I believe," the old man said casting a sidelong glance at the magazine thrown in the middle of the desk. "Alexandra Markum. She is my granddaughter."

"That horrendous name means Alex?" Ian questioned. "That was not in the article."

"Alex would never allow a publication of any kind to use her tribal given name. She is a direct descendant of centuries of tribal chiefs. She is also the chosen one for our people. The u-ne:-g ya'-n'-s-si' is a strong and powerful sign to our people. Especially sacred to our people, she represents high spirituality, wisdom, and wealth."

Putting his hand to his head, Ian took a very deep breath. "My humblest apologies, sir, for drawing my weapon. You took me quite by surprise. I had no way of knowing who you were."

"No apologies are necessary, Sheriff Valin," the man replied, drawing out Ian's last name slowly so as to pronounce it correctly. "My granddaughter has always had the ability to make even the most sane man crumble when forced to endure her ways." Then a playful furrow crossed his brown as the visitor paused and added, "Her stubborn streak, however, is one to be reckoned with. Personally, I believe that particular part of her came from her father's side of the family. Her mother, my daughter, was the most even-tempered being that ever lived."

"How do you know my name?" Ian said slowly, suspiciously.

"Not by the means you think," the old man laughed as a twinkle lit devilishly in his eyes. "I have received many e-mails from my granddaughter and your name was listed prominently in most of them. I am aware of your troubles here and have come to help. I only hope that I am not too late."

"I'm sure that her messages did not give you a shining representation of my character."

A warm-hearted chuckle emanated from the elderly man. "That would be an accurate statement on your part. There were other things that disturbed me greatly from her accounts. If they are accurate, she will need some help from us all."

"You'll forgive me, but I haven't had the luxury of your e-mails. Your name is…? And just how do you think that I can help?"

"I am known to my people as Lightning Horse. I believe that you will also find my name in that article, although I was little more than a spectator," the older man replied as he pointed to the rolled up magazine on top of the desk. Ian noticed that the old man avoided the other question entirely. He decided to let it alone for the moment.

"Please forgive my initial greeting of you, sir."

"There is no *sir*. Lightning Horse, or if you prefer, L.H."

"L. H.?"

"This is shorter than my given name; at least the one that you can pronounce. We must all do our little part to preserve harmony and balance."

"Hmm. Oh yeah, Lightning Horse. Anyway, depending on how much or how little you know, things have been very…well, for lack of a better word, strange here. I'm sorry, I find that I am just not myself."

"No apologies are necessary. I am well aware that you have had many problems here. The air of your town carries the fragrance of misfortune throughout. No one needs to speak, one can feel it if the senses are opened to the vibrations."

"What can I help you with, sir? Sorry, Lightning Horse."

"I am, as people of your generation might say, in need of a lift. I have just gotten off a bus and need some directions in order to get to the hotel."

"I'll be glad to drive you there," Ian offered, as he grabbed his coat from the back of the chair."

"That would be most welcome. I am weary after the hours spent on the bus."

Ian moved from behind the desk, and the phone rang.

"Please, sit down," Ian said gesturing towards a chair in the office. "This should not take long. At a time like this, all phone calls could be important."

"Understood. And thank you." The older man walked across to the group of chairs and, selecting one, sat down.

"Sheriff's office, this is Valin."

"Thank goodness," came the reply on the other end of the line.

"Is that you, Jack?"

"Yes. My hostess, Jennie Thomas, has disappeared from the restaurant."

"Are you sure?"

"Of course, I'm sure," came the panicked voice. "She is a most dedicated worker and her shift is not over for another four hours yet. Please help find her; she has never done anything like this before. I fear that something has happened to her. I am especially concerned after the disappearances in town of late. What will I tell her parents? After all, as her employer, she is my responsibility while she is here."

"Calm down, Jack. I'll make every effort to find her. I'll be right over for the details."

"Thanks, Sheriff."

"And I know just the person to help me, too," Ian said, glancing at his guest while hanging up the phone receiver.

"I take it that there will be a minor stop along the way," Lightning Horse said.

"If you don't mind," Ian said. "It is really right on our way, but it might take you a little longer to get where you are going."

"You mean where *we* are going."

"Right. Where *we* are going."

* * *

The sheriff's cruiser pulled up outside The Blue Ram; Ian turned towards his occupant in the passenger side of the front seat.

"Sir…er um…Lightning Horse," Ian stammered. "Why don't you just stay here in the cruiser while I go and talk to Mr. Darwin for a moment."

"That will be fine."

Ian disappeared into the restaurant, and Lightning Horse opened his door and climbed out, crossing over to the building. This enabled him to get a better look inside the restaurant window. He was glad that he had opted to stay outside. The interior of the building seemed dark to him. There were clouds hanging from the ceiling courtesy of the smoking patrons and the picture depicting The Blue Ram on the wall did not give him a comfortable feeling.

* * *

A twig snapping in the distance caught Lightning Horse's immediate attention and he turned quickly to his right, straining to see something in the dark. When he looked back inside, Ian Valin had stopped talking to the tall, dark man and had begun to question a very young girl that obviously was employed there judging from her uniform. Another twig snapped, this time more closely. Reaching inside his shirt, he drew out a silver talisman and placed it to the outside of his shirt. It bore the markings of an eagle in flight. Just to the right, from behind the building, he thought he could see the outline of a wolf darting out of sight and into the tree line. A small sigh escaped him as he realized that the evil that he had come to help seek out had found him first.

30

Drawers were ripped out of desks. Pillows were torn through with a sharp knife, spewing feathers everywhere. It was searching for something. Something important. Piles of papers were thrown up in the air only to fall scattered on the floor, revealing nothing. Books were pulled out of the bookcase and left in heaps on the floor.

It breathed heavily as it hurried from room to room in the hotel. Time was running out for the search. The women would be home soon, and it was not yet time. The idea of the delicious main event was not far off. The torment that he had planned was still yet to take place. The thought of the future events brought a twisted and evil grin to his face. There was still so much pleasure to experience before the kill. A lightning fast glance toward a front window told the being that time was up. Racing to the back door the shaman figure shifted its shape and became a large rogue wolf, the familiar of the evil one.

*   *   *

The women entered the hotel lobby and were shocked at the obvious vandalism done to their property.

"Dare we call the sheriff?" Sarah asked.

"I don't think so," Alex replied. I think that the sheriff has seen enough of us the past few days. Come to think of it, I can't even guarantee that the sheriff did not do this."

"Well," Sarah said with hesitation. "I think, ignoring that last remark, that this can wait until tomorrow to clean up. I am simply too tired."

"Me too."

"What do you think they were searching for?"

"They?"

"It would take more than one person to make all this mess!"

"I wouldn't count on that if I were you," Alex replied. "I think whoever it was, they were looking for something important. Let's think about this as rationally as we can."

"It has to be something we have recently come into possession of."

"Correct. The reason being that otherwise this would have happened much sooner."

"That only leaves one thing, doesn't it?"

"Right, Sarah. It has to be the talisman. I hope you have it hidden somewhere safe."

"I have. It's hanging around my neck," Sarah said.

"Around your neck?" Alex screamed. "Take that thing off and hide it well, until I tell you otherwise."

"Well, if I hadn't been wearing it, they might have found it."

"Sarah," Alex said as she grasped her by the shoulders. "I am concerned for your well-being. For me, because you are my best friend, please take it off and hide it."

"Okay."

"You'll promise me?"

"Yes, I promise."

"Good, let's go get sleepyhead out of the truck and put her to bed."

"That sounds like a great idea!"

* * *

"Well, she is finally in bed and fast asleep," Sarah said to Alex as she swept her palms together in a brushing motion.

"Good."

"Tell me now, Alex. You really don't think that Ian has anything to do with this."

"Sarah, I don't know what to think, but it is too much of a coincidence to write off," Alex said, withdrawing the photo of Graham Valin from her purse.

She stared into the lifeless eyes of the photograph, and they seemed to bore a hole right into her. It hurt her to think that this man might actually be the evil one. Toying with her at every turn. Trying to worm his way into her circle as a friend. Awaiting his chance to destroy her and her *family* utterly.

"It's spooky, isn't it?" Sarah asked, breaking the silence.

"What is?"

"That these two people look so much alike. Enough to be twins in fact."

"Sarah, what if they are not look-alikes."

"I know you said that before, but it can't be Ian."

"Why can't it? Do you think just because he's the sheriff that he can't do bad things?"

"No," Sarah replied softly. "I think because my friend took an instant liking to him that he simply could not be the one."

"Sarah, you were married to a cop. How can your instinct be so awful? I can be wrong. I've made mistakes before," Alex said sadly, then very softly she added, "Only never on such a grand scale."

"I think that we all need a good night's rest. Let's follow Kendra's example and turn in."

"I'll try. I am exhausted," Alex replied, rising from the couch and setting the photo down on the coffee table. She yawned and stretched as she headed for the stairs.

"Goodnight," Sarah called after her.

"Aren't you coming?" Alex asked.

"Just want to turn off some of these lights. I wonder why Alfred left them all on?"

"Oh, he's probably just afraid of the dark. He was as a kid; maybe he just never grew out of it."

"Say, where is Alfred anyhow?"

"He is most likely playing it safe. There is no doubt in my mind that he is bunking with the horses."

"Really?"

"They are a great alarm system."

"I suppose you're right. I'll be up momentarily," Sarah said, calling after her friend.

Roaming from room to room, Sarah turned off some twenty lamps. Heaven help them when the electric bill came. Sarah could not help chuckling to herself; she secretly wished she were still here and alive when the next electric bill arrived. One never knew if they would survive from one day to the next around this place. Sarah found it funny how her perspective had changed in the last few weeks. She reentered the lobby in front of the staircase and picked up the old photo from the table. Sitting sideways in a big armchair with her legs flipped over one big rolled arm, Sarah assumed her favorite way to flop in comfort. She looked at the photo. Maybe this time she might see something that would give her a clue. She didn't care how many times Alex said it was possible, she just could not believe in her heart that Ian was a killer. Sarah could tell that Alex was not totally convinced one way or the other. If Sarah was any judge of character, and she felt that she was, the man in the photo was not a killer. But if it wasn't him, then who could it be? They were running out of possibilities.

Sarah nodded off in the chair. Her dreams ran wild, changing course and plunging to the dark side of that which nightmares are made of.

She was awakened by a noise, which turned out to be a soft rapping at the door. Turning on the porch light she was startled to see Ian's face in the window of the door. She was so startled that she screamed and jumped back from the door.

"Well, I didn't think my unshaven face was that bad," Ian said as he turned to his elderly companion.

"Let me try," Lightning Horse said. "She has known me for many years, and I think, that no matter her state, she will trust me."

Ian stood aside. The windowpane filled with the image of another face; this one was well known to Sarah and her panic subsided.

"Sarah, it is L. H.," he said.

Sarah stopped shaking. Still hiding behind the door, she took in a sharp breath of courage. She listened, and again the voice outside spoke to her. With a dawn of realization, Sarah understood that it was, indeed, Alex's grandfather on the other side of the door. Cautiously, she undid the deadbolt and opened the door.

"Why have you brought him?" she asked sharply.

"I needed a ride," Lightning Horse said. "The sheriff's office is one of the few things open at this time of night."

"Why are you here?" Sarah asked Lightning Horse, as she shot a cool look to Ian. "I know Alex wanted to send you Kendra tomorrow."

"Kendra? Oh yes, her ward," the older man replied.

"May we come in?" Ian asked.

"Sure," Sarah replied.

The pair walked into the interior of the house, and Ian set down the older man's travel pack.

"What has happened here?" L.H. asked.

"Wow, this place really is a mess, is everything okay?" Ian asked.

"Alex got home and just couldn't stand any of this stuff any longer so we're going to redecorate."

"Hmm," L.H. muttered.

"Is Alex awake?" Ian asked.

"She is not," Sarah replied, coldly. "And, I'm not going to wake her either."

Confused by the woman's behavior, Ian just decided to ask her outright what the problem was.

"Look, I know I have not been the most welcomed person at this household lately, but would you mind telling me what you are all steamed up at me about? I can understand why Miss Markum is upset with me and, while I can not claim to comprehend exactly what she is, I know that many things that I said to her were way out of line."

"I hardly think she will care what you have to say to her now," Sarah said icily.

"If it was just for my benefit, I'd forget the entire thing, but I don't want to speak to her for myself. I need her to use her talents for another missing girl."

"Oh, no, not another girl!" Then Sarah bristled and continued, "I think you would know as well as anyone here, Sheriff, just what has happened to that girl."

"Would you please make sense! I'm very tired and don't have time to cipher these puzzles that you and Miss Markum delight in throwing at me."

"I believe she means this," Lightning Horse said, interrupting their conversation and holding up the picture of Graham Valin.

"Don't," Sarah cried out.

"Forgive me," Ian said as he took the picture from the old man's hand. "What has a picture of my great-grandfather got to do with all of this?"

"They do not believe that this is your ancestor," Lightning Horse replied. Seeing the confused look on Ian's face he continued, "They believe that this is you."

"Me?" Ian exclaimed.

"Am I correct?" Lightning Horse asked turning in Sarah's direction.

"Well, that is," Sarah hemmed nervously, "Well, yes. As a matter of fact we do."

"What? You think that I…" He indicated the picture and them himself, and then he lost his temper. "That I had anything to do with…That's it! You and your small-minded friend have gone too far this time."

"Really, further than accusing Alex of killing Janey Stevenson?" Sarah shot back.

"I never said that!" Ian yelled back.

"You implied it. It is the same thing."

"May I make a suggestion?" Lightning Horse said.

"Sure," Ian said curtly.

"This is not helping the girl that we need to find."

"You're right," Ian conceded as he wiped his hand over his mouth in thought.

"And you, young lady," Lightning Horse said admonishingly. "You must set your quibbling aside until later and not fight Alex's battles for her. Whether anyone wants to admit it or not, I know that this is the soul mate for u-ne:-g ya'-n'-s-si', I have seen it since I first entered his office. Childish prattling will get none of us anywhere, except perhaps all killed."

Both Ian and Sarah stared at the old man with their mouths open. Ian was the only one of the two turning slightly red under his unshaven cheeks.

"What's going on down here?" Kendra asked, as she rubbed her left eye to remove the sleep. "What's all the yelling about? Who are you? Are you a ghost, too?"

"It is about two full-grown adults acting like little children; thank goodness the third child is in bed," Lightning Horse replied. "You must be Kendra."

"And you must be Lightning Horse," she replied sleepily, descending the stairs. "Wow, you really do exist, and I think, from what little I'm hearing, I'm glad that you're here."

Kendra got to the foot of the stairs and noticed that no one was even paying attention to her. Instead, they were looking almost directly above her.

"What are you looking at?" Kendra said. Turning, her eyes fell on a misty shadow floating about six inches above the floor and silently moving down the visible staircase hallway. The seconds ticked by, and her facial features became more distinguished. Her body took a more defined shape, and even the lines of her dress were visible. Once the figure became fully visible, the ghostly body decayed in stages. Blood spattered the walls, and the woman's body was ravaged before their eyes. Finally, it reached the stage of looking as though she had been physically torn apart. All of the occupants found that their clothes were spattered heavily with blood. Then the ghost vanished utterly along with the bloodstains. Kendra was crying and ran to Sarah for comfort.

"What…what the hell was that?" Ian stammered.

"That, my friend, is just a sampling of what we see almost three times daily here at the hotel," Sarah replied. "Actually, that and worse."

"I don't believe it," Ian whispered.

"That is why you fail," Lightning Horse commented quietly.

Ian gave him an odd look and then said, "Like grandfather, like granddaughter."

*   *   *

Their silence was broken by a bone-chilling scream. It shattered the air around them. It was the scream of someone being tortured.

"Oh my god," Sarah shouted as she bolted for the stairs. "Alex!"

Sarah was quick, but Ian was faster and passed her on the stairs. Taking three stairs at a time, he threw open the door hiding the nightmarish screams. There, in her own room where anyone should feel secure, was Alex, lying on her bed. Blood steadily streamed from her eyes. Her body was struggling against invisible bonds that held her in place. She writhed in pain at an invisible attacker, taking blows received from somewhere beyond. Bruises formed on her skin as if she had been struck violently. Her clothing tore, and bloody rivulets trickled outward, soaking the strips of material.

"What the hell?" Ian crossed the room to be at her side.

Sarah reached the doorframe only seconds before Kendra, who began to cry hysterically again and ran back into the hallway. Ian was just about to touch Alex with his outstretched hand when Lightning Horse stopped him.

"Do not touch her!" he commanded.

Alex screamed again. The sound was pure pain. A growing red blotch began to appear over her heart region, soaking through her shirt.

"I have to help her!" Ian shouted back desperately.

"You cannot help her. What you do may endanger her life," Lightning Horse replied.

"She's in so much pain; can't we help her somehow?" Sarah cried.

More low moaning emanated from the girl lying on the bed.

"There must be something we can do," Ian insisted.

"She is in a rare empathic trance with someone else. She is feeling someone else's pain. Experiencing another person's horror. Bleeding someone else's tears. What she does is very dangerous. She is taking the pain into herself for the other. The spell must be broken correctly or you will endanger her life and lose them both. It must also be done quickly, the other must be near the end."

Quietly, the old man advanced. His murmurings were low and almost inaudible. Not that it would have mattered if he had spoken up. Ian recognized the quiet words he spoke as more of the Cherokee dialect he had heard earlier in the evening. His eyes were closed, and he advanced to the stricken woman. Sarah came up even with Ian.

"Was this how it was before with the blood?" she whispered to him.

"Yes, but not nearly this much," he whispered back with concern. "She just went out cold, not all this screaming and sobbing. I was worried before but this makes the other attack, or whatever it is look like a picnic."

"What's he saying?" Sarah whispered again.

"Great, I was going to ask you that question."

"What makes you think I know Cherokee?"

"It is a prayer to save your soul," came a tired voice from the bed. "And even if you knew Cherokee, you still couldn't make out the words. He is speaking in an ancient tribal Cherokee dialect."

"Alex?" Sarah said hopefully.

"Are you one, my child?" Lightning Horse asked.

"Yes, Grandfather, but I feel very tired."

"You must not move yet; we will take turns watching vigils over you."

"I'll take the first," Ian said.

"I knew that you would," Lightning Horse replied. "You must keep her talking right now."

"Talking about what?" Ian asked.

"Anything at all. You must do the majority of the speaking. Reading to her is ideal." Then he warned Ian, shaking his finger at him. "Do not upset her or argue with her. If she is unreasonable, let her be so. Argue with her later."

"Understood."

"I must attend to the tenderhearted one in the hallway," Lightning Horse said. With that, he walked out into the hallway to take care of a nearly hysterical Kendra.

Sarah turned to follow him and then turned back towards Ian and Alex.

"Ian, I'm so sorry."

"For what?"

"For attacking you the way I did. I should not have made the accusations I made. My imagination ran off with me in a nightmare. It was totally out of place; you just frightened me, showing up at the door like that so late. I should have known you couldn't do anything like this. The concern you showed for her after she took off the other day..."

"Yeah...some concern. I wanted to beat her senseless for running off with some fool notion in her head."

"Nonetheless, the feelings were genuine. I think she knows it, even if she won't admit it to you or anyone else."

"It's all right. I probably had it coming for being such a jerk to begin with. That's something I hope to rectify soon."

"Could you please stop talking like I'm not here!" said a tired voice from the bed.

"Sorry, Alex," Sarah said. "Feel better, okay?"

"Okay, chief," Alex replied, adding a tired smile to the red, tearstained face.

Sarah turned, walked through the doorframe, and left.

Ian dragged a wooden chair up to the side of the bed and sat down. "So, little girl," he began, "since the only books in this room are computer manuals or books on horsemanship, I guess I'll have to make up a story. What would you rather hear, Goldilocks and the Three Bears or Jack and the Beanstalk?"

"Goldilocks."

"I suppose you want characterization voices, too?"

"I can't wait to hear you do Goldilocks."

"Just wait until you get better!"

Alex relaxed and listened to Ian's comforting voice as he began to tell the story.

"Once upon a time, in the woods, there lived three bears," he began. "Do I really have to do the voices?"

"I want you to turn in the best damn performance you've ever done."

"A papa bear, a mama bear, and a little baby bear," he reenacted, in three various voices.

The inaneness of the story was helping to ease her mind. It could have easily been gibberish, but Alex was enjoying putting Ian through the wringer. All she really needed was to hear a voice, one that would take her away from the hurt inside. One that could help her forget the immediate pain of the joining with the victim. Once she had mended her psyche, she could return to normal and speak of what had befallen the latest victim.

31

Everyone had slept in late. Everyone, that is, except for Ian. It was his own fault; he did not want to leave Alex's side. He spoke to her until well into the wee hours of the morning. His voice became scratchy, but he convinced himself that he was making a difference. He wanted to believe that she would be more at ease with him now, more than ever before. Ian wanted to take advantage of the situation, to try and rectify some of the rotten things he had said to her since she arrived. He hoped, selfishly, to ease his battered conscious. Very quietly, the door to the room swung open, and in tiptoed Sarah with a hot cup of tea.

"It has honey in it for your throat," she whispered as she pointed at her own throat.

"Thank you," he mouthed.

"I can relieve you if you would like to take a shower or something," Sarah offered.

"I suppose she would look on me in better favor if I showered and shaved," he replied.

He began to leave the room, and Sarah sat down and soothingly began to read from one of the computer manuals sitting on her desk.

"She seems to prefer Goldilocks and the Three Bears the most," Ian whispered as he poked his head back inside the doorframe.

"She will have to settle for an Adobe Photoshop program manual. I don't do voices very well," Sarah whispered back. "Besides, she wanted to have more time to sit down and learn this new program. Perhaps she can pick up things in her sleep."

"You've been listening at the door!" Ian chastised her quietly.

"Only a little. But you certainly do a wicked Baby Bear!"

"Very funny!"

An hour later, Lightning Horse entered the room. He motioned for Sarah to continue to read, but asked her to lower her voice to a whisper. Another chair was brought to her bedside and he sat, propping his elbows on his knees. Leaning slightly forward he interlocked his fingers and studied Alex for a few moments. Reaching in his pocket, he produced an item and pressed it into Alex's hand."

"What's that?" Sarah asked.

"A powerful, healing citrine crystal."

"Oh," said Sarah, no wiser than before she asked the question.

Ian reappeared in the doorway, clean-shaven, and gestured to Sarah that he would like to continue. He had brought another book into the room. She recognized it immediately. It was the book from her nightstand; a science fiction novel called Nyceegam, which Alex herself had picked out for her. Sarah smiled when she remembered that Alex had once said that the relationship of the two main characters reminded her of the relationship she had with Sarah.

He sat down to read and then asked, "What's with the rock?"

"That's a citrine crystal," Sarah said.

"And that means…?" he asked.

"Well, it's a healing crystal," she replied.

"Okay, sure. That certainly explains everything."

Lightning Horse smiled at their exchange.

Sarah moved close to Lightning Horse and whispered into his ear. He nodded in compliance, and Sarah scurried off, only to return minutes later with a washbowl and cloth. She began to gently wipe off the bloody smears that stained her friend's face. She took great care in wringing the cloth out into the washbowl. When she was done, the water looked like a bowl of blood. After a gesture from Lightning Horse, she went and sat in the corner. Lightning Horse bent forward and began to whisper to Ian.

"I am going to ask her some questions," he said quietly. "I want you to continue to read until she wakes up."

"I will," Ian whispered, sneaking in his answer between the lines of the science fiction text.

"Be prepared. When she comes to, she is liable to do anything."

"Anything, like what?"

"She may be hysterical. She may be violent. She could be both. She could also have temporary insanity. She will have a tendency to act and think irrationally at times. You must be ready for whatever happens."

"What should I do for any of those choices?"

"You must follow your heart. Despite the fact that you are a white man, your heart is genuine."

"Thanks, I think," Ian replied sarcastically.

Turning from Ian, Lightning Horse concentrated on the still form of his granddaughter.

"Who are you?" he asked her.

"There was a muffled, inaudible reply."

"Again," he demanded more parentally. "Who are you?"

"Jennie Thomas."

Ian was startled and ceased reading. The voice did not belong to Alex. This was a voice he had heard often enough. Every time he went to The Blue Ram, Jennie had said hello to him. She was a nice, seventeen-year-old kid, responsible enough to get good grades and keep a part-time job too.

"Continue," Lightning Horse injected quickly. "Alex needs the comfort of your voice to keep her from the edge."

"But that doesn't sound like Alex."

"It matters not. Read!"

Quickly, Ian looked down and continued with the passages in the book.

"Where are you?" continued her grandfather, in a low, almost monotone voice.

"I…I do not know where I am."

"Can you describe it?"

"There are many large trees and several large stones," Alex/Jennie continued in an audible whisper.

"How did you get there?"

"I don't remember exactly. Someone hit me over the head in the kitchen at the Ram. When I woke up, I was here."

"Can you get up and leave?"

"No. I'm tied down. Why am I tied down?"

"Jennie, the person that took you wants to hurt you. Can you tell me who that person is?"

"No," the response was more frightened this time. She was beginning to cry at this point.

"I can't get loose," she continued as she pulled against invisible restraints. "Why would someone want to hurt me?"

"Do you see anyone?"

"No, there is no one here. There are some markings on one of the stones here. I don't know what they mean."

Ian cast Sarah a sideways glance, but never deviated from his reading.

"Wait, someone is coming out from behind the stones." The voice emanating from Alex began to sob again, growing hysterical. "His face is painted half black and half red. He has this really long knife in his hands. It is wavy looking. Please, keep him away from me!"

Tears brimmed in Sarah's eyes when she heard the fright in the voice emanating from her friend. This story was beginning to sound uncomfortably familiar.

"Somebody help me," she pleaded. "Please keep him away. I'm very frightened."

"You must be brave, Jennie. The only thing I can do now is help you to cross over."

"His eyes are so evil. They are filled with hate. He is raising his knife. No!" the voice screamed.

"You must face him."

"Stop! Who are you?" Jennie's voice shouted in terror. "Please don't hurt me. I'll do anything, only, please, let me go."

Jennie/Alex was sobbing hysterically now.

"You must be brave, Jennie. Help me to help you. You must relive the entire episode in order to move on to a better purpose."

"I can't!" she cried out. "I'm too frightened."

"You must be strong or you will take an innocent soul with you."

"No, not Alex," Sarah whispered from the corner as she abruptly stood and then froze.

Ian looked up at the old man in shock, but never stopped his reading.

"I am told that you are a fine girl, Jennie Thomas. I know that you would not hurt another for your own gain," Lightning Horse said.

"No. I don't want to."

"Then you must do as I say."

"I will try," she said more calmly.

"Good," he said soothingly. "Let's try again, shall we, Jennie?"

"He is coming closer to me."

"Can you tell who he is?"

"No. Yet there is something familiar about him."

"What is he doing now?"

"He is making some motion with his knife hand towards the carved stone. His back is to me; I can't see very well."

"Continue."

"He has turned around again and is headed for me. I can see the reflection of the fires in his knife and in his eyes. Can't you help me?"

"I am helping you the only way possible, Jennie Thomas. I am helping your soul to depart for heaven. Otherwise, you will lead a tortured, earth-bound existence here. Your hurt and terror were cushioned for you by the one with which you are now linked. You must take your place in the circle of life."

"Can he hurt me anymore?"

"No, Jennie. There is nothing more he can do to you unless you force yourself to remain here."

"Okay. He is raising the knife. God, I'm so frightened. He is slicing off my skin. Peeling it back. It's so horrible, but you're right I feel nothing. How can that be?"

"Because, Jennie, you have already endured the pain of the injuries. This man has killed you. You are already dead. You must continue."

"I'm dead?" she questioned. "Strange, I don't feel dead."

"The body that you are feeling is the body of another. She is the one who was there giving you strength so that you could make it through the rite. She is the one who gave you the courage you needed. Now your spirit must let go of her or you will drag her down with you."

"I don't want to hurt anyone."

"I know you don't."

"He is pulling apart my ribs and reaching into my chest. I can feel him touch my heart. He is caressing it and I can feel a power, like small electric shocks, rushing through his skin as it touches mine. Then…" she screamed and was gone. A gust of wind blew strongly through the room. There was white mist at first, and then it dissipated.

Alex's body snapped upright in a quick, forward motion. Ian dropped the book on the floor, crossed quickly to her and held her quietly in his arms as she began lightly sobbing. Her tears, thankfully, were normal this time.

"Will she be all right?" Sarah asked through her own tears.

"The connection is broken," answered Lightning Horse. She will recover in a time that is normal for her. Only she can decide how much time is needed."

* * *

Time passed quickly for Ian; so much had happened to him in such a short span of time. It was early evening before he knew it. Alex had slept soundly through the entire day. His conscious nagged at him that he should be out looking for Jennie Thomas. He knew now in his heart that the girl, Jennie, was truly gone from this life. He had been present to watch her spirit depart; Ian also knew that he would find no more trace of her physical body than he did of Rita or Janey. What he could do, however, was stand guard over the living. Supernatural or not, this being would have to go through him first in order to get to anyone else in this house.

Lightning Horse had warned him that it would be quite possible for Alex to awaken and remember nothing of what had transpired. It no longer mattered to Ian; he was content to be at peace within himself. The question of whether such things really do exist would at least be an arguable point from here forward. The next time she had any kind of input, he promised himself that he would listen.

Ian had just about dozed off in the comfortable, blue easy chair in Alex's room when he heard a faint sobbing. Snapping into full-awake mode, he checked on the sleeping woman. After further scrutiny, he was convinced that the noise had not come from the sleeping figure. Opening the door and peering into the hallway, the muffled sound intensified in Ian's ears. Glancing back, Ian could see that Alex had not stirred from her slumber. He turned back toward the sound, and something caught his attention out of the corner of his eye. It was Sarah.

"You hear it too?" Sarah asked.

"What is that?" he replied.

"That is one of our resident ghosts, and perhaps our most shy one."

"Why do you say that it's shy?"

"Because it never forms; it stays in the form of mist all of the time."

From behind them, Lightning Horse now joined them with Kendra in tow.

"Is this one of your residents you told me about?" Lightning Horse asked.

"Yes, it always comes from the same, unfinished suite," Sarah replied.

As the foursome crept slowly down the hallway, Ian stopped and faced Alex's grandfather.

"Will she be all right? Maybe Sarah or Kendra should stay with her?" Ian asked

"She will be fine. If more spiritual activity begins, she will not be able to sleep anyway."

Sarah's hand hesitated and shook when it reached out for the doorknob. She could hear the bumping, scraping noises that had become commonplace in this suite. Then came the gentle sobbing. Trying the door, Sarah found it to be stuck. Ian stepped forward to get directly behind Sarah and withdrew his gun.

"That will not work in this instance," Lightning Horse said and he gently laid his weathered hand upon the barrel.

"Right, I forgot," Ian, replied as he snapped on the safety. "Old habits die hard it seems. Here, Sarah. Allow me."

Stepping in front of Sarah, Ian grasped the door handle.

"Careful," Sarah warned. "Last time I had to throw my whole self into the door in order to open it."

He prepared to push hard. Something told him at the last minute to gently turn the knob instead. He did so, and the door to the unfinished suite swung wide open without complaint.

A bright white light engulfed the room just as it had done before on numerous occasions. The group entered the room. Sarah no longer felt alone in her solitude. Now more people were finally witnessing the transformation of the strange room. The cobwebs and dusty furniture faded from sight, and, in their place, came forward the vision of a beautiful room from yesteryear. The bed was decorated in the same sea foam blue, velveteen-looking coverlet that Sarah remembered from the previous encounters. Everything transformed like before, from the throw pillows to the blood red cover of the Victorian platform rocker.

Curtains billowed out from painted shut windows and the sobbing became more intense. The mist that normally enveloped the chair was settling in and taking a more recognizable shape than it ever had before. A quick glance to the doorframe area revealed that Alex had joined the foursome.

"Alex!" A happy Kendra exclaimed, in unison with Sarah.

"You must be still," Lightning Horse warned.

"Why?" they both whispered in unison.

"She is now more in tune with the spirits of this place than ever before. They should appear more real to us. Communicate more with her."

"I don't know if I like that arrangement," Ian growled.

"You have no choice. If she does not help these wandering souls, she will be plagued with them the rest of her life. They will follow her wherever she goes."

"You mean," Sarah said, "what she told us is true. That we could all leave here, but she could never leave because the dead would follow her."

"That is the blessing and the curse of this gift. At least Alex is stronger than her mother."

"Alex's mother?" Sarah asked. "You know, in all the years that I have known her, she has never spoken of her."

"Alex's mother was a gifted seer, as is Alex. Her downfall was that she was too tenderhearted. In a situation of trying to save the souls in a haunting, she suddenly and inexplicably lost her nerve."

"Did something frighten her?"

"We believe that is so."

"What happened to her mother?" asked Ian.

"That split moment of indecision was too much for her. She was committed to a mental hospital. The doctors," he shook his head. "They think they have all the answers. They deemed she had schizophrenia. What she really carried was the souls of the haunting within herself. She absorbed them after she joined with them."

"Like Alex did with Jennie?" Sarah asked.

"Yes, exactly like that," he replied.

"Alex's mother, what happened to her?" Kendra asked.

"She died in the hospital," the old man replied. "Alex would not speak for a year after that."

"But Alex will be all right?" Ian questioned.

"From Jennie, yes. Thankfully I was here in time to help her."

"Would it have been different if you had not been?" Ian asked.

"Maybe yes, maybe no. It takes weeks to recover from such a bonding. With my outside help and her inner strength, anything is possible."

"I'm not sure I like the way you said *from Jennie, yes,*" Ian added suddenly.

"I do not yet know all of what we are up against. Since I have arrived, I have learned much. There are still many unanswered questions. I must have the answers to in order to know."

"Look!" Kendra exclaimed as she pointed towards the rocker. "The shy ghost is beginning to take shape."

"Now this makes sense," Sarah said nodding.

"You know who that is?" Ian asked.

"Yes, her husband haunts our barn every morning. From the photographs Alex and I looked at with Ron Van Allen yesterday, I would say that without a doubt, this is the ghost of Mildred Conrad."

On cue, the features became more defined. There was no malevolence in her manner. Alex began to cross the room towards the spectral white woman. Ian began to intercede, but Lightning Horse pulled him back. The look from Ian provoked Lightning Horse to respond.

"Let her go to this one," he whispered. "She means her no harm."

The lips of the ghost moved, but no one could hear. Alex suddenly dropped from her trancelike state. Her body language told her friends that she had returned to her former state of being. She dropped to her knees in front of the vision. She looked up at her with a kind of childlike awe.

"She is so sad," Alex said.

"What can she tell you, Granddaughter?" Lightning Horse asked.

"There is something in this room which gives her great consternation. If we can discover the secret, we can free her spirit from this room and her soul can forever rest."

Nodding in approval, the glowing ghost smiled and was suddenly gone. She left with a note of hope in her face. You could tell that she wished this to be her last visit.

In the blink of an eye, the room returned to the cobwebs and dirt that were really there all the time.

"We must look," Alex said as she turned toward the rest of them.

"Look? For what?" Sarah said.

"Couldn't she tell you?" Kendra asked.

"The spirits are not allowed to tell us things directly. We must be clever enough to decipher their clues," Alex replied.

"Seems stupid to me," Kendra said.

"It is a trial of worth, isn't it?" Ian asked.

"There is hope for you yet, Sheriff," Alex said. Then she did a double take and squinted at Ian. "That is you, isn't it, Sheriff?"

"It is."

"What are you doing here?" Alex asked suspiciously.

"I just dropped off this man who came to town to see you."

"Grandfather!" she exclaimed, running towards him and giving him a hug. "When did you get here?"

"I have not been here long."

"She doesn't remember," Sarah whispered to Ian.

"No. Lightning Horse said that she might not."

"What are you two conspiring about?" Alex said.

"It was nothing important, I assure you," Ian answered.

"See that it isn't," Alex shot back at Sarah. Afterwards she turned and gave Ian another dirty look. "You know, Sheriff, as long as you are here, you might as well help us look."

"My pleasure, ma'am," he replied with a smirk.

The group fanned out to search the room. They checked every square inch and at the end of their search came up empty.

"I don't understand it," Alex said with frustration.

"Where else could we look?" Kendra asked.

"I'm not sure," Alex replied. "I know! Let's ask our chief resident detective. Okay, Sheriff, there are stolen jewels in this room. Where would you look for them?"

Ian had no retort for her. He no longer wanted to bait her. He remained leaning up against the wall, fingering the bed frame.

"Hmm…no answer," Alex said. "What are you smirking about, Grandfather?"

"Me? Nothing?" Lightning Horse said innocently.

During this exchange, Ian had absently twisted off the finial on the leg of the bed frame. Doing a quick double take he glanced down into what was a hollow leg and saw that there was something inside.

"You did that!" Alex exclaimed, pointing a finger at her Grandfather.

"I did nothing, child. Ian has done this on his own. You must recognize him for his worth. He is a part of this. Just as much as you, yourself, are. It is his great-grandfather who began this investigation many years ago."

"How did you…? I really do have some missing time from my memory," Alex said with a tired sigh.

"It will pass," Lightning Horse assured her. "Given time, you will remember some, if not all, of the last several hours."

"Well, look what I have here," Ian announced as he held up a rolled oil painting cut from the original frame. "It seems that I'm not the only one in town with a vintage twin!"

A sharp gasp emitted from all three women as they looked at the face staring back at them from the portrait. There was no mistaking it; the scowl on the face was pure evil. There had been plenty of years for him to practice being charming. This was the missing picture that Alex had searched for at the library.

The portrait of Jonathan Conrad smiled back at her in mockery. Alex knew that the fight had just begun.

* * *

Evil eyes snapped open in its lair. His identity was now known. The showdown was imminent. How he reveled in anticipation. He had been planning this show for the last few days, breaking the will of the seer. He had paid homage to his god of the Morning Star with the life of Jennie Thomas. Alexandra Markum had just been along for the ride on that one. The next time he planned to make her the main event.

32

"I don't understand," Kendra exclaimed. "You mean to tell me that he is Jonathan Conrad, reincarnated?"

"No, he is not," Alex replied.

"Wait. Now I don't understand," Ian said.

"I'm afraid that you've lost me as well," Sarah said sighing heavily.

"You must tell them of the u-yo du-ye'-du Ka-no-he-s-gi," Lightning Horse stated.

"Who?" Kendra uttered, confused.

"That last part is one of her tribal given names," Ian whispered to Kendra quietly behind the back of his hand. "I recognize it from one of the first phrases Lightning Horse spoke to me in my office. It means truth declarer, or something like that."

Giving Ian a decidedly dirty look, Alex replied to her grandfather in a long series of Cherokee sentences. The language barrier caused confusion for everyone else in the room. Her grandfather countered. It was clear to the three outsiders that they were witnessing a strong difference of opinion that they would never understand in the present format without the aide of a skilled interpreter. Whether the words were known to them or not, the intonation and body language between the two was unmistakable. What no one knew was that Alfred was hovering just outside the door to the suite.

"Wa-hya' uwe t lu gu," Alfred uttered as he entered the room.

"Will you all, *please* speak English!" Ian shouted. "I'm not sure what the problem is, but we have all come this far together. I, for one, would like to know what you are debating so heatedly."

"Sure, I'll tell you," Alfred said, ignoring the angry glare that he received from his cousin. "Ian is right, Alex. He has come this far. They are all at risk. They need to know."

"To Alfred, you will listen," Lightning Horse agreed.

"What do you mean, at risk?" Kendra whispered in a frightened tone.

"It seems that I will have no choice," Alex replied, clearly irritated. "What my cousin has not told you is that this is not a reincarnation of the man you now hold the picture of. This is the original, Jonathan Conrad."

"But, that's impossible," Ian said slowly.

"How many things, young man," Lightning Horse said, "have you seen in the last twenty-four hours that were possible."

Taken aback by the statement, Ian was silent. Then slowly, he began to nod his head in agreement.

"But…that would make him," Sarah stammered.

"Well over one hundred and seventy years old," Ian said.

"Who needs my help?" Alex uttered.

"The man in the hallway," Alfred replied.

"Wait, now I've missed something," Ian said, confused.

"The statement that Alfred made as he came in the door," Lightning Horse explained, "wa-hya' u-we t lu gu, means that someone is in trouble and calling for help."

With Alex and Alfred in the lead, the entire group went back into the hallway of the great house. They approached the landing, and the apparition of the hanging ghost appeared to them. Shaking his hands in the age-old message that the girls had become all too familiar with.

* * *

"This is who needs your help," Alfred stated.

"What does he mean, Grandfather?" Alex asked, turning her head toward him.

"Who is that?" Kendra asked.

"Alex," Lightning Horse admonished, shaking his head back and forth. "Always playing with the animals and never studying."

"I recognize it," Alfred offered.

Lightning Horse turned and gave Alfred a look that meant for him to remain silent. Alfred knew that look, he had seen it often enough through his growing up years, and he wisely chose to remain silent.

"Where have *you* seen it before?" Alex exclaimed.

"Besides my studies?" Alfred teased, as he purposely sought to push the barb a little further into the already opened wound. "I just saw it done by the gentleman in the barn. He seemed relieved that I understood him. When I said it out loud, he smiled and then disappeared."

"So, what does it mean?" Ian said, now getting annoyed that the answer was taking so long."

"You saw the man in the barn alone?" Alex asked, ignoring Ian.

Alfred just nodded his head, bearing a large smirk on his face.

"It means," Lightning Horse interjected, obviously tired of the bantering of words, "Bad Pawnee."

"Pawnee!" Alex exclaimed as she raised the fingertips of her right hand to her forehead. "Of course. Why didn't I see it before?"

"You have become too deeply involved to be objective," Lightning Horse scolded. "The evil one has clouded your reasoning by incorporating you into the equation."

"I'm sorry," Sarah said interrupting. "I don't understand any of this. I always thought that the Pawnee were considered friendly to the white man."

"It is said," Lightning Horse stated, "that the Pawnee migrated from the south to the north. The beginning of their culture was formed by many of the Aztec beliefs."

"You mentioned the Aztecs once before. Remember that day on the hill?" Ian said to Alex.

"How could I forget!" came the sarcastic reply.

"Alex!" Lightning Horse exclaimed quite sharply. "That will be quite enough! U-yo ni-tsi-l' s-tah-ne!"

"Forgive me, Grandfather."

"It is not my forgiveness you need."

"You are correct," Alex replied apologetically. Then, after a rather uncomfortable silence for Alex, she added, "Forgive me, Ian."

"It's okay," Ian assured.

"No!" exclaimed the old man. "Your forgiveness is necessary. Something evil has tainted her outlook. Clouded her judgment. It has infiltrated her mind and she needs to purge it from her system."

"I think," Ian said. "That it could be caused by the fact that I gave her much too hard of a time during our first meeting."

"Was that the time at the altar?" Lightning Horse asked.

"Yes."

"That is when the evil one first attacked her mind. If you said things that you did not wish to, then perhaps it had momentarily tainted you as well," Lightning Horse replied.

"Please continue, Grandfather," Alex said softly.

"As I began to explain," Lightning Horse continued, "the Aztecs, often thought of as the mentors of the Pawnee race, worshipped the Morning

Star. They made sacrifices to it. Since the Pawnee originated in the south and slowly progressed northwards over the years, this became a practice that was followed by many Pawnee until the end of the 1800s. It was often told in our stories that there could have been a renegade band of Pawnee contained here in the Rock River area."

"The Morning Star, Grandfather?"

"The drawing that you sent me, Alex. The two ovals with all of the cross marks inside of them. That is proposed to be the star chart, used by the shamans of the Pawnee to call the spirit father."

"Tirawa."

"Yes, Alfred. Tirawa. Like the Aztecs, the Pawnee worshipped the sun and the moon. The tribes were known for their many secret societies, each with their own elaborate rituals."

"The red and black face. Grandfather, I have been so blind."

"Not blind my child, but blinded."

"The meaning is the same," Alex said. She picked her head up from the slightly bent forward position. Ian could clearly see the tears forming in her eyes. She turned toward the ghostly apparition still hanging behind them and muttered a Cherokee prayer for the soul. At the conclusion of the prayer, the figure dissolved.

"Who was that?" Kendra whispered in a near hysterical voice.

"That was…" Alex began and then broke off to look at Ian. "Ian, I'm very sorry for everything. I should have guessed that this ghost was your great-grandfather, Graham Valin."

"What?" Sarah exclaimed.

"That ghost was my great-grandfather?" Ian exclaimed incredulously.

"It is obvious that Jonathan Conrad hung him here," Alex answered. "He allowed that poor man to rot here, just to suit his purpose. He used him, so that people would think that it was he who had died here. He let your ancestor take the blame for things that he did himself. Your great-grandfather, Ian, must have finally learned the truth, and this was how he was repaid. How your family was repaid. Your ancestors must have suffered for this indignation. Of course, the reason you have stayed here, continued on in the family tradition, is so that you might clear his name."

"Well, yes. That is true," Ian stammered.

"I should have seen it," Alex replied sadly. "I hope that in time, you might forgive the terrible accusations I have made against you. When I saw the photo of your great-grandfather, I grew suspicious of how much you look like him. If it is any consolation, I privately hoped that I was wrong."

"You did what?"

"I know that you are angry now and I also know that you have every right to be. In time, you may understand that I really am very, very sorry. It was my fault that Sarah got that notion planted in her head. If I had kept it to myself, where it belonged, you would never have known and...and...Why are you smiling?" Alex stammered curiously.

"Never mind, I'll tell you later," Ian replied.

The look of confusion grew on Alex's face, and her grandfather continued with his explanation. "The sacrifice of the half-and-half face requires a maiden. This accounts for the poor women that have been brutalized over the last hundred-plus years in the surrounding community. The participants would paint half of their face red for day and the other half black for the night. The maiden was then tied into a rectangular frame in the fields outside of the village. As the Morning Star rose, three priests would perform the horrible murder of the victim. They used an arrow, a knife, and a torch. Their religious ceremonies often centered around cosmic forces. The Pawnee looked upon the lightning, rain, wind and thunder as the messengers of Tirawa. Their secret societies believed in the function of supernatural animals. I have seen this myself. On our way here last night, outside of The Blue Ram, I spotted a wolf. And painted on the walls inside the pub was a golden ram that had been painted over in blue to hide the original."

"A wolf and ram?" Sarah said absently.

"Could the wolf possibly be mistaken for a very large dog from a distance?" Ian asked.

"Yes. The golden ram is an evil Pawnee symbol," Lightning Horse replied.

"About the religious ceremony you began to tell us about, why did they do it?" Alfred asked.

"The real reason it was begun here is unknown to me. I know that without the blood ritual the deities would perish. Their life flows from the death of others."

"I think I'm going to be sick," Kendra murmured.

Unable to find a response, Alex grabbed the girl and gave her a reassuring hug.

"I think I might have an answer to how this began," Sarah whispered breathlessly.

"Go on," Lightning Horse said with encouragement.

"The history that Alex and I found at the library said that the first murders committed in town were the parents of Jonathan Conrad."

"Revenge?" Ian questioned. "This whole record of hundreds of missing persons was built on revenge?"

"I think that the young Conrad set out to avenge the deaths of his parents, and it got out of hand. The deity that had gotten hold of his soul twisted him. It used him and turned him into, well…for lack of a better word, a high priest to the Pawnee rights," Alex theorized.

"You are probably right, Alex," Lightning Horse said. "The ceremony you described to me with the arrow under the victims arms. The multiple arrows. Setting her on fire. The cutting out of her heart and the ritual of blood being wiped across the shaman's face all point to the Pawnee ritual. The women and children counting coup afterwards, and the smoke ascended in the sky, all of the people prayed to Tirawa."

"Setting her on fire?" Ian said as the detective in him picked up on a clue. "Alex, how did you get those charred clothes you were wearing the other day?"

"Charred clothes?" Lightning Horse asked angrily. "You joined with someone else and you did not tell me."

"She was from long ago, Grandfather," Alex explained. "It was more of an ancient rerun. I don't think that I was in any danger…"

"That is the problem! You discount the danger because she was from the past," Lightning Horse replied warning her sternly. "You may yet be carrying the impression of her soul with you. It could be a weakness, one that could be exploited when you must confront this entity. I might remind you that he is also from the same era as the woman. He will be very dangerous."

"How do you mean, she joined with her?" Ian asked. "Like she joined with Jennie Thomas, joined with her?"

"That is correct, Ian," Lightning Horse explained. "She and the other exchanged places for a short time. That soul's impression could be used against you, Granddaughter."

"Confront the entity?" Sarah added. "Does she have to? Isn't there another way?"

"No, Sarah," Alex replied. "There is no other way. It is as I have told you all along."

"Well, this is the first that I've heard about it," Ian interjected disgustedly.

"All of you must leave," Alex said slowly. "I must confront him alone. That is something that I have been trying to get across to Sarah for some time now."

"Alex, I've told you before, I stand with you," Sarah stated.

"Count me in," Ian added.

"You don't understand," Alex sighed. "Just like he can use any soul impressions I carry with me, the man formally known as Jonathan Conrad can also use you against me."

"Is that true?" Ian asked of Lightning Horse.

"There is no way to know for sure," Lightning Horse answered, "but he is a strong presence. It would be a possibility that should not be overlooked.

"It is better to be safe and believe it to be so," Alex said. "Otherwise, I would have your deaths on my hands. A fact that my spirit could not deal with."

"If we both die, you won't know the difference," Ian blasted back at her.

"We are so different," Alex sighed. "For my people, the spirit lives forever. That is a long time to deal with the guilt of your death, Ian. Or your death, Sarah. I cannot take that chance."

"We are not as different as you might think, Alex," Ian argued. "If you die, and I do nothing, then you are condemning my soul to live with the fact that I might have saved you. I might have been the difference between your living, and dying. How will your spirit deal with the fact that you will have ruined what is left of my life?"

Alex opened her mouth and closed it several times as she intended to come back with a crushing reply, but found nothing that she could say in support of her argument.

"You are twisting my beliefs around to suit your purpose!" Alex exclaimed.

"I believe on several occasions that there has been quite a bit of character analysis of me on your part. I suggest that you take it any way that you want, but I'm going to stick by your side like glue, Ms. Markum. This is still my town. My people being hurt. And to add insult to injury, it has been my family that has been forced to pay for all of it," Ian argued. "You just try and stop me."

For once in her life, Alex found herself speechless.

"Wow," Kendra exclaimed. "Alex, I think you just found someone that is as stubborn as you are. Ian, I'm impressed."

"Kendra, you haven't seen anything yet!"

33

Ian sat comfortably on the bale of hay and thought back to the last time that he had been sitting here in this exact spot in the barn. Unaccustomed to horses, he was amazed to discover just how much time horses took with their daily, routine care. Alex and Alfred both worked tirelessly, steadily, as if neither had a care in the world, through the brushing, the bucket scrubbing, and the endless necessity of cleaning the stalls. Still, in the face of danger, it was amazing to see Alex interact with these animals. Upon reflection, it seemed to Ian that the horse Alex had been riding the other day on the hill could actually read her mind.

He was a person of action, and sitting around on a bale of hay was not his idea of preparing for the upcoming confrontation. Ian found that he could not argue with logic. Lightning Horse had been so perfect in his analysis of the situation. The evil one would come to them when the time was ready, trying to force them into action. To seek him out would be worse. He would strike out like a cornered, angry animal. If he is allowed to make his plans then he may become over confident. Lightning Horse felt that it was possible that this might be a weakness that could be exploited. Perhaps it would give them a better chance of winning.

"You look deep in thought, Ian," Alfred said, startling him.

"I'm…I guess I don't know how I feel," Ian replied. "I am unaccustomed to waiting, yet I am hesitant to want this to begin. I know that Tirawa struck fear into the hearts of the Pawnee, but tell me, who is this Tirawa, that Lightning Horse spoke of?"

"Tirawa is considered their supreme god," Alex said. "He is spoken of as the father of the sun. According to the legend, Tirawa and Mother Earth conceived Morning Star, the god of vegetation. There are many rituals surrounding this god. Jonathan Conrad has chosen the bloodiest of them all for his revenge. Among the Pawnee bands, their shamans represented a large and powerful class. They composed a priesthood that possessed symbolic reminders of the southwestern Uto-Aztecan culture. The Morning Star ceremony was begun in the Aztec cultures and moved north and west up the Mississippi valley. Historians had guessed that this culture ending up somewhere around here."

"It appears that they were correct."

The slam of the barn door being flung open grabbed everyone's attention and startled the horses.

"She's gone, Alex!" Sarah wailed.

"Sarah, slow down. What do you mean she's gone," Alex said.

"Alex, I'm so sorry. I just turned my back for a minute, and...Kendra. She's missing. I can't find her anywhere."

Fury stormed into the eyes of Alex. The normally bright green had turned dark and turbulent. A flash of heat lightning sizzled outside, emphasizing the moment.

With no words, the seer grabbed her bridle off the hook outside of Peverell's stall and quickly began to tack up the big horse.

"Just where do you think you are going?" Ian exclaimed.

"I am going to get Kendra. I would think you of all people here might understand my actions the best."

"Not without me you're not!"

"I do not have time to argue with you now—Kendra's life is at stake," Alex replied. "Besides, I only have one horse that is able to quickly cover that kind of distance cross country, and even if I did..."

"Even if you did have another, you don't feel that I could ride and keep up with you."

"I know that you couldn't," Alex said as she dropped the reins off in the open hand of Alfred so he could finish putting the saddle on Peverell. Knowing this to be a discussion that he should stay out of, Alfred chose the better part of valor and said nothing.

"I cannot protect you both."

"Well, who says that I need protection?" Ian said defensively.

"I do," Alex said shouting as she drew right up into the sheriff's face.

With that, Alex swiftly drew her arm out from behind her back, and Sarah gasped as she saw what her friend held. Ian turned toward Sarah's unexpected reaction and did not see the set of horseshoes that Alex held in her hand. He barely felt the steel hit him in the head as she swung her arm to connect with him. The world went suddenly black for Ian and he slumped to the floor.

"He's not going to like that one little bit when he wakes up, cousin," Alfred scolded.

"I don't care. At least he'll be alive to hate me. Remind him that it is a curse to think evil of the dead."

"Alex!" Sarah exclaimed.

"Don't argue with me! Give me the talisman, now!"

"But, Alex, you can't touch the thing!"

"Only at the right time I can, and this is that time. Give it to me," she commanded.

Sarah drew her hands to the nape of her neck and fumbled for the clasp.

"I thought I told you not to wear that thing."

"I'm sorry, Alex. I didn't think that it was hidden well enough so I put it back on yesterday," Sarah whined, handing the talisman over.

"That's okay, Sarah. I'm sorry that I snapped at you. It doesn't even matter now. The fact is, that I only wanted you to be far enough away from this thing to be protected. I just didn't want anything to happen to you in case…well, I don't know what he can do with the power of this thing."

"Alex,"

"Yes, Sarah," Alex replied as she settled the talisman in place around her neck.

"Be careful."

"I intend to be just careful enough to get Kendra back alive!"

"And yourself?"

She got no response; Alex took the reins from Alfred and mounted Peverell on the fly, bursting out the barn door. Sarah and Alfred ran to the door behind the departing pair. They could already see the big horse opening up into his large and powerful cross-country stride that had made him a legend in Olympic circles. Sarah could remember just a few days back when Alex and Peverell had galloped down the very hill they were now disappearing over. She had felt relieved then, and Alex had approached the barn fully intact. She wished she could feel that now; all that she could feel was dread. She feared she might never see Alex alive again.

* * *

Her mind raced as the powerful equine legs churned underneath her. The talisman, neatly tucked under her sleeveless black polo shirt, seemed to pulse against her skin. It was an unnerving sensation, but she was comforted by the fact that she had been able to grasp the artifact without any ill effects. Somewhat to her surprise, there had been no crippling electric pulses to run through her body when she had grasped the talisman this time.

The sky was beginning to darken, and soon it would storm. The lightning was already visible on the not-too-distant horizon, and the gentle roll of thunder was announcing the approaching weather front. It seemed ironic how she had always slept so well during a gentle thunderstorm. The sounds had been a comfort to her many evenings in the past. Now, the minion of Tirawa had called to the father of lightning, thunder, and storms to help him in his quest to kill her.

On her way home from her last trip to the altar, Alex had found a shortcut through a shallow forest. Ahead of her, she spotted the turnoff; there was a large, fallen tree over the path, blocking the entrance. The tree trunk had landed at such an angle that the jump over it was a good five-plus feet. Not that the horse had never jumped five feet before, but he had always jumped well-manicured obstacles that were designed for safety. The tree looked okay, but could have an unstable base. No time to risk looking it over now; time meant everything. The horse and rider turned toward the fallen tree base, and the rain began to patter quietly, then grew quickly in steady increments. The jump effort by Peverell was tremendous. For a fleeting second the professional equestrian wished that she had it on tape to see a replay. Her mouth gave a sarcastic little smile when she realized that she would probably never live to see it. By the time Peverell had landed on the other side and had begun to gallop up the overgrown path, the gentle rain had turned into a torrential downpour.

The steep path became slick quickly, and a few times Alex thought that the normally graceful horse might slip and fall before she could reach Kendra in time; she had not had time to screw the grip-holding studs into the treads of his shoes. Just before bursting from the cover of the forest, Alex glanced to her left and, with dread, spotted a white owl sitting on a branch. The ancient Native American symbol of death was so close that, if she had dared, she could have reached out and stroked it.

The altar was now in sight; from where she was, it seemed to be illuminated. Another skill of Jonathan's, she supposed. When she drew up to the altar, Alex was relieved to see that, although bound, Kendra was still very much alive.

From the top of the horse, Alex could feel Peverell's sides rise and fall like a bellows.

"Steady, my friend," Alex said as she tried to settle the unstrung animal. "Soon it will be over, and you will be back in your stall, happily munching oats and getting fat." Not taking her words to heart, Peverell continued to dance around in excitement. Alex withdrew her knife from the top of her boot and began to cut the bonds of the nearly hysterical girl.

An ugly clap of thunder and accompanying bolt of lightning proved too much for the stressed out animal, and he reared just as Alex was reaching for the last strand of rope to cut. Peverell settled back to earth, and a menacing figure came out from behind the rock. His face was painted half red and half black. In his hand was the sacrificial dagger, the one that so many women in the past had died from. Though the blade had been wiped clean, the stains of the sins it had committed remained there for all to see. It gleamed wickedly in the lightning, and Kendra screamed when she caught sight of him and the horrible blade.

"Conrad," Alex shouted. "You will let the girl go. This is between us."

"Clever girl," he oozed. "What makes you think that I intend to give either of you up? My lord will be very pleased with me over this."

"You will never be able to go back to your life after tonight, evil one. Too many people know of you."

"All the more to send on to Tirawa. You, Alex, have doomed them all," Conrad said provokingly. "I'm really quite shocked that you did not catch on until it was too late."

"Too late for you, you mean!" Alex shouted, challenging him.

Reaching behind her with cat-like reflexes, Alex withdrew a Cherokee dagger that had been blessed by the tribal shaman in the name of the blessed three Red Thunder Beings. With one fluid movement, the dagger sang quickly through the air and lodged itself in the place where Jonathan Conrad's heart should have been. He screamed in pain as the dagger sunk deeply into his flesh. The holy knife burned in him like a hot poker, and from the wound poured a tremendous amount of hot steam and smoke.

Alex took this opportunity to continue with the other knife she had carried with her and cut the last remaining strands of the ropes that held Kendra to the sacrificial altar. Grabbing the girl roughly by the arm, Alex pulled her up into the saddle in front of her. Vaulting off the back end of Peverell, she called out commands to the horse in Cherokee and, with a slap on the hindquarters, sent the horse full tilt back toward the hotel grounds.

His hoof beats rang out between raindrops until they drew too far to be heard.

"Goodbye, my friend," Alex whispered sadly.

"That was very brave. How sad!" Conrad said mocking her.

"You would never understand since you have no heart."

"I don't need one of my own for soon I will have yours. I shall collect her later and finish the job," replied the oily voice.

"I don't think you will," Alex said.

"What makes you so certain, seer?" he said, sneering.

"This!" Alex expounded as she drew the talisman from underneath her shirt. Surprised, Conrad took a step back from her. Alex thought that this might be the small edge she had hoped for.

"The talisman will help you not, woman. You must have the knowledge to know of its many uses."

"I do not have to have much knowledge to know that soon I will be dead."

He laughed at that.

"And I intend to take you with me!"

"You! A mere mortal with one puny lifetime would be able to take my life? I think not!

"You might only believe in one lifetime. It all depends upon how you look at it."

"I have the power of Tirawa on my side, and you will succumb to his wishes. I shall sacrifice you and resurrect you as my bride. You will serve my lord as do I."

"No!" Alex exclaimed in utter distaste.

"Yes!" He hissed in delight at her fear. "You and I will continue on in his wishes here. Destroying life. Reveling in their fear. Tasting their blood. You will find, my dear, how glorious it is to serve my master."

"Glorious! Do you feel glorious? You, who was once the real Jonathan Conrad. Do you know how the souls of your parents have suffered because of you. They have not rested in peace for one moment since you have walked down this path."

"You lie!" he said and snarled as he lunged closer with his weaponry. "Their souls have been avenged. These simple townsfolk killed them because of fright, jealously, and greed."

"Wrong again, Conrad, or do you prefer being called Darwin? Jonathan or Jack? Your parents make a daily appearance at my hotel trying to warn everyone about you. To them you have become an embarrassment, one that keeps their eternal souls from finding peace."

A hideously low, and menacing growl emanated from the man. His eyes took on a golden glow and he began to advance toward Alex.

"Jennie Thomas," Alex shouted as she dodged a hatchet blow. "What did she ever do to your parents? Or how about Janey Stevenson? Did either of these girls hurt your long-dead parents?"

"These girls were in tribute to Tirawa. He made it possible for me to avenge my parents."

"Yet he still craves blood? What kind of god is that?"

"The best kind. A corrupt god is strong. Bow on your knees to Tirawa!" shouted Conrad as he swung his outstretched fingertips towards her. A crackle of lightning sizzled overhead, and another unnatural bolt flowed out of Conrad's fingertips. Alex found that his newly unleashed weapon knocked her backward with supernatural force. After flying through the air, Alex hit one of the large stones that surrounded the altar, and she swore that she could feel one of her ribs give way. A searing pain tore through the left side of her body, sending her into agony. He approached her prone figure, lying at the foot of the stone; Alex summoned her powers and, at the last second, tumbled left over her tender ribs to miss a hatchet blow meant to end her existence. A grimace crossed her face, and Alex rolled up into a kneeling position to face her attacker. Alex's eyes focused on the hatchet head buried deeply in the earth. Instead of Conrad, she found a large and menacing wolf staring her down. The growl was one of rage, the hatred flowed from the creature, and Alex took a deep breath, preparing for what was to happen next.

34

It was all that Kendra could do to hang on. Her muscles were sore from being bound, and her wrists were raw from where the ropes had dug into her flesh. Tears flowed freely down her cheeks and intermingled with the rain, which stung her face. The steep trail down the hilltop was slippery and treacherous but no amount of pleading with the horse would slow him in his resolve to follow out his mistresses last instructions—to return to the barn. When the large, fallen tree first appeared in Kendra's sight, she thought that she was seeing things. Approaching the tree, she noted how it seemed to grow in size quickly and Kendra tried to plead with Peverell.

"Please, Pev! Pull up! I've never jumped anything," she said.

Peverell lengthened his stride about three strides out from the obstacle, ignoring the caterwauling of his passenger.

Kendra grabbed a handful of mane in each hand, closed her eyes, and hugged her body as close to the big horse's neck as possible. When they landed on the other side she was still screaming. One stride away from the fallen tree, the horse shifted his weight and compensated for his passenger who was flopping off slightly to the right.

* * *

"God. What hit me?" Ian moaned as he regained consciousness and began to rub his head.

"Alex," was Alfred's only response.

"She packs quite a wallop for a girl," Ian replied, trying to be humorous.

"A girl with a set of steel horseshoes in her hand," Sarah said.

"Steel horseshoes!" Ian exclaimed. "No wonder I feel as though I had been kicked by a mule. Or maybe, that is, a mule holding steel horseshoes."

"Here's the ice, Sarah," Lightning Horse said, entering the barn holding an ice bag.

"There isn't enough ice in the continent of Antarctica to fix this," Ian moaned. "Where is she anyhow? Just wait until I get my hands on her again!"

No one said anything and Ian looked from Sarah to Alfred to Lightning Horse and back again.

"Well, where is she?" he demanded.

"Did you hear something?" Sarah asked, trying to look away from Ian.

"Don't try and evade the issue!" clamored Ian. "I said…"

"There it is. I hear it now, too!" Alfred said.

"It's Peverell, and he is carrying Kendra," Lightning Horse said with closed, concentrating eyes.

The three of them hurried outside, and each of them could hear the hoof beats as they drew nearer and nearer to the barn.

"Alex!" Ian shouted.

No answer came. In the darkness, the nearly exhausted Peverell could barely make out the figures of the people and ended up almost running over the three of them.

"Look at the froth on that horse," Alfred shouted. "He had to have been running his heart out."

"Kendra!" Sarah exclaimed.

Ian reached up for the girl and felt for her pulse.

"She's alive, but she's out cold," he reported. He tried to lift her out of the saddle but found that her fingers and hands were frozen, each desperately clamping down on a large handful of Peverell's black, course mane. Ian tried to bring the girl around by lightly slapping her cheeks, but was met with no response.

"Kendra," he called lightly

"Any luck?" Sarah asked.

"None."

"I can't get her hands free," Ian said, struggling with the frozen digits. "Get some scissors."

"Bring the horse inside so that we may see," Alfred said, running back into the barn and grabbing a pair of scissors from the peg near the hay bales.

Leading the exhausted horse inside the barn, Ian noticed the changes in the horses' demeanor. Although his nostrils were dilated enough for a person to fit his fist in, Peverell seemed changed. He hated to admit that the horse seemed sad, like he had lost his best friend.

With the scissors, Alfred quickly cut the unconscious girl loose from the exhausted animal. All three of them worked as a team to walk the animal out, place a cooler on him, put the animal away quickly so he would not get sick, and simultaneously put Kendra to bed in the house.

"This is crazy, I'm going after her!" Ian shouted angrily, storming out of Kendra's room.

"Are you sure you know where to look, Ian?" Sarah asked as she stood from Kendra's bedside.

"I've got a pretty good guess."

"I must go with you."

All eyes turned to Lightning Horse.

"Now wait a minute," Ian began. "That's pretty rough terrain up there."

"I am more agile than you believe me to be," Lightning Horse responded.

"No time for arguments," Ian said exasperatedly. "Just know that if you must stop, I leave you to help her if it is not too late already."

Before any objections could be made, they were gone. Sarah and Alfred looked at each other in silence and then turned toward the unconscious girl lying in the bed.

35

The war raged on and the stone altar area looked more like a battlefield. So far, Alex had managed not to get any appendages snapped off by the half-crazed wolf. It seemed incredible to her that her blessed knife did no extensive damage to Conrad. Hell, she thought, it hadn't even slowed him down for longer than a few seconds. She reached up to take the ancient talisman in hand and was sent flying as something struck her from behind.

Her reflexes were all slowing down with fatigue, and she barely got her hands up in front of her face before the wolf was upon her, snapping and biting. Her legs, powerful from all the years of riding, drew underneath the wolf and sent him sailing backwards through the air. He landed on his feet, snarling, blood running from his mouth.

Alex drew her hands up in front of her, and she could see that they were bleeding severely. She reached up and grasped the talisman in her hand. With her blood as a trigger, she found that the talisman began to glow strongly and it burned her, but she would not relinquish her hold on it.

A sharp cry of pain rang out from the wolf, and through bleary eyes, Alex could see that Conrad was having difficulty holding his animal form.

Alex felt she had a chance at victory and smiled while she planned her next move.

36

A loud scream rang through the hallways of the Grand Detour, and Alfred sprinted up the stairs to the room where he knew that he would find Sarah and Kendra. Near hysteria, Kendra cried in Sarah's arms for comfort. Her hands still grasped the wads of black mane.

"Alex!" Kendra wailed loudly.

"Easy, Kendra," Sarah soothed her as she rocked the girl.

"We have to help her," Kendra cried. "It was terrible."

"Ian and Lightning Horse have gone to help her, Kendra," Sarah said.

She pulled away from Sarah, and the tears ran down her face like a waterfall. Glancing at her hands, which were full of dark horse hair, she looked up at Sarah with her unasked question.

"When Pev brought you in, we couldn't get you to let go of his mane. We had to cut you loose."

"She," Kendra gasped in between rushes of air. "She should have gone with me! Why did she stay behind?"

"To assure herself that you would be safe," Alfred said.

"But…but now she is there with that horrible man…thing…whatever he is. What are you looking at?"

"Sarah," Alfred whispered softly as he became silent and staring. "Look at that would you."

Sarah followed Alfred's pointing finger out of the picture window frame, and, as she did so, a startled intake of air escaped from her lips. On the far horizon of the woods, huge spires of light shot up from the tree line. They could both see shards of lightning striking trees down the middle. It looked a lightning bolt had been tied to the earth and was having a temper tantrum because it was unable to get free.

"What is it? What's going on?" Kendra said. She sat up and strained to look. As emotionally exhausted as she was, all that she could do was open her eyes widely in amazement.

"What do you think that is?" Sarah asked Alfred.

"That," he gulped, "could only be one thing. It is a final confrontation between good and evil. That is a war being raged between Alex and Conrad, each supported by their gods."

"Let's hope that Alex's god is stronger," Sarah whispered.

37

"Do you see anything?" Ian asked.

"There," Lightning Horse said as he pointed out of the squad car window. "The light is where we will find what we seek."

"You know," Ian added, "after I go save her, I'm going to kill her for hitting me with those horseshoes!"

Lightning Horse smiled at him and returned, "I hope that you get a chance to. And that I will be around to see it."

The rest of the short ride was traveled in silence as both men concentrated on what lay ahead of them. When they could go no further by car, Ian and Lightning Horse continued on by foot. There was still a fairly steep climb ahead of them.

* * *

"Uhalotega, Atunutitsu, Usgohula," Alex's voice thundered down the hillside.

"What is she saying?" Ian said as he puffed out of breath on the way to the altar area.

"She is calling for the Chota-auhnele-eh, the Great One and the Great One's two children."

"These are your gods then?" Ian asked.

"She prays for the help of the beings that came down from the heavens and formed Mother Earth. To help her to rid their world of this human monster."

"Does it work?" Ian queried.

"I do not have any idea. It has never been needed before in the history of our people. I know not of these things; they are, as you might say, undiscovered country."

"Great!"

"Alex is from the Ani-Waya."

"The Ani-What?"

"Ani-Waya," Lightning Horse said as he struggled to keep up with the younger man.

"It's not much further; can you make it all right?" Ian said.

"I will make it. The Ani-Waya is the Wolf Clan, keepers of the wolves, known as warriors. She has a chance."

"A-ki-na-lv'. De-ni-n'-di'-s-ga!" The sound thundered angrily down the hillside to Ian's ears.

He looked at Lightning Horse, who looked grim.

"She says that she is angry and that they will cross over."

"Cross over? Cross over to where?"

"A place I think you would deem as…Hell."

"Not if I can help it! Come on! Hurry!"

* * *

The sight in the clearing was more than either one of them expected to see. Shards of lightning pushed the two adversaries back and forth like rag dolls. Although the pendant was glowing like it was radioactive, it didn't take long for Ian to see that Alex was losing. It stunned Ian to see the use of power that was involved in this confrontation and he was trying to think of something that he could do to help. Conrad still looked strong, as if he was reserving some of his power to finish the fight. Alex was pale, bleeding, and had fallen to her knees. It appeared that she no longer had the power to return to the standing position. Ian was ready to charge out and face the music, but Lightning Horse held him back with a strong hand.

"What's the deal?" Ian snapped.

"Now is not the time," Lightning Horse replied softly.

"What do you mean now is not the time? She looks like she could use some help right about now."

"Trust me. To go now would throw both of your lives away for nothing. Conrad would strike down the rest of the town before dawn. None of us will probably survive this, but we need to make our sacrifice count for the life of others."

"I won't wait long."

"You won't have to."

*   *   *

"How are you now, my pretty?" Conrad snarled.

"A-gwe-s-ta-ne!" Alex cried out in agony.

"Yes," responded Conrad to the Cherokee. "I bet that you *are* in a great deal of pain, my dear. It is not easy to go up against a god, is it?"

"U-yo!"

"Is that the best you can do, you contemptuous little half-breed?" Conrad laughed. "Certainly, I am evil. That's what makes the whole thing so delicious!"

Alex screamed again; she became surrounded by a very real ring of fire and she could feel the flames lick at her outstretched hands and arms. She was frightened, and Conrad took advantage of his newfound leverage.

"Remember the fire?" Conrad said viciously. "Do you remember how it burned you? How frightened you were?"

*   *   *

"What's wrong with her?" Ian asked.

"It is as I feared," Lightning Horse replied. "The one she bonded with before, the woman from the past. He is exploiting the weakness she carries inside her."

Alex screamed in agony. Her arms were thrust out to her sides, and slightly above her head, as if she had again been tied into the Morning Star ritual torture frame.

"This time, I have not cushioned the pain, my dear," Conrad cooed. "This time you will feel every bit of anguish and terror!"

Ian began to get up from his place, but felt an arm once again pull him back down into place. Shrugging off Lightning Horse's hand, Ian pulled out his revolver and fired pointblank at Conrad.

"Oh look," Conrad said. "I do believe that your boyfriend has arrived. Now you can watch him die first."

"No!" she cried.

A bolt of lightning flew from Conrad's fingertips and he swung his targeting from Alex to Ian. At the last second, Ian jumped to the side, taking Lighting Horse with him as the boulder that they had been hiding behind shattered into millions of small pieces and rained down upon them. Conrad returned his attention to Alex.

The flames intensified, and Alex's breathing became ragged. The sensation of searing pain that had taken place before returned to invade Alex's body. She was surprised when the torturous sensations were relayed to her neural senses, and the invisible entity stabbed her repeatedly with the invisible ritual knife. The entire ceremony took no more than a few moments.

"Oh, Gi daw da, Oh, E lo he no, Oh, Uhalotega,alsdeliha ayv ayostanohvsga hi a uyo," Alex commanded.

Recovering from the downpour of rocks, Ian rose and was frozen in horror at the scene unfolded in front of him.

"She calls for our gods to help her destroy this evil one," said Lightning Horse.

Alex felt her last breath exhale; she gazed skyward. She could see a fine mist over her head and felt the welcome throes of death encircle her.

"Forgive me, Great One," she whispered through her final tears, "for I have failed all whose trust I held."

Conrad laughed cruelly as Alex slumped forward. He was enjoying himself so fully that he did not notice the fine mist forming above her head.

"No!" Ian yelled.

"Now!" Lightning Horse encouraged.

"Now?" Ian asked. "And just what am I supposed to do now?"

"Give her a diversion."

"A diversion?" Ian said, snapping back angrily. "A diversion for her now that she is dead? That makes no sense!"

"You will see. You must forget Alex; your diversion is for the Great One, above her."

"Forget Alex? That patch of fog? Don't get me wrong, I don't mind dying, but I can think of better causes than a patch of fog!"

"You must trust. If you honored her, you must fight for what she believed in."

"Well, I guess I can't argue with that logic," Ian replied in exasperation. With that, Ian stepped forth into the clearing.

* * *

"You're under arrest," Ian began a little nervously.

"What? Oh, it's the boyfriend again! Aren't you dead yet? Well, do not worry, I can aid you in your little journey to join your newly departed girlfriend." Conrad's laughter was filled with evil and he confidently shared it with them.

"You have the right to remain silent, and I wish to Christ you would," Ian said, the anger creeping back into his voice.

"Or what, Sheriff? You'll take away my liquor license?" Conrad grinned at Ian with his suddenly enhanced, razor-sharp teeth.

Conrad's eyes began to take on the glow of change, from brown to a golden color. His irises narrowed and Ian could only watch as he began to shape-shift slowly into the form of a wolf. A quick glance to the fallen Alex gave Ian a glimmer of hope. He saw the mist envelope and enter Alex, enabling her to stand. And with it, other shapes began to take form behind her. The numbers alone were astonishing to him, and he struggled to maintain his poker face.

"No actually, I thought that I might let them take care of your punishment," Ian said, stalling for time.

"Who?" Conrad asked, "I don't fall for those tiresome children's games".

"Them," Ian replied as he pointed toward the now-standing Alex and the souls that had formed behind her.

"You'll never live to see it," snarled the man/wolf as he hurled a bolt of lightning toward Ian. The bolt hit Ian square and knocked him up in the air, blowing him back some sixty feet. Ian landed as far back as the tree line from where he had emerged only moments before. The last thing he saw before he blacked out was the meditating form of Lightning Horse.

* * *

"You will kneel before us!" commanded the powerful voice now emanating from Alex.

"I kneel to no one!" Conrad shouted back as he tried to hide the sound of fear in his voice.

"These beings behind me are all of your victims, one who calls himself god. They have implored me to put an end to their suffering, and to those who would follow them. Along with this girl, whose body I now engulf, who sought to give her life to such an outcome. I, Uhalotega, cannot let these people suffer any longer at your hands."

"You do not have the power to stop me!" Conrad said, raging.

"Ah, but I do. You forget the talisman. The half-breed, as you called her, perhaps could not use it to the full capacity, but I know that I can. And shall. And so do you. I can feel your fear. How does it feel to share something with all of your victims, evil one? Where is your god, Tirawa, now? Your god fails you in your moment of need. He abandons you when he knows that you cannot possibly win. He has thrown you to the wolves. They are a hungry pack, and their retribution is one to be reckoned with. Retribution day is at hand, Conrad. Are you ready to pay for your past?"

"No!" he screamed.

A bright shaft of blue light emanated from the talisman and threw a large flood of light into the entire area. The beam narrowed and wrapped around the figure of Jonathan Conrad/Jack Darwin. It was a light from which he knew he had no escape. It held him there, pinning him as he writhed in pain. Lightning Horse had to throw his arm over his eyes in order to block out the blinding rays of the gods.

38

Ian woke to find a strange-looking scene before him.

"Are you well, Ian?" Lightning Horse asked. "Can you stand?"

"Yes, that is, I think that I can stand. Why?"

"You also must confront Conrad now that the Great One has arrived."

"But, Alex."

"She is gone from us, Ian. You must come to terms with it. She did what she felt was best for everyone. You must finish the release of your ancestor, Graham Valin."

"But his spirit was released at the house. I saw Alex do that myself."

"I refer to the part of him that you carry within you. You have a desire to keep him alive in your heart; it is carried over from your need to right the wrong done to him and your family all those years ago. He has been released from the house, but he must also be released from you. If you look to the left of Uhalotega, you will see him there."

One look told Ian that Lightning Horse was right. His great-grandfather was there, and Ian was amazed at the startling resemblance between the two of them.

"Go, now," urged Lightning Horse. "Release that which you hold in your heart."

Ian stepped forward from the bushes and made eye contact with the transparent figure of his great-grandfather. For once, Ian found that he was able to smile at the man. To know in his heart that all had finally been settled officially for the record. That is, for the family record. None of this could ever make the official police record, besides who would have believed it?

"You have no more hold on me, Conrad," Ian shouted at the prone figure held within the light bubble. "Beyond a shadow of a doubt, I can now release the fixation my family has held of the question of my ancestor's guilt or lack thereof. I now see you for what you are and the pain that you have inflicted on him and others like him. His name will be cleared."

Conrad could only growl and hiss demonically in response. Ian backed away and glanced back quickly, it was a relief to see the look of serenity that crossed his great-grandfather's face. The light, which held Conrad, began to ascend, and as it did so, the transparent figures of days past and not-so-past gathered beneath him. They all raised their hands to Uhalotega, and the light began to increase in brightness. Trapped within the confines of the light bubble, Conrad felt the pain intensify as the temperature increased. Below, he could see the many faces from his past. They were the Lives that he had stolen in order to pay homage to a god. Not just any god, but his god, a god who had beseeched him in his time of trouble, a false god that lived off agony and fear as Conrad had provided it. Lastly, Thomas and Mildred Conrad came out from behind Uhalotega. Conrad's eyes widened, as he was able to take in the sight of his parents for the last time. The light became unbearably blinding, once more forcing Ian and Lightning Horse to cover their eyes. When it dissipated, Conrad was gone, even his final screams were fading from their memories. The ghosts of all the yesterdays were gone. Ian and Lightning Horse surveyed the surroundings and the only thing that they could find was the crumpled body of Alexandra Markum, lying as she had collapsed just before the coming of Uhalotega. The two men said nothing as Ian scooped up Alex's limp body and began the trek back down the hillside, towards the patrol car waiting below.

* * *

It was dawn as the patrol car reached the hotel. The occupants rode in an uneasy silence, both looking as though they had been through a war. It would not be an easy task for Ian to face Sarah and Kendra.

The women had looked so hopeful upon his return. Both had tearfully gone to their room, and there had not been another sound from either of them.

Alfred had sadly left the house, claiming the horses were in need of attention. He returned later and silently climbed the stairs to his room. Even Lightning Horse had quietly gone to his room to rest. Ian was left alone to contemplate how quickly something he had held so dear for such a short time had been stripped away from him. All the rapid changes that had been made in his persona had not helped the situation. Alex had relieved for him the one thing that always made him so bitter. The smear on his family had forever been removed. There was emptiness inside of him, and he picked up the highly decorated decanter of liquor and poured some of the contents into one of the matching glasses. So weary that he could no longer stand, Ian picked out the large easy chair in the lobby area and rested his feet on the equestrian-decorated coffee table. He smiled and reminisced about what Alex might have said about having his muddy shoes on her hand-painted table.

Before he knew it, he had drifted off into a restless slumber. The final scene between Alex and Conrad played over and over in his mind. While he felt guilty, as if he should have tried to do more to affect the outcome of the situation, his heart sank each time as he realized that the outcome would never change. Each time after the final blow to Conrad, Ian would wake only to find himself sweating violently. Unable to sleep any more, Ian walked into the kitchen to check out the barn area from the window. He entered the dark kitchen and rubbed his eyes in disbelief when he saw a fine white mist begin to take form. First, it was in front of him, in the kitchen, and then he watched it as it traveled to the door and dissipated through the door seams, only to reappear outside.

Cautiously, he stepped outside to follow the mist. Staying a healthy distance, Ian was frightened when the mist began to take on the shape of a ghostly white wolf.

"Be calm," emanated a female voice. "I am the leader of the Ani-Waya."

"The..." Ian stammered.

"The leader of the Wolf Clan of the Cherokee people."

"Why..." Ian said, continuing in a shaky voice, "are you here?"

"I have returned to earth momentarily at the request of Uhalotega. It is she, the Great One, which commands me."

Unable to answer or comment, Ian fought with his emotions. Then finally, he had the answer he had been looking for. "Can you take me to be with her? With Alex, I mean...not Uhalotega?"

"That is the purpose of my brief visit here: to seek you out and reunite you with the one for whom you were meant."

Ian gulped heavily, closed his eyes as if waiting for some kind of pain and then said, "I will not be afraid. I will endure any trial or hardship that is involved in order to be with her, one way or another."

The vision smiled slightly, confusing Ian. "There is no need for any more suffering. The Great One was correct, you are honorable even though you are not Cherokee. The circle of life continues and so shall you continue with Ka-no-he-s-gi."

"But…that's not possible," Ian said flustered. "I saw her. I watched as she endured great pain. She fought with all she had and more. I watched her…I watched her die."

"Uhalotega bids me to tell you that she is not dead. Ka-no-he-s-gi has fought bravely and is renewing herself with a powerful Cherokee healing trance. What Ka-no-he-s-gi tried to do was self-sacrificing. She chose to honor her friends, her family, and her love to save all. Her selflessness has saved her spirit. Go to her now. Look into your heart, and she will return to you."

The white wolf returned to the form of the white mist and then gradually disappeared. Ian, figuring that he had been sleepwalking turned and walked back through the hotel door.

"There is only one solution," Ian muttered to himself. "I am quite simply losing my mind."

Entering the kitchen, Ian crossed to the refrigerator and, opening the door, grabbed a large bag of carrots. Letting himself back out into the yard between the kitchen and the barn, Ian silently walked toward the barn. Emptiness began to fill his heart as he realized how empty his life would now be without the bullheaded, Cherokee woman. It was this empty feeling, he assured himself, that had made him hallucinate the white wolf. After all that had happened today, he knew that just wishing never made anything so. Alex was gone from him, the only thing he could do was to try to face the facts. Ian's mind wandered, as he opened the barn door and flicked on the light switch. His heart nearly broke when he saw Peverell quickly swing in his direction. The look of disappointment shone greatly in the big horse's soft, sad eyes.

"I know, fella," Ian said. "I miss her too. I brought you some carrots though."

Ian crossed over to the stall door and, flipping the latch, slid open Peverell's door. To Ian's dismay, he saw that the horse had not touched his hay, grain, or water. When he tried, the carrots were met with the same lack of enthusiasm.

"You can't give up," Ian said empathizing with the big black horse. "I know that I'm not one to talk, but Alex would not want you to act this way."

Disturbed by the horse's lack of enthusiasm, Ian fetched the expensive looking wooden brush box with Peverell's name on it and spent some time currying the saddened animal. It gave Ian a great deal of comfort to have something to do with himself. Now he understood why all those horsewomen had said that horses were their source of therapy. He had watched

Alex brush the horse and now repeated her sequence of currycomb, grooming mitt, hard brush, soft brush, face brush, comb, and finally, the hoof pick. Although Peverell did not look any shinier, Ian felt a sense of accomplishment.

"You know, Pev," Ian said sheepishly since, after all, he was talking with a horse and expected no reply. "It is amazing to me what difference a few weeks can make in someone's life. I'm only sorry now that I fought with her in the beginning. I don't know how I'm supposed to feel now. My life's purpose in this town is over. Alex is gone. I don't know what I'm supposed to do now."

Amazingly, Peverell reached over and nuzzled Ian comfortingly at the nape of his neck. Then down went the broad but chiseled head and grabbed up one of the carrots that Ian had tossed into the large tumbleweed of hay in the stall. The big teeth crunched happily and with a smile, Ian reached over the big horses withers and gave Peverell a half-hug, half-pat.

"Are you attempting to steal my horse?" said a voice from the doorway.

Ian spun around to the doorframe and froze as he saw a figure that could only be a ghost.

"You're dead!" he whispered under his breath.

"I was in a deep healing trance. I only looked dead."

"And I just bet that you stood there in that doorway and listened to all the nice things I had to say about you before you let me know you were here."

"You said nice things about me?" Alex inquired sarcastically, crossing over to the horse's stall.

"Well, I'm glad you're back, for Pev's sake."

"Just Pev's sake?" Alex asked arching an eyebrow.

"No, not just for Pev's sake." Ian exhaled a relieved sigh as he closed his arms around her and hugged her.

"Did you really ask to die to be with me?" Alex asked.

"What?"

"The leader of the Ani-Waya said that you did."

"You know, weeks ago, I would have denied any of this, but I think that I have changed. I confess: I did."

"Ian."

"Yes?"

"There's hope for you yet. By the way, who got mud all over my coffee table?"

978-0-595-33902-0
0-595-33902-6

Printed in the United States
48089LVS00005B/67-114